SOUTHERN JUSTICE

SOUTHERN JUSTICE

Arkansas Knights

Bill Kinkade

Rev. date: 12/08/2015

To order additional copies of this book, contact:
Xlibris
1-888-795-4274
www.Xlibris.com
Orders@Xlibris.com
727728

All meaningful journeys go to new places,
achieve new things, then end up at—

CHAPTER 1

The Beginning

The first rays from the rising sun came through the sliding door into the bedroom and penetrated his closed eyelids. He moved involuntarily and untangled himself from the arm and leg that were draped over him and opened one eye. At that angle, he could see the outline of the hills to the east and a half-circle of the sun as it slowly rose over the southern end of the Ozark Mountains.

Blake Stevens opened his other eye, and for a moment, he beheld the beauty of another sunrise over Hot Springs, Arkansas. He looked to his left at another vision of beauty. Gabby was on her side, facing him, and the sight of her still filled him with a sense of excitement and awe.

Gabrielle Fleming was a vision of beauty; asleep or awake, she was perfect. Her tanned skin was so smooth and soft, and her honey-blond hair always framed her perfectly shaped face. Her eyes were vividly blue, and when she flashed her knowing smile, Blake always felt as if he were falling into those deep-blue pools.

He had been smitten by Gabrielle from the first time he saw her at the Spa here in Hot Springs. On that day, he had followed her to her house, just through the woods from the Spa, and made love to her like he had never done to any other woman he had ever known. When he was away from her, he constantly visualized her and sensed the touch and scent of her. When he was back with her, he was consumed by her presence.

Certainly, her physical beauty and her sensuousness were unlike anything he had ever experienced, but he quickly learned to appreciate her intellect and quick sense of perception.

Too soon, Gabrielle had to return to Kansas City and perform her role as the hostess for a series of business parties where she would charm her husband's business contacts and help him add to his already-notable wealth.

It turned out that the hectic social schedule and the stress around consummating some of his pending business contracts were more than his weak heart could handle. The deadly attack had occurred in his office, and he was rushed to Baptist Memorial. He had lasted a couple of days before the doctors in intensive care stopped their extraordinary efforts and acknowledged death as the victor, which it always was, ultimately.

Blake had driven up to Kansas City, desperate to see her, and, upon his arrival, learned of the pending medical crisis. He rushed to Baptist Memorial in time to be at her side when she got the news from the doctors.

A few months later, Gabrielle had liquidated her husband's business interests, moved the proceeds into a variety of trusts and negotiable bonds, and had a sizable bank account. She had become, by anyone's standards, a very wealthy widow.

She never hesitated in her decision to go back to Hot Springs to be with Blake, and he felt sure they would be together the rest of their lives.

Blake's business relationship with the shadowy men from Memphis, New Orleans, and other places that kept slipping into his awareness was mushrooming.

In what seemed like a very short period, they had built a motel next to the old country tavern and then the elegant casino and hotel here in Hot Springs.

* * *

Blake pulled on a robe and went out to the great room of the suite they now occupied at the hotel they and their partners had built adjacent to the casino. He started a pot of coffee, and his thoughts went back ten years. Gabrielle had invested a portion of her wealth in the Hot Springs project because she wanted to be a part of Blake's life, and it was important to her to feel she had paid her own way. The passion between them was just as important to her as it was to him, but in Gabrielle's experience—and as Blake had learned—business was separate from passion.

The hotel and casino was a good investment, and over the decade, the two lovers had put away a lot of money in three different banks. An officer in one of those banks had advised Blake on the process of making the money invisible to prying eyes.

The partners Blake had acquired just before he met Gabrielle were definitely a plus—and a minus. The conflicts in his relationship with them pushed and pulled at Blake every day.

The partners had bought into the countryside roadhouse called Blake's Place. The deal they offered was a no-brainer. They would put up the money for the casino and hotel in Hot Springs. In addition, they would fund the construction of a small motel adjacent to the roadhouse. Despite the remote location, in terms of highway traffic, its proximity to Fort Chaffee made it an ideal place for soldiers to gather in for recreational relief from their training. The proposal from his partners allowed Blake to leverage his position in a country roadhouse to a significant stake in a business worth five times more than Blake's Place with no out-of-pocket expense. The partners were smart men who made their business decisions based strictly on how much money they could make in return. In their wisdom, they knew they needed a front-man partner to avoid attracting the attention of various law enforcement agencies ranging from the FBI, DEA, ABI (Arkansas Bureau of Investigation), and last but not the least, the IRS.

How legal or illegal their business practices were was a minor distraction to them that could be fixed with some of the cash flow.

Each year, it seemed more illegal activities and corruption in general crept into the operation, and with each additional such practice, Blake felt he was being pulled deeper into a whirlpool. Recently, his thoughts touched on the concept that the day would come when he would probably fight for his life to get out of the pool.

* * *

He checked his watch and went to the door to the hall and, opening it, found a tray sitting on a folding stand just outside the door. The restaurant had sent up the usual morning treat—a basket of biscuits, scones, and assorted fruit awaited his appetite.

Blake carried the tray into the kitchen area, picked up the coffeepot, and went out to the balcony and set everything on a small round table. He plugged the pot into an outside receptacle to make sure it was still hot when Gabby went out.

The breakfast was perfect, as usual, and he looked down at the hotel's pool, which was flanked by umbrella tables, where a few of the guests had started to gather for their nourishment and morning sun before going back into the casino to deliver a slice of their wealth into Blake's bank account.

His attention was pulled back to the balcony by the sound of the sliding door.

Gabby, looking like a high-fashion model, was in a full-length peach-colored silk gown that clung to her in front and flowed behind. "My god, what a beautiful sunny morning! A table of delicacies, a pot of coffee, and a handsome man—what more could a girl want?"

Blake smiled as he poured a second cup. "Whatever it is, my dear girl, just name it and I'll move heaven and earth to get it for you."

Gabby stood, taking in the view, and said, "Tell me honestly, sweetheart, will we ever tire of this? What if someday we say we've had enough, we want to do something else?"

Blake's smile faded as he spoke, "If we ever feel that way, Gabby, we'll find a way to do it. I do think about it from time to time. I tell myself it's not as if we were in prison here, but when I think about making substantial changes, I realize how difficult it might be. You've put the bulk of your assets in capable hands with people in Kansas City, so no problem there. We have the arrangement with the banks in Little Rock, Memphis, and New Orleans. I feel pretty sure they will fulfill the anonymity that they've promised. However, I damn well know how powerful our partners can be. When they want some information, they usually get it."

Gabby went to the table and sat in the chair next to Blake. "I'm sorry, darling, I didn't mean to put you in a funk and start worrying about things that haven't yet occurred. Let's just have our breakfast, and I'll tell you about the man that came to my bed last night and made fabulous love to me until I was exhausted. I wish you could've been there!"

CHAPTER 2

Governors Never Retire

Glenn Wiggs sat on the veranda of his stately home, enjoying one of his less-productive activities since his retirement.

While most houses of this vintage had a front porch, when Glenn designed this house and had it built, he told the builder that he wanted a large porch to be built across the entire east side. This would afford him adequate space to entertain friends and, just as importantly, in his more solitude moments, to sit and contemplate the view of the mighty Mississippi River, which flowed directly toward him and then made a sharp bend to the south and proceeded on its whimsical path to New Orleans in constantly changing patterns.

After his second term as governor, he had decided that while most of the people still liked him, it was a good time to step down and find other interests. He contemplated going back into the ministry and finding a church that he could pastor and make significant contributions to people's lives. However, starting immediately after his retirement, he was in heavy demand as a speaker to both civic and religious groups. That had kept him in the public eye, and increasingly, the new governor had appointed him to one commission after another.

Eventually, he had sensed that God was leading him in a different direction than that of a pastor. His contributions to the different groups that he headed, or contributed to, made his activities have a greater impact on more people's lives than he could ever do as a church pastor. Well, maybe not greater in the larger sense. Nevertheless, it was an area that he was good at and a service that needed to be done.

A few months back, the first woman governor of Arkansas, Lorna Summers, Republican, had called him and asked him if he would consent to becoming a member of a regional crime task force.

He jokingly replied, "That may not work, Governor Summers. I don't think I commit enough crimes to qualify for a commission."

Lorna Summers had laughed and said, "I'm sure that's true, Governor Wiggs. So I guess we'll have to call it an anticrime commission. Does that work for you?

"I think I would be more comfortable with that," Glenn replied.

Governor Summers continued, "You have a reputation in our state and beyond of being a serious fighter against crime and corruption. That kind of reputation is going to be important to establish the legitimacy of this commission. I have submitted your name, and each of the governors of the states involved has unanimously agreed to your appointment."

"Thank you, Governor. I'll await your next call." He replaced the phone receiver and began to contemplate the possible responsibilities of such an undertaking. An effort to reduce crime in the river states from St. Louis to New Orleans would be a major undertaking.

A movement in the corner of his vision snapped his attention back to the river.

One of the fascinating things to him about the river was watching the huge barge trains make their way up and down the treacherous currents and the constantly changing channel.

Glenn likened the Mississippi River to an interstate highway with no lane markers. The professional captains were trained on the navigation rules of the river and were 95 percent successful at staying in the channel and avoiding collisions with other vessels.

The two unpredictable factors that kept it from being 100 percent were novice pleasure boat operators and the sudden, powerful shifts in the river's currents that might cause a collision with another vessel or a bridge piling.

Such events would be catastrophic and were avoided with all possible efforts. That kind of mishap could render the busy river unusable for a painfully long time.

The Mississippi River begins its journey to the Gulf of Mexico at Lake Itasca, Minnesota, and meanders 2,300 to 2,500 miles before it spills into the Gulf of Mexico at New Orleans. At Lake Itasca, the river is a mere twenty to thirty feet wide, but at Lake Winnibigoshish in Minnesota, it spans more than eleven miles in width.

The combination of the Mississippi, Missouri, and Ohio River systems makes it the fourth largest in the world. By the time the Ohio River works into the system, it contains the collected soils of some of the richest farmlands in the United States. Its slow rate of movement has aided in the river's ability to drop the rich soil particles during floods, creating the rich farmlands on either side of the river in Illinois, Missouri, Arkansas, Tennessee, and Kentucky.

Over the centuries, and with the assistance of numerous earthquakes spawned by the New Madrid geological fault, the Mississippi River has developed a dizzying series of changes in direction: sharp turns and horseshoe bends, creating great conflicts in the currents and challenging the trains of barges to handle the turns and stay in the channel.

The job of keeping the barges from going aground on the many sandbars that the currents constantly build and then carry away and then reestablish in new, sometimes unexpected locations falls to the powerful tugboats or, as they are often referred to by rivermen, push boats. The dynamics of the old tugboats that used to drag the trains up and down the river were not capable of applying the right thrust at the right time to manage the ever-increasingly longer and wider trains. Technology had contributed with new hull designs and strategically placed side-thrusting engines and jets, fore and aft, that dramatically enhanced the boats agility and power to combat the sudden attacks of the changing currents.

Glenn's attention was now focused on the nose of the lead barge of the approaching train as it dug into the muddy waters while the push boat struggled to change directions and avoid the sandbars that waited on the left and the right. There were eight barges rafted together, two wide and four long, and the push boat was adding power and pushing the back of the barges out to the right to accomplish the left-hand turn. The powerful engines roared, and the side thrusters created their own mini whirlpools as they pushed the powerful vessel to one side in response to the captain's commands. With expert precision, the barge train completed the turn and then moved to the far side of the channel to accommodate another train that was approaching them from the south.

Glenn Wiggs finished his iced tea as he watched the skilled maneuvering of the captain of the push boat as it straightened in the elusive channel. It was a good finish to a session of river-watching, and Glenn got up to go in and see how Mary was doing as she prepared dinner.

"Well, did another river captain safely bring his barges around the point?" Mary asked as she kissed him on the cheek. "If you want to set the table, I'll have dinner ready by the time you're done."

As he was setting the table with plates and silverware, he looked back in the kitchen at Mary doing the final prep on their dinner. He thought back to their first date; it wasn't even a real date. They were just two people in a group of kids going out for Sunday brunch after church. It was as if God had sent him a message: "Mary will be a perfect wife for you. She will be the mother of your children and your constant companion to support you and encourage you in the life I have planned for you."

Glenn and Mary had built a life based on mutual support and encouragement. Before the children, she was the perfect partner, always interested in what he was doing and what he was saying. It still amazed him that when their son and daughter joined the family, Mary's abilities expanded and allowed her to continue to be his partner and supporter in his varied pursuits and yet also be a perfect mother. Maybe the most remarkable thing was, after two children and the other burdens of their changing lives, she was just as beautiful as ever and was always kind to everyone.

CHAPTER 3

Riding the River

The wet deck shifted suddenly, causing the deckhand to momentarily lose his footing. He managed to grab a railing and avoid falling down, but the momentary feeling of no control brought another wave of nausea. He made his way toward the stern of the boat, and when he was sure no one was watching, he hung his head over the side and threw up what little was left in his stomach.

Carl Hoffman had signed on with the barge line in St. Louis over two weeks ago. He had taken his discharge from the United States Army three months before and had spent much of the time since wandering aimlessly around St. Louis, getting drunk every night, and sleeping it off every day. When his savings started to run pretty low, Carl realized he needed to get a job.

A drinking buddy had told him he should go to the barge line. They always needed hands; the pay was good, and the idea of working two weeks straight and then a week off sounded good to him. Two weeks ago he had come aboard the *Mary Lynn*, and his dream job had become a nightmare.

Stationed in Korea by the United States Army, Carl had driven a big supply truck, delivering supplies from the ships to the forward command posts. The lurching and pitching of the big army truck on the poorly constructed Korean roads never caused Carl any motion sickness, but the boat was a very different vehicle. Maybe it was because he had never done much boating in his life and had not developed any trust in the watercraft's abilities.

His working in supply was a cushy job, but boring most of the time. Driving a truck from supply added a little excitement in that he was always alert to a possible mortar attack or watched the road carefully for mines that might have been installed the night before.

The Pentagon was generous with the quantity and variety of supplies they shipped into the strange little country. In spite of the total number of goods that came in, soldiers seemed to always be short on what they needed and oversupplied with things they didn't use.

Carl quickly figured out the items that would be in short supply and high demand. He would siphon those items off in small quantities and hide them away until he had buyers. His supplemented income made it possible to buy the best booze and the best-looking whores Seoul, Korea, had to offer.

Initially, he resisted fraternizing with any woman with dark shades to her skin—brown, black, or yellow—but eventually, he decided they were just whores. So it didn't matter.

Carl, the youngest of three children, had grown up in East St. Louis. His parents had immigrated to the United States from Germany after World War II. They passed along to him and his two sisters an attitude of distrust and contempt for people of dark skin. Carl had little use for Mexicans and a special dislike for blacks.

In Korea he had become a first-rate driver of big trucks. His duties of hauling supplies never brought him closer to a boat than unloading equipment or supplies into a warehouse in close proximity to a dock.

When the *Mary Lynn* finally reached the dock where her cargo would be off-loaded, Carl would be eligible for a week of shore leave. He had decided he would spend that week in New Orleans and then sign on to another boat going back north.

The cargo on this trip was wheat, picked up from giant grain elevators in Minnesota and Iowa. They would off-load the cargo into a similar giant elevator, where it would be held until it was resold and then be augered into a ship headed for one of the Middle East countries or Japan.

It was late afternoon when they finally pushed the barges up to the grain dock. Docks like this operated 24-7, so the unloading began as soon as the equipment was moved into place. It was past midnight by the time the last barge was emptied and Carl went off duty. He stopped by the kitchen of the push boat and got a leftover plate of pork chops and some mashed potatoes smothered in gravy. By the time he finished, fatigue had really set in on him, so he decided to just go to his cabin and get some sleep. Time enough tomorrow to see what pleasures New Orleans had to offer.

He slept hard. Even the loud sounds of a busy dock did not wake him the next morning, but eventually, the hand on his shoulder shook him back to consciousness.

The first mate told him that he had to get off the boat so they could move to a different dock for a load going back north. He dressed hurriedly, grabbed his duffel bag, and carried it across the wharf to the barge company's small office. He signed the necessary papers and picked up his check: $635 after taxes. That was more money than Carl had had since he was mustered out of the army and got his back pay, which had accumulated while he was in Korea.

* * *

The music was southern country with the bayou accent and was coming from a jukebox, which was unusual for New Orleans. It was okay with Carl as long as the sound and the beat were there; he wasn't a connoisseur of live music. He had spent the afternoon walking around in the French Quarter, getting into the New Orleans mood. The musicians were out on almost every corner, playing their instruments. Everything from guitars, banjos, and horns—lots and lots of horns—the whining voices sending out the news of how much they'd suffered and how bad they had the blues.

Carl figured, if you were down on your luck and hadn't gotten laid in a couple of months, it was crazy to sit down and write a song about it. Pathetic bastards. Just needed to go out and find somebody and get the job done.

He took a sip of the dark-amber liquid and followed it with a long pull from the beer bottle that sat next to the small glass. B and B was what he called the drink. Not the fancy liquor B and B. Beam and beer were what he had when he wanted to get drunk. He worked on his third B and B and was just about as drunk as he wanted to get by himself. He looked over in the direction of the blonde sitting alone at a table beside the dance floor.

He had been watching her for a while. She had turned down two requests to dance, but he had a feeling that she just didn't like the looks of the two that asked. He signaled to the bartender. "Whatever that lady at the table by the dance floor is having, send her another one and take it out of my stash." Carl pushed a five out of the change lying on the bar in front of him.

Carl watched as a waitress and the blonde exchanged words, and then the waitress set the drink in front of her. The woman raised the glass toward Carl and tipped him a salute. Carl nodded then picked up his drink and walked to her table.

"My name's Carl. Mind if I join you?"

The woman looked up and said, "Hell no, I don't mind at all. Fact is, we'll find out whether that chair is broken or not. You're the first one that wanted to sit in it all night."

Carl pulled it back from the table and sat down in the questionable chair. "I haven't fallen on my ass yet, so it must be okay."

The woman smiled and revealed a glimpse of what she might have looked like a few years before. Her hair might have been blond originally—that is, before the years advanced—and it had darkened, and she began using a store-bought bottle that promised it would stabilize and preserve the blond. Her eyes were a pale blue, dull when she looked sad, but when she smiled, a bit of the sparkle came back.

Carl pulled his chair up closer and said, "I didn't catch your name."

"That's because I didn't give my name. What do you think I am, some broad that broadcasts her name all over the place?" The smile came back to her face. "Alice, Alice Swenson, that's my name, and I'm glad to meet you, Carl."

"I'm glad to meet you, Alice. I got tired of sitting all alone at the bar, so I thought to myself, why don't you just go over and see if that lady would let you sit at her table? That way the two of us can drink twice as much."

Alice laughed and slapped the table with her hand. "That's a good one, Carl. You got a sense of humor, and you're not too hard to look at."

They continued the chatter through two rounds of drinks. Carl said, "Alice, what do you say about us getting a bottle and going somewhere private to drink it? You good for that?"

She brought back the smile. "Yes, sir, Mr. Carl, that sounds like a damn good idea. I could use some fresh air anyway."

They walked out on the street, which was still busy with people of every shape and description coming out of one party and heading to another.

Alice snaked her right arm through his left and looked up at him. "There's a package store half block up and to the right."

Standing up, Alice gave Carl a better picture of what she had to offer. She was about five feet seven and looked like she would weigh in at about 135 pounds. She was full-figured, top and bottom, and Carl began to look forward to a good evening.

They turned off the street busy with pedestrians milling about and, in the middle of the block, found the small package store.

"Well, you know your way around town. The liquor store is right where you said it would be. Wait right here and I'll go in and get something."

Carl went inside the liquor store. It was different from any liquor store he had ever seen. All the merchandise was on shelves behind an L-shaped counter. No thief was going to get anything here unless he brought a gun.

The tall gaunt man stood up from his stool and said, "Okay, buddy, what's it gonna be?"

"Let me have a fifth of Southern Comfort and a large bottle of Coke."

Back out on the street, Carl did not see Alice. He looked back toward the busy street and then turned to his left. There she was with her back against the wall and her right foot cocked back just under her butt. She was humming something that sounded blues and rocking side to side.

"Come here, Carl, and show Alice what you got in the bag."

When she pulled the Southern Comfort up high enough to tell what it was, she dropped it back into the sack and leaned forward against him. She put both arms around him and pulled him tight against her. "I just love a man that knows how to treat a lady, and I think I've found one. Let's you and me keep going down the street about three blocks. I'll show you where I live."

For the next three blocks, Alice walked with her arm around Carl's waist, occasionally dropping her hand and squeezing him on the buttock.

Alice's place was up a flight of stairs that had been scabbed on the outside wall of the house. In its heyday, this house had been the home of someone important who had entertained other important people frequently. However, as time passed, the important people moved to other parts of the city, and the house had been occupied by people who didn't care about its history, only its cash flow value; it looked like the house had been divided into numerous apartments. They made their way up the stairs and through the makeshift door into one of two rooms. The front room was big enough for the sofa, an overstuffed chair to the left, and a small table and kitchenette to the right.

Wanda took the sack and set it on the table and turned back to Carl. She reached up with both arms around his neck and began to press herself against him, moving in a way that left no doubt in Carl's mind what was coming. Then she pulled back, kissed him deeply on the mouth, lingering long enough, and then whispered in his ear, "Let's have a sample of what you got in that bottle."

She got two low-ball glasses out of the drain on the kitchen counter, wiped them with a dish towel, and poured each of them half-full. She handed him the glass and then pointed her glass against his in a toast. "Here's to new friends and good whiskey!"

They sat on the sofa, sipping the drinks. The tasty bourbon quickly worked its magic on both drinkers.

Alice began to nuzzle him on the neck while one hand began to unbutton his shirt. She ran her hand inside the shirt and began to explore him. "You've got a good body in there, mister. It feels so good."

Carl took a swallow of his drink and set the glass down. Her dress was buttoned in the front from the neckline to her knee. When the dress had opened wide enough, he saw she had no bra on. His hand slid inside, and he found a hard nipple. He brushed his hand over it and then took it in his fingers and squeezed. Wanda let out a low moan and tugged at his belt with one hand while the other reached between his legs.

"Come on, big boy, let's go in the other room, where we can do this right." They left a trail of clothes through the door and into the small bedroom. For just a moment, each of them studied the other's nakedness and then fell into the bed.

Their lovemaking was sudden and rough, expressing a hunger that was built up in both. They were side by side, facing each other, exploring everything. Then Wanda pushed Carl over on his back and climbed on top of him. Her full breasts were on each side of his mouth, and he took turns with them with his mouth and tongue until her moans ran together. She moved down, and he felt his erection slide into her. She began to move up and down, forward and back until they both exploded.

"My god," she said as she caught her breath, "that was by far the best screwing I've ever had."

They both lay on their backs until their breathing returned to normal and then drifted off into sleep.

About an hour later, a strange sensation caused Carl to awaken and start to sit up. Alice was sitting beside him, wiping his body with a damp cloth and a dry towel.

"What the hell are you doing?" Carl asked.

"Just cleaning you up, baby. We made a big mess, and I thought it would make you feel good to wake up clean."

Wanda finished wiping him off and threw the towels on the floor. She lay down next to him and ran her hand over his chest and stomach.

"Hey, knock it off! You've had enough for now. Let's get some sleep." Carl turned with his back toward her. Alice moved, her breasts pressing against his back. Her left hand hovered over his hip, and she began to fondle him. Carl started to protest further but then felt the sensation between his legs. In seconds, he was as erect and hard as the first time. He turned back to her, taking a breast in his right hand and moving over it. She kissed him, her tongue searching and stimulating. For the next half-hour, they tested the limits and imagination of each other until they finally consumed their passion once again.

* * *

Carl was back on the boat. The storm was fierce, and the waters of the Mississippi River were angry, pitching the boat to and fro, the deck constantly slipping beneath his feet. Then the light from another boat was so bright it blinded. The other boat was headed right at them, and the light grew brighter; it seemed there was nothing he could do to avoid the collision.

Carl opened his eyes. The morning sun was coming through the window. He reached and pulled the shade down to block out the light.

His mouth was dry, and his head hurt like hell. He looked around the small room, at the meager furnishings and possessions. Alice was nowhere in sight, and when he called out to her, there was no response. He lay still and thought about going back to sleep, but the headache caused him to get out of bed and look for the aspirin bottle. He found it in the cluttered small bathroom, on the bottom shelf of the medicine cabinet. He swallowed four of the white tablets and went back into the bedroom. He was putting on his briefs and beginning to pull his jeans up when he heard the front door open.

"Carl, are you awake? Come on, sleepyhead. I brought you some breakfast. You want it in bed?"

"Naw, I'll be out in a minute." He found his shirt near the door and pulled it on as he walked out into the living room.

Alice was wearing a pale-green sundress with broad straps over her shoulders. She had fixed her hair, put on makeup, and was looking pretty good. She was putting butter on two scones, and there were other pastries on a plate, which she had purchased from a street vendor nearby. Suddenly, Carl was hungry.

"I got two large coffees with chicory. Have you ever tasted it?"

"Never heard of it. What the hell is chicory?"

"I don't know for sure, but it's some kind of seed they grind up and mix with the coffee, and then they put milk and sugar in it. It's the best coffee you'll ever drink. Try it."

The first taste caused Carl to set the mug back down in protest to its bitterness. Alice urged him to take another taste, and soon it started to taste good. He had never had scones before, and soon he had eaten two and drunk all the coffee.

"That was a damn good breakfast. Let me give you some money for it."

"Don't worry about it, Carl. I took twenty bucks out of your wallet. Here's your change." Alice held out three rumpled one-dollar bills.

"Goddamnit, I don't like people going into my wallet and getting my money!" Carl grabbed the bills from her and pulled out his wallet.

"Fuck you, Carl. I saw you had a big wad of money in there, but I only took a twenty. I'm not a thief. I was just trying to do something nice for you."

Carl kept hanging out at Alice's place over the weekend. They would fight once in a while, but mostly they got along pretty good. Carl bought another bottle of Southern Comfort, and each night, they would have a few shots and then go in the bedroom and see if they could screw each other's lights out.

Sunday night, after they had finished their lovemaking, Wanda asked Carl how he made his money.

Carl told her about the riverboat and his motion sickness. "The pay was good, and the work was hard but not too bad. I'd rather be driving a truck instead of trying to walk on that deck. I haven't decided if I'm going back next weekend or not."

Alice was standing at the sink, smoking a cigarette, and she turned to him and studied him for a moment. "I know some people. If you're not too picky about whom you work for but like to make some real money, they would probably put you on as a truck driver."

"What kind of weird business are they in?"

Alice considered her response. "I don't know everything about them, but every once in a while, when I have the money, I buy a little pot or cocaine from a dealer I know. He gets his stuff from an operator down on the waterfront. He tells me his contact is a big operator. If I ask him, he would probably connect you and see if they have a job for you."

"What makes you think they would trust someone they don't know to bring them a driver?" Carl sneered.

"They would trust my friend, and my friend will trust me," Alice said as she walked off into the bathroom.

Carl followed her to the bathroom door and said, "I'm interested. Make a phone call and see if you can get me an appointment."

* * *

It was just after 4:00 p.m. when the taxi stopped in front of the Jolly Roger Bar and Grill. Carl gave the driver a $10 bill and asked him to keep the meter running and wait. The Jolly Roger sat right on Front Street, looking out at the docks. The fishy, oily smell of the docks followed them in the door.

The saloon was narrow, with a mahogany bar starting from the front and running down toward the back, a good twenty-five feet with a mirrored backbar. Behind the bartender, a row of small tables ran along the left wall and led to another dozen tables arranged off the end of the bar toward the rear.

Carl and Alice stopped at the bar.

The bartender approached them and asked, "What'll it be, folks? Name your poison."

Carl looked around the place. A few customers were at the tables and a few more at the bar. He leaned toward the bartender. "We're supposed to see Fred. Carl and Alice, here to see Fred."

The bartender smiled and turned to a phone on the backbar. A few words later, he turned back to Carl. "Go on through the back and up the stairs."

The bar had a general rundown look to it. The stairs squeaked with every step, and Carl had begun to doubt whether the man they were going to see was such a big shot or not.

The door they approached upstairs was labeled Office, and when he knocked, he realized the door was made of heavy steel. He heard the sound of a bolt being pulled, and the door opened. It was like walking into a different world.

The walls were mahogany wainscoting up about three feet from the floor, and the area above the wood paneling was adorned with paintings of everything, from matadors, beautiful women, bullfights, and a parade going down a cobblestone street led by three men playing horns and guitars. A mahogany desk, eight feet across by four feet deep with silver caps on each corner, was the centerpiece of the room.

The man in a high-back chair behind the desk stood up and carefully watched Carl and Alice as they walked toward him. The man's skin was dark olive, and his coal-black hair was combed straight back and glistened with wax that held it in place. His mustache matched his hair but was neatly trimmed, and his white teeth glistened through his smile as he reached across his desk. "Good evening and welcome to my humble office. Sit down, both of you, and tell me your names."

After they sat down, Carl's eyes adjusted to the light in the room, which came from can lights in the ceiling and sconce lights mounted between the paintings on the wall. Some of the can lights were floods that highlighted the paintings.

Now Carl could make out the two other men in the room. Each one was standing in the shadows, one on the right and one on the left, slightly behind the man at the desk.

"I'm Carl Hoffman, and this is my friend Alice. I believe you were expecting us."

The man at the desk smiled, and the other two men chuckled. "If I weren't expecting you, you would not be here, but never mind that. The information I have says that you have driven a large military truck in Korea. I am informed that it takes a skilled driver to handle such a truck, am I correct?"

Carl relaxed a little and said, "I'd say that's true, especially on the kind of roads they have in Korea."

A boisterous laugh came from the man, and the two men behind him chuckled. "Well, my trucks are much easier to drive, and the roads are in much better condition. It is also important to me that my drivers concentrate on delivering their cargo, not worrying about the content. Is that something you would be comfortable with, Carl?"

Carl looked straight into the man's eyes and said, "If the pay is good, I will only worry about my truck and the safe delivery of my cargo, whatever it is."

"Are you new to New Orleans, Mr. Hoffman? I do not detect an accent that would indicate you are a native."

Carl squirmed in his chair. "Yes, sir. I arrived in New Orleans last Friday as a crew member for a barge line. I signed onto the boat in St. Louis, and by the time I had reached New Orleans, I was ready to find a new job. I can drive a truck, and I've spent many hours in an airplane, but that was my first boat ride. I puked up everything I ate for two weeks."

The man took a large cigar from a wooden box on his desk. He ran his tongue over it from one end to the other. Then, taking a small silver clip from his desk, he cut a small piece off one end and put it in his mouth. He flipped a propane lighter and touched the flame to the Cuban tobacco. When it was sufficiently started, he inhaled deeply and blew the smoke toward the ceiling. He made an appreciating sigh and pushed a button under his desktop. "Orlando, come into my office, *por favor.*"

A door behind one of the two men swung open, and another man with similar hair, mustache, and skin color as Fred went in and stood at Fred's elbow.

Fred spoke, "Mr. Carl Hoffman, I want to introduce you to Orlando Perez. Mr. Perez will assign you your duties and deliver your pay each week. I want you to feel free to confide in Mr. Perez and ask any questions you may have. At this time, do you have any questions for me?"

Carl replied, "You've mentioned pay two or three times, but so far I don't know how much my pay will be."

Fred's eyes lit up, and his smile showed off his white teeth again. "An excellent question, Carl. I have learned to never trust a man that doesn't worry about the money. Your pay will start at $500 per week. Most of your expenses will be paid for in advance or reimbursed the next time you see Orlando. For tonight, I am giving you three $100 bills, which you should use to buy some new clothes that will be appropriate for a truck driver. What extra money you have left, you should use it to take this beautiful lady out for a nice dinner."

The two men standing in the shadows chuckled again.

Orlando accompanied them downstairs and gave him a card that read "Latin Imports, 320 Gulf Street, New Orleans, Louisiana."

"This is the address of our warehouse. It is three blocks west of here and one block north. In the middle of the block is an alley, and the numbers 320 are stenciled on the side of the building adjacent to the alley. Halfway up the alley you will see an overhead door. Push the button next to the door, and it will be opened. If you will take tomorrow to do the errands that have been recommended, you will report to the warehouse the next morning at six a.m. sharp." He turned to Alice and said, "I hope you have a very nice dinner, senora."

The taxi was still waiting, and Carl directed it back to Wanda's apartment.

On the boat ride down to New Orleans, Carl had overheard the crew talking about the nightlife, and more than once, they had mentioned the name of the restaurant the Court of Two Sisters. When Carl asked Alice if she would like to go there for dinner, she hugged him and kissed him and ran to the bedroom to change clothes.

The restaurant might not have been the number-one pick of the hotsy-totsy set, but it was better than anything Carl had ever experienced. The maître d' escorted them through the restaurant and into the courtyard and seated them at a table for two with a white linen tablecloth draped over. Carl ordered champagne and two selections from the Cajun menu recommended by their waiter. After they had finished their meal and drunk the last of the champagne, Carl asked the waiter to recommend a good dessert wine. They took their time with the dessert wine, and both felt they had moved into high society, if only for a couple of hours.

Back at Alice's place, she poured a little Southern Comfort into two glasses. They toasted to Carl's new job and went off to the bedroom to practice the new ritual of losing themselves in their passion.

The next morning, they walked to the French Quarter, and at a mall near the convention center, Carl bought new shoes, socks, two pairs of khaki pants, knit shirts to match, and a pair of coveralls.

They called the cab driver from last night, and he went over to pick them up outside the mall. Alice instructed the cabbie to take them to Sam's Crab Shack for lunch. They drove west out of the city into one of the sparsely populated parishes. Sam's occupied an old building built on cedar logs, which floated in the bayou and was tied to the land by steel cables and a wooden walkway. On the back side of the building was a deck where Alice and Carl were shown to a crude small wooden table.

The waiter brought two frosted mugs of draft beer and then came back with a small bucket heaped with steaming crawdads and a roll of paper towels. Alice tore off enough of the paper towels and laid them on the tabletop. She then tipped the bucket and poured out a golden pile of boiled crawdads. The empty bucket was set to one side, and a bowl of red Cajun sauce was placed next to the pile of delicacies. For the next hour and a half, they consumed the pile of crawfish and two steins of beer each; they were stuffed!

CHAPTER 4

New Roads, New People

It was one minute before 6:00 a.m. Carl was sitting in the backseat of the taxi, watching as the red Chevrolet pickup pulled up to the gate marked with a small sign that read Latin Imports, and the driver got out. The gate was connected on each end to strings of chain-link fence that stood eight feet tall and enclosed a paved apron of parking in front of the warehouse. An eighteen-inch extension of military-grade barbed wire extended from the top of the fence outward at an angle of 120 degrees. It was obvious that the management wanted to ensure that everyone who went to this place entered through the gate and the front door.

Sometime during the night, a line of clouds had swept over the dock area, dropping an inch of rain then moving on north toward Baton Rouge. For the moment, the new-fallen rain gave off a clean, fresh smell and hid most of the other odors of the dock.

The driver of the pickup worked a key in the padlock and then slid the gate open, and as he turned back to the truck, Carl recognized Orlando. The four floodlights near the top of the building provided excellent illumination of the front lot, and the closed-circuit TV cameras ensured instant awareness by the people inside of visitors.

Satisfied that everything was in order, Carl reached over the back of the driver's seat, and the man extracted the $20 bill from between Carl's fingers. Carl got out and started toward the warehouse.

There were two pedestrian doors on the front of the building. One door was adjacent to the overhead door, and the other was about twenty feet to the right, with a window close by. Carl correctly assumed that one led directly into the warehouse and the other into an office. He walked to the office door and found it unlocked. He pulled it outward and walked into a small office.

Orlando Perez rose from behind one of the desks. "Good morning, Carl. You are exactly on time and, I assume, ready to go to work. Being on time is very important in our business. If you arrive at your destination too early, it might raise suspicions. On the other hand, if you arrive too late, it might cost us a lot of money, or you might be dead!"

Carl replied, "I'll remind myself to be just on time for my appointments. Thanks for the advice."

Orlando started a pot of coffee on a counter next to a sink. "The coffee will be ready in five minutes. Let's go in the warehouse and I'll show you around."

The warehouse was about fifty feet, square, and was divided into two distinct areas of operation. On the left were wood pallets stacked on top of one another, and to the right of the pallets were a number of fifty-gallon steel barrels. On the other side of the warehouse was an assortment of tables constructed of two-by-fours for legs and frames with four-by-eight sheets of plywood for a top.

Orlando talked as they walked. "You should know that we have checked your background very carefully and have verified that everything you told Frederico seems to be true, and there was no bad information, except that in your military records, there are indications you had a behavior problem."

Orlando continued the orientation. "As you can see, our warehouse is very simple. Your cargo will consist of two items: One item that is not important will be bulky and intended for the curiosity that a police officer might have from time to time. The second item in your cargo is very important, and it is what we never want the police to see or know about. Most often, this item will be secreted inside one of the barrels among an item of much less importance. Oftentimes, that substance will be identified on your bill of lading and on the sides of the barrels as toxic to discourage a curious officer of the law from wanting to open the lid for a closer look."

Carl heard voices back toward the front of the warehouse, though he had not observed anyone entering. The engine of a forklift motor drowned out the Spanish phrases. The driver of the forklift proceeded to move pallets and barrels to get a load ready. He moved a tall stack of pallets to one side and revealed a wooden crate standing in front of three other identical crates. A worker approached the crate with a pry bar, and in a few seconds, they lifted the top of the crate.

The labels on the outside of the crate indicated it contained Bad Fish. The bill of lading and the shipping label showed the cartons were to be delivered to Aqua Gardens Fertilizer Company. The smells coming from the crates confirmed that the fish were, indeed, spoiled, and it was going to take a dedicated state official at the weigh station to insist on inspecting the contents.

Orlando paused and gave Carl time to absorb his new information, then he said, "I will now show you your truck. It is a new Chevrolet cab-over with a cargo box fourteen feet long and eight feet tall on the outside. If you look carefully, you'll notice that the inside doesn't appear to be fourteen feet. That's because it isn't. A false wall has been constructed at the eleven-foot mark, creating a hidden compartment just short of three feet deep. I will now show you how we access the front compartment."

Orlando nodded to two of the men who had left their duties at the pallets and approached the truck. They walked, one on either side of the truck, and stopped at the space between the cab and the front part of the cargo bed. Each man dropped a hand beneath the truck and gripped a handle. When they pulled the handles toward themselves, the cab tipped forward, and two panels opened, the one on the left jutting forward two inches while the right one slid behind. The four-foot-wide door gave ample access to the concealed forward compartment.

"That's the damnedest thing I have ever seen. Even the army never came up with anything like it," Carl said through the big grin on his face.

"One of our people in Panama designed it and supervised its construction in a machine shop there and shipped it to us," Orlando said with a strong sense of pride.

Carl climbed up into the cab of the truck. His eyes swept over the instrument panel, and he was sure if anything began to malfunction with the motor or the refrigeration unit on top of the cargo box, he would get instant notification. Satisfied with his inspection, he reached for the door handle, but before he could pull it up, his eyes focused on an odd feature just below the dash to his right. It was about two feet wide, molded plastic with a push button in the middle. There was a keyslot centered in the push button, and when Carl reached over and pushed the button, the molded plastic dropped down about six inches to a thirty-degree angle. Mounted in spring clips on the plastic drawer was a Mossberg double-barreled shotgun. The stock of the gun had been replaced with a pistol grip, and the barrels had been sawed off to eighteen inches. In a molded compartment above and to the left of the gun was a box of twelve-gauged, double-aught ammunition. Carl pushed the plastic shelf up to its original position and heard the lock click.

Carl looked down at Orlando and said, "Looks like you guys thought of everything except dancing girls."

Orlando shrugged. "Let's go in the office and check your papers so you can get started."

CHAPTER 5

The Deliveryman

Getting out of New Orleans in a ground vehicle was not an easy task, but after a few wrong turns, Carl got around Lake Pontchartrain and headed north to Baton Rouge. He crossed the Mississippi River and headed north. Passing by Pine Bluff, Arkansas, he pulled off the road and stopped at a cluster of businesses. A sign in front of one of the buildings caught his eye: "Uncle Bob's Barbecue: The Best Thing That Ever Happened to a Pig."

He sat on the bench at an outdoor table, eating the pork sandwich. "I don't know how the pig feels about it, but it's the best thing that happened to me since breakfast."

Back in the truck, Carl was careful to obey the speed limit and watched for the turnoff. He turned off where US 65 went back into Pine Bluff and turned left on US Highway 270 toward Sheridan. The countryside was sparsely populated, with older farmhouses widely scattered.

"No nosy neighbors to deal with out here," Carl muttered and then applied the brakes sharply as he saw the sign Razorback Road—Private.

He turned south on the unpaved, private road and kept the truck slowed to accommodate the chuckholes. He drove about two miles before he saw the cluster of buildings beyond a large grove of trees. The house was old and tired and suffered from lack of maintenance. Fifty yards behind and to the right of the old house stood the barn, which didn't appear to have been the recipient of any repairs and maintenance for a long time.

The barn appeared to be two stories tall in the middle, with one story attachments on each side.

A man, in bib overalls, went out the back door of the house and walked over to the truck. "Hey, how's it going?" the man asked Carl through the open window of the truck.

"I'm not sure. I'm trying to find a meatpacking plant. Seems I may have taken a wrong turn."

The man's eyes opened wider, and he flashed a quick smile at Carl and said, "I'll open the gate, and you can pull the truck straight in when the sliding door opens. Pull into the middle and keep the truck to the right to make room for the fork truck."

As Carl drove the truck to the middle of the barn, an electric motor reversed directions and began closing the big door. Two men in tan khaki pants and matching shirts waved him to a stop and stood near the door while he climbed down. Before exiting the truck, Carl had observed a cluster of long tables with four or five women standing around each. The tables had longer legs than normal, standing about three and a half feet above the floor, and the women standing as they worked appeared to be less than five feet in height.

The women were short, with dark-brown skin and long black hair. *Another import from across the Gulf of Mexico?* Carl wondered.

The men quickly opened the panel in the front wall of the box and unloaded the barrels. When the kilo-sized packages of drugs were removed, the spoiled fish were put back in the barrels, lids tightened. A tractor and flatbed trailer stood at the back of the warehouse, and one of the men backed the trailer up to the truck, and all the barrels of fish were unloaded onto the trailer.

Carl turned to the man who seemed to be in charge and asked, "Where's he going with that crap?"

"About one hundred yards back behind the barn is another building. It's all set up to take the fish through processing and turn them into garden fertilizer," the man replied.

"You've got to be shitting me," Carl said with disbelief.

"I'm telling you straight. The guys in New Orleans were afraid that the smell from the fish would attract too much attention if we tried to bury it. Somebody said fish was a good fertilizer and people with gardens would probably pay good money for it, so we went into the fertilizer business. Is that funny or what?"

The man in charge picked up a clipboard and held it out to Carl. "You need to sign this paper that says we took delivery of the 'fish' and be sure to date it and put down the time. The man in New Orleans is real fussy about timing."

Carl finished signing the papers and then asked the man, "You have any information on what I'm supposed to pick up for return load?"

The man referred to the papers on the clipboard and pulled out the bottom sheet. "Yeah, you're supposed to run on over to Memphis and pick up a fork truck and take it to the warehouse in New Orleans. The address there is for a motel down by the river. The fork truck is only a few blocks from there. You can pick it up in the morning."

Carl said, "That's good. By the time I get to Memphis, it will feel like that truck seat is coming up through my ass!"

* * *

Carl guided the truck through the eastbound lanes of the I-55 bridge into the south end of Memphis. He took the first exit and stayed to the right down to the riverfront. As his direction instructions had stated, he spotted the Channel Marker motel sign and turned into the parking lot. He parked the truck in a space alongside the office.

The man at the desk looked up as the door opened, and a small bell tinkled, announcing his arrival.

"My name is Carl Hoffman with Latin Imports. Do you have a reservation for me?"

The desk clerk's attitude changed immediately as he put on his customer service smile and reached under the counter. His hand came up with the key, which he handed to Carl.

"That's the key to unit 38. It's all ready for you, and please drop the key back here at the office when you check out."

Carl had taken a pen from its holder on the counter, but the clerk shook his head. "You don't need to register, Mr. Hoffman. The bill has been taken care of, and I hope you find the room satisfactory."

Carl threw his duffel on the bed and quickly surveyed the room and the bath. On the nightstand next to the bed were a lamp, a clock, a telephone, and a pint bottle of Jim Beam. He unscrewed the cap and took a healthy swallow. He turned on the TV and lay down on the bed.

The local news was on. And pretty soon, the long day caught up and he fell asleep.

He dreamed fitful scenarios that didn't make sense. They came and went without connecting. Then he was back in Korea and his truck was under attack from many soldiers with yellow skin and large cat eyes. He was fighting them, and suddenly, a new character appeared, pointing a gun straight at him, and it began to fire. He heard the staccato of the Russian-made machine gun but felt no pain. He opened his eyes and saw the wheel turning and clicking as it went from one prize to the other, finally resting on the $2,500 label.

"Fucking wheel of fortune!" Carl muttered as he rolled out of the bed and headed for the bathroom.

It was 6:45 p.m. Carl had slept almost two hours, and after splashing cold water on his face, he realized he felt much better.

He walked out to the street in front of the motel and, to his left, saw a sign that read, River Rat Bar and Grill. Carl started walking in that direction.

Inside the River Rat, the lighting was dim (drunks don't tolerate bright lights), but as Carl's eyes adjusted to accommodate the low light level, he could see there was a long bar to the left, and on the right side were tables and chairs and a jukebox against the back wall.

A waitress who looked to be in her twenties was headed to one of the tables, where four men waited for the drinks she carried on a tray.

"You can sit at the bar or at a table, but if you want food, grab a table and I'll be right with you," the waitress said over her shoulder as she headed toward the table of four.

Carl sat down at a table and picked up the paper menu and began reading.

The waitress had set the drinks in front of each of the four men and replied to a comment from one. All the men broke into a loud laugh, and the waitress turned and went toward Carl's table.

She had a good walk, except for one exaggerated way she picked up her feet, as if she were stepping over the rows of cotton on her daddy's farm. She was dressed in a short black skirt and white blouse that buttoned up front. Carl noticed the top three buttons were not fastened and the walk accentuated the movement of her hips and a slight bounce of her breasts.

"What can I do for you?" she asked through her smile.

Carl smiled back. "That's a dangerous question to ask a man who has been on the road, driving a truck all day."

"You don't look too dangerous, but I'll change my question. What can I get you to drink, and since you're looking at the menu, you want something to eat?"

"You got a good steak back there in the kitchen?" Carl asked, still holding the menu.

"Corn-fed beef, Kansas City sirloin." She raised her eyebrows, and Carl noticed her eyes were a rich brown and matched her short-cut hair.

"Can your cook fix one of those, medium rare, and take it off the grill before it turns to shoe leather?"

The brown eyes swept over Carl appreciatively. "I haven't had a complaint since I've worked here."

"How long has that been?" Carl asked curiously.

She responded proudly, "Six months and two weeks as of tomorrow."

"Well, you ought to be celebrating. Six months is a long time. What's your name?" Carl asked, turning to face the girl.

She replied quickly, "Cindy, Cindy Murphy. What's yours?"

"Carl, just call me Carl, but be sure and call me." Carl laughed at his own joke, and Cindy joined him.

"What can I bring you while you wait for your steak, Carl?"

"Bring me a double Jim Beam and a mug of your best draft beer."

Cindy made a note on her pad and said, "That oughta get your appetite going. Let me turn this into the kitchen, and I'll be right back with your drink."

The steak was not the best he had ever eaten, but it was not the worst. Cindy stopped by his table at least three times to see if he was okay or wanted anything more. Finally, he told her she could take his plate if she would return with a Jim Beam and 7-Up in a tall glass.

It was a weeknight, and business was slow. Twice, Cindy had sat at the table with Carl. He learned she had graduated from high school six years ago at Hayti, Missouri, and married her boyfriend, who had graduated from the same high school three years prior. She said the sex had always been good prior to the marriage, but a few months into the marriage, the new husband started feeling like he was trapped. He began going out with the boys after work and getting drunk, coming home at two o'clock in the morning, wanting to have sex with her.

In his condition, her husband was often unable to perform, so he began to knock her around. Cindy had gotten a job at the local Dairy Queen, making minimum wage and no tips. One day, she finally realized that if she stayed where she was, she would keep getting what she was getting or he would kill her. She packed her clothes in a bag, took what little money there was in the bank, and got on a southbound bus headed for Memphis.

By 11:00 p.m., Carl and a man at the bar were the only customers left. Cindy did a last call for alcohol.

"Carl, do you want another drink before we shut this place down?"

"Yeah, Cindy, but I've got a bottle of good stuff in my room at the motel. Maybe you'd like to come over and help me drink it."

Cindy went to the bar and talked to the bartender, who waved his hand in agreement to what she was saying. She handed him the two twenties she had gotten from Carl and went back to the table with a sweater over her arm and his change in her hand.

"The change is yours. Are you ready to go?"

Cindy's eyes softened along with her voice. "I'm ready anytime you are, Carl."

Outside, she pulled her sweater on against the night air, and they walked toward the motel.

Inside room 38, Carl put ice in two glasses and poured each half-full of Jim Beam and added 7-Up. He sat down in the chair next to the bed, and Cindy pulled her sweater off, carried her drink over, and slid into his lap.

Three tips of her glass, and her drink was gone. She leaned over backward and set her glass on the floor.

"Your drinks are almost as good as the ones I serve," she giggled as she looked up at Carl.

Carl slid his hand under her blouse and began to loosen the remaining buttons. His hand found her breasts, small but firm with hard, pointed nipples, and he began to explore.

Cindy moved into a sitting position and began to nuzzle his neck and ear.

Carl picked her up and carried her to the bed. As he lowered her, she looped both hands around his neck and pulled him down with her, undressing him on the way.

She was an uninhibited lover who didn't have all the sophistication of an older woman but made up for it with her youthful energy and wild imagination.

One and a half hours after they had gone to the bed, they finished their third session. Carl lay on his back, still breathing hard, and Cindy was curled up, facing him with her eyes closed. In two minutes, they were both sleep.

The next morning, the alarm clock in Carl's head went off at seven o'clock.

Carl went in the bathroom and turned on the shower. The hot water felt good and relaxing, but when he had finished, he turned the handle to cold. One minute under the cold shower speeded up his metabolism, and when he had toweled off, his energy level had peaked, and he was ready to face the day.

Cindy had pulled the sheet over her head and, in her muffled voice, asked, "Has anyone ever told you you have a mean, cruel streak?"

"You're the first one. Everyone else has always told me I was a soft, cuddly teddy bear."

Cindy giggled under the cover and then pulled the sheet down from her face. "Seriously, why are you out of bed, making all that noise?"

"Number-one rule in my business: be on time!"

Cindy added, "Well, the number-one rule in my business is get plenty of sleep."

Carl picked up his bag, stopped at the foot of the bed, and said, "Get all the sleep you want. The room's paid for until noon. I gotta hit the road, but when I get back this way, I'll look you up. It's been fun." Carl hung the Do Not Disturb sign on the outside handle and closed the door.

Thirty minutes later, the fish fertilizer was unloaded, and the fork truck was loaded and tied down. Carl drove the truck away from the warehouse and breathed a sigh of relief. None of the workers had noticed or asked about any discrepancy in the depths of the truck's box.

CHAPTER 6

Preparing for War

Glenn Wiggs walked up Bienville Street in New Orleans, and in the middle of the 800 Block, he spotted the name of the restaurant etched in the glass panel above the front door. A tiled, inlaid plaque confirmed the name above: Arnaud's Main Entrance, which directed him through the double doors crafted from heavy oak timber with a frosted glass panel centered in each door.

Arnaud's had been a flagship of New Orleans restaurants since 1918. Glenn had been to the restaurant once before when he was governor of Arkansas. He remembered it as one of the best dining experiences he had ever had, although he thought he probably wasted at least part of the experience since he did not go to its famous bar for the exotic drinks and fine cigars.

He pulled the door open and walked into the foyer, where he was greeted by the maître d', who looked as if he might have just gotten off the plane from Paris and went straight to work. He stood only about five feet six and was slender to the point of almost skinny. His hair was shiny black with a sharp, receding hairline on each side, and the pencil mustache matched the jelled hair, combed straight back, with no part.

"Good evening, sir. Would you like a table, and how many will be in your party?"

"My name is Wiggs, and I believe we have a private room reserved under the name Boudreau."

Without referring to any notes, the maître d' replied, "Indeed, Mr. Wiggs. I am Jason, and we have been expecting you. If you will follow me, I will show you to your room. Some of your party has already arrived."

Glenn followed the maître d' down a hallway toward the back of the restaurant. Just before going out into the courtyard, which every respectable restaurant in New Orleans had, Jason turned to the right and opened a door. Arnaud's had fourteen private dining rooms, and this one was small but adequate. A round table was centered in the room with six chairs evenly spaced. Two men and a woman were already seated at the table, and they rose to greet Glenn.

Glenn walked around the table and shook hands with Clint Parker, Amos Boudreau, and the woman whom he had never met. Clint Parker did the introduction. "Governor Glenn Wiggs, I'd like you to say hello to Sarah Goodwin. Sarah will be acting as secretary during our meetings and managing the commission's office here in New Orleans."

The heavy oak door opened again, and two men entered. Bill Gooding, chairman of the board of Real Southern Fried, a multistate chain of restaurants, and Chester Abernathy, an attorney from Pass Christian, Mississippi. Pass Christian is an exclusive small residential community in the Gulfport-Biloxi area. Everyone shook hands, and as if on cue, a waiter entered the room and asked if he could take drink orders. The other four men ordered cocktails, and Sarah Goodwin and Glenn ordered a glass of white wine.

Clint Parker opened the meeting. "Good morning, everyone, I think all of you have had a chance to get acquainted. We have name tents that will direct you to your seat, and if you all don't already know one another, that will help stick the name in your memory. I'm Clint Parker, FBI agent based in Little Rock, and the gentleman seated to my left is my counterpart in New Orleans, Amos Boudreau. To begin with, I'm going to put some statistics on the screen to give each of you a full picture of the problem you're going to be dealing with."

The slide presentation presented each of the past five years in side-by-side columns. The categories were drug-related arrests in each of the three states, Louisiana, Mississippi, and Arkansas. The members were further broken down by the dollar size of the bust, individual hustlers on the street, arrests by local cops, raids on distribution centers, and interdiction raids on incoming shipments, including boats and airplanes along the Gulf Coast.

Chet Abernathy raised his hand. "Looks like the number of boats apprehended coming into the coast have declined, while a growing number of planes are being found along the coast. Would one of you like to educate us about how that has occurred and if it's important?"

Clint Parker stepped back to the microphone at the podium. "The answer to the last part of your question is yes, and the first part is more complicated. I'm going to have Amos come up and address the first part of your question."

Boudreau walked to the podium with a three-ring binder in his hand. "The answer to the first part of your question is multifaceted and calls for a brief history lesson on some of the activities we have been encountering along the gulf. Ever since drug smuggling became a significant problem in the US 48, the coast guard has played a prominent role in intersecting and apprehending."

Boudreau continued, "The methods used by the smugglers have ranged from large pleasure boats coming into harbors along each of the two states of Louisiana and Mississippi, as well as Florida. When it appeared we had that method coming under control, the importers shifted to high-speed boats that initially could outrun the coast guard. The coast guard bought faster boats, but we have learned that the cartels are nothing if not creative, thus the airplanes we are now finding throughout the Everglades.

"Another commission like this was organized a few years back, and it focused primarily on Florida and a couple of states to the north. We have asked that they share their information with you, and you with them, to compare incidents and detect any connections that would be helpful to both groups.

"As the coast guard and the FBI became more successful in pursuing the pleasure boat activity, the cartels shifted to high-speed, shallow draft boats that often outran the coast guard, and then the boats were beached on remote stretches of coastline and off-loaded into vehicles. That method was abandoned pretty much after the coast guard simply bought new and faster boats.

"The latest technique seems to be the use of older DC-3s and similar kinds of airplanes. The DC-3s were the workhorse airplane during the latter half of World War II, and Douglas Aircraft had become very good at manufacturing them, lots of them. Then, when the war ended, there were more DC-3s than people could find uses for. Some were used to start up new commuter-type airlines, and after a few years of that kind of use, they were still good machines. And the next market was primarily in Latin America, where they were very effective at flying freight into the backcountry areas where the runways were often short and the mountains tall.

"When the market value for these planes became cheap enough, the drug cartels spotted them as an ideal way to haul large cargoes that justified writing the planes off on a one-way trip. Their pilots have become pretty successful in avoiding radar while crossing the gulf and performing controlled crash landings in the marshlands along the Gulf Coast, especially in the Florida Everglades and the bayous adjacent to the mouth of the Mississippi River. The cargo is then off-loaded from the wrecked plane into either airboats and/or ground vehicles that can successfully move through the swamps."

Glenn Wiggs raised his hand, and Amos Boudreau nodded toward him. "Glenn."

"This is all good information for us to know, but I think you need to tell us what kind of actions this group will take to assist you and other agencies in the field."

At this point, Clint Parker stood and turned to the group. "We'll be getting specific requests from Washington as we go along, but at this point, it's important that you gentlemen understand your value to this effort. First, all of you are very active in your communities, your state, and the entire southeast region. Your backgrounds and present activities equip you with a unique understanding of the nature of this problem and the steps we need to take to get it under control. Glenn had a taste of law enforcement after becoming governor of Arkansas and demonstrated his commitment to the cause then and presently. I'm sure most of you are familiar with the Orville Carson episode in Arkansas.

"Bill Gooding has been a strong supporter of law enforcement and clean government everywhere he has opened new restaurants, and Chet Abernathy has made his reputation dealing with the federal grand jury out of Biloxi."

Amos Boudreau was rejoined by Clint at the head of the table. "A press release will be issued from Washington, DC, following our meeting today. It will announce the formation of this commission with brief biographies on each of the members. This publicity will help this commission and the staff working with you attract attention. You'll all get the usual pat on the back for good work from your leading citizens, but it's our hope that you'll also be contacted by citizens aware of activities they want this commission to know about. Initially, your duties will be to collect information of known or suspected criminal activities in the tristate areas then, through investigation, boil that information down to proven or disproven status and, finally, to recommend action to law enforcement groups as well as to legislative groups recommending action that may need to be taken and to formulate new laws needed to deal with the identified problems."

The rest of the meeting dealt mostly with the minutia that accompanies every government operation. Glenn was confirmed as chairman of the commission and Sarah Goodwin as secretary while serving as office manager in the New Orleans office. A three-inch binder was presented to each of the commission members that summarized the current areas of concern on the part of the FBI. Protocol for day-to-day communications was reviewed, and everyone agreed they would have their next meeting in one week.

CHAPTER 7

Carl Hoffman picked up speed as he climbed the ramp up to the bridge over the Mississippi River into Arkansas. The fork truck was tied down in the back and seemed to be riding okay; that was one thing the crew at the warehouse didn't screw up. He was still pissed off at the dockworker that moved the steel ramp in place from the dock to his truck. He had misjudged the alignment and slid the plate under the truck, taking out a taillight on the right rear. It was daylight now, and Carl didn't think it would be a big deal; he'd get it fixed in New Orleans after he unloaded.

It was near noon on Friday, and Carl was surprised that the traffic was as heavy as it seemed to be. Summer tourists, he guessed, trying to get to the coast for the weekend or maybe over to Baton Rouge and New Orleans for a little riverboat gambling. He held the truck steady at sixty, occasionally having to pass a slower car but mostly staying even with the traffic. It was about one thirty in the afternoon, and he hadn't eaten since the little amount of breakfast he'd had, and he started looking for a place to go off the road. Five miles later, he saw a sign for a Stuckey's. You couldn't go far in the south without finding a Stuckey's restaurant and gas stop. As he neared the exit, he touched the brakes to slow down and turned on his right signal.

The car immediately in front of Carl decided at the last minute that he too needed to get off here. He cut quickly in front of Carl to get on the off-ramp. Carl had to use his brakes again to avoid bumping into the damn fool. In the parking lot, the car went straight ahead into a parking slot for restaurant patrons. Carl took one of the bigger slots for the truck in the second row of parking. He shut off the motor and hit the door lock button as he stepped down from the cab.

A voice from behind startled him. "Hold up there a minute, fella!"

Carl did a one-eighty turn and saw an Arkansas State Police car had pulled in behind the truck, and the driver was just exiting the car. "Are you talking to me, Officer?"

The patrolman adjusted his cowboy hat as he approached. "Yes, sir, I'm talking to you. You got your driver's license and papers on the truck handy? Oh, and if you're carrying cargo, I need to see a bill of lading."

"Well, I'm not carrying any real cargo, but I do have a fork truck back there that I'm taking back to New Orleans, and I got a bill for it. What's the problem? Did I do something wrong?"

"You came pretty close to bumping that car on the off-ramp, and I noticed that you have a taillight out and the signal didn't work when you got off. Were you aware you had a busted tail and signal light?"

Carl's face flushed with anger. "Yeah, I'm aware. Some stupid asshole at the dock hit it with a steel plate that he used to drive the fork truck into my cargo hold. I need to be back in New Orleans before five, so I was going to wait till I get there to fix it."

The patrolman studied Carl's facial expressions and saw his nervousness. *What the hell*, he thought. *Lots of guys get nervous when a uniform approaches them.* "You want to get the back door open and let me have a look?"

Carl stepped up on the back bumper and rolled the door open then stepped down and away. "Like I told you, that's the only cargo I'm hauling today."

"What kind of cargo do you usually haul?"

Carl hesitated then said, "Uh . . . fish. Seafood, that kind of stuff."

The patrolman looked at Carl's license and the receipt for the fork truck and looked up at Carl. "I'm just going to give you a warning ticket today. You're left taillight and brake light are working okay, but if you get into an accident because of that broken right light, you're gonna have serious troubles. You better not put off getting that light fixed very long."

Carl's head was bent down with a hangdog look on his face. "No, sir, I understand. I'll get it fixed right away."

The highway patrolman took one last look inside the truck and seemed satisfied that everything except the taillight was in order. He handed the papers and the license back to Carl and said, "Okay, I think we understand each other. Y'all have a nice day."

Inside Stuckey's, Carl ordered a hot dog and a Pepsi and nervously ate his lunch. As he drove out of the restaurant / truck stop area, he looked both ways and saw no sign of the state patrol. He relaxed as he headed for New Orleans.

* * *

Driving the opposite direction, Arkansas State trooper Stan Murphy glanced at the clock in his dash and saw that his tour only had an hour and a half to go. Murphy had been with the Arkansas State Police for nearly four years, and he was still learning new techniques and sharpening the skills he had been taught from the beginning. He was very intuitive, and his training sergeant had told him before his training completed that his intuition was something he did not create and could not control. However, the sergeant had urged him to pay attention to his intuition. The best police officers often add a sense of intuition to a greater or lesser degree. The trick was to learn how to read the intuitions. Sometimes they were right, and sometimes they were wrong, but he should always acknowledge them.

The image of the fish truck would not go out of his mind. He didn't see anything wrong, but he knew there was something. He was just tired, he thought. Even though his eyes didn't see anything wrong, his brain did. A good night's sleep and tomorrow it would come to him.

At the patrol station just south of Little Rock, Stan Murphy checked in his patrol car, wrote his reports, and called his wife, Alice. "You can start dinner, honey. I'm on my way home and am pretty beat, but tell Ricky I'll play Lego with him when I get there."

* * *

It was 6:30 p.m. when Stan Murphy pulled into his driveway, punched the remote button on his sun visor, and pulled into his garage. Most of the time, his job was not tiring, at least not in the physical sense. He had made up his mind in high school that he would work in law enforcement at some level. After graduating from high school in Little Rock, he enrolled in the law enforcement curriculum at the community college. Stan wasn't a mental giant, but he would rank in the top twenty-five percentile, and with hard work and long study hours, he pulled a B+ average and received his degree.

Stan and Alice met during his junior year, and after two or three dates, they both knew they would make their future together. Alice was one year younger and wanted to get her degree in education, so they postponed any wedding plans. Stan went to all the law enforcement agencies—sheriff, city police in Little Rock and all its suburbs, and the state police. It didn't take long, although it seemed like it did at the time, before he got the call from the Arkansas State Police. They had an opening for patrolman, and he would be based in the Little Rock area. After he finished his training, he was assigned as patrolman for an area southeast of the city, the district patrol office along the interstate south of town, and his patrol car became his workplace.

Glenn Wiggs was still governor when Stan joined the patrol, and the high standards that Governor Wiggs had infused into the state police was obvious to Stan and prompted him to do his job as well or better than any other patrolman in the state.

He and Alice were married shortly after her graduation. She took a job in an elementary school in the southeast area of Little Rock, teaching first graders. She took great pride in the fact that she was preparing young minds to become responsible and well-informed adults. The kids loved her!

They postponed having children, and between the two salaries, they were able to establish a respectable savings account at the bank. Eventually, they began talking about buying a house, and it didn't take long to find the three-bedroom, two-bath ranch with a two-car garage. Moving into their own house gave them a huge shot of pride and satisfaction that they had their lives going in the right direction. It was about three years later that they decided it was time to add to the family. Ricky was born a year later.

Stan went through the door from the garage into the kitchen, and Alice turned from the stove to greet him. "Hi, handsome. Welcome home." She put her arms around him and kissed him to confirm the welcome then leaned back and asked, "Did you remember to get milk?"

"Do you think I would forget something as important as milk? How's our son going to grow up and be a star football player at ASU if he doesn't drink lots of milk? Is he in his room?"

Alice turned back to the stove to resume preparations for dinner. "No, he has his construction toys in the living room. The last time I checked him, he had built a truck stop, a state police headquarters, and was in the process of putting the wheels on a truck. You better go see if he needs any help."

Stan walked into the living room and was amazed at the mess as well as the success Ricky was having in constructing a scene that would connect him with the job his daddy went to every day. Ever since he was two or three years old, he had expressed an interest in where Stan went each day to do his work. For the last two years, it had become a routine for him and Stan to review the day's activities, so it was not surprising to see the things he was creating with his toy kits. Truck stops and patrol headquarters were symbolic to Ricky of what his dad did and where he went.

"Hi, buddy! Whatcha building?"

Ricky jumped to his feet and ran to Stan and leapt into his arms. After a big hug and a kiss on his forehead, Stan set Ricky down and turned his attention on to the construction.

Stan and Ricky reviewed all the details and challenges involved in the project. Ricky explained the process and the importance of each feature of the buildings right up to the gas pumps at the truck stop. Ricky picked up a truck and held it out to Stan for his examination. "I'm not finished with the truck, Dad, but he has to get some gas."

Stan inspected the truck and was impressed at the job Ricky had done on the assembly. "This is a great truck, Ricky, but I don't understand why this wall of the truck is there." The sidewalls in the wall on each end of the truck bed were properly done, but then another wall went across the truck a few inches back from the front. "What is this wall for?"

Ricky looked down and studied his feet for a few seconds and then looked up. "I put it in the wrong place, Dad, and then I put it in the right place but didn't take the wrong one out. After I put in the right one, I couldn't get the wrong one out without taking it all apart."

Stan smiled knowingly at his son and was reminded that patience was not one of his strong virtues. "Do you want me to help you take the wrong wall out?"

"Yeah, Dad, that would be great!"

In less than a minute, Stan had removed the interior wall and put the pieces back on, completing the outer wall of the truck. "What about the top, Ricky? Are you going to put a top on it?"

A serious look from Ricky and he said, "I want to put a top on it, Dad, but I haven't figured out how yet. Will you help me?"

Stan got down on the floor and, in short order, figured out how to put the top on the truck. Ricky was happy and looked at his dad with a look that every dad wants from their son: sheer, unadulterated pride.

"Dinner's ready!" Alice called out from the kitchen, and the father and son headed for the table.

After dinner, the family went back into the living room. Ricky went back to the truck stop, and Alice and Stan sat in matching stuffed chairs with a lamp between them and began their usual recapping of the day each of them had experienced. Alice had stopped teaching because they both agreed that Ricky would progress much better in the care of a parent than in the custody of a day care center operator. Alice loved her young son, and she took great pride in operating her one-student classroom five days a week.

Stan was giving Alice a rundown on his day's routine and had just come to the part where he had pulled the truck over at the Stuckey's truck stop. Ricky heard the words *truck stop* and immediately picked up his truck and showed it to his mom and explained how his dad had fixed the bad wall.

Alice responded in typical schoolteacher mode, interested in each detail and looking over the parts of the truck as Ricky talked.

Suddenly, Stan set forward in his chair and looked at the truck in his wife's hands. "Well, I'll be! Ricky, you have just helped me solve a dilemma that I came home from work with in my head."

Alice frowned. "What is it, Stan?"

"I was just starting to tell you about the truck that I followed off the interstate into the Stuckey's. The driver came to my attention because he didn't put on his signal light when he turned off the highway, and then a driver ahead of him made a delayed decision to get off at the exit and swerved in front of the truck. I could tell by the movement of the truck that the driver applied his brakes, but just like the signal light, the brake light didn't come on. So I followed him into the parking lot, and as we are supposed to, I did a cursory inspection of the truck to see if there were any other infractions that needed to be addressed. The only cargo he was carrying was a fork truck that was properly tied down, and I let the driver go with a warning ticket to get the light fixed. I left him and the truck and went back on patrol, and then my shift ended shortly and I drove back to the station. The strange part was, after I left Stuckey's, I kept thinking about the truck and that something didn't seem right. But I had not seen anything irregular and I kept thinking about it until I checked out of my shift. I couldn't reconcile my thoughts to what my eyes had seen until now."

Alice smiled. "And Ricky helped you figure out your dilemma?"

Stan put his hands under his chin, steepling his forefingers while he ran the pictures back through his mind. "I think so. I think the incongruity of the view inside the truck matched against the outside of the truck was the difference in dimension. I can't say for sure because I didn't measure it, but I'm pretty certain that the depth of the box inside was shorter than the dimension of the box on the outside. That by itself wouldn't break any law, but it would sure prompt me and any law enforcement officer to investigate further and find out why such a difference would exist."

Alice commented, "Could it have to do with special equipment that needed to be separated from the cargo and that equipment might be built in to the space in front?"

Stan smiled at his wife and replied, "It could be, but I don't think so. It was a refrigerated truck, marked Latin Imports, and the refrigeration units were mounted on the top. Anyway, I didn't check it, so I will probably never know, and it probably isn't anything important."

However, Stan resolved to himself that tomorrow he was going to put that information as an amendment to his report.

CHAPTER 8

The next morning, Stan Murphy was at his desk, writing his additional notes to his report of the previous day. One of the young cadets in training to become a patrolman walked up to his desk with a sheaf of papers in his hand and laid one on Stan's desk. Glancing at the paper, Stan saw it was a copy of a bulletin from the FBI. A hunch prompted him to stop his typing and read the bulletin:

> Please be advised that as of this date, a federal task force has been appointed by the president of the United States for the purpose of investigating and prosecuting individuals and organizations involved in smuggling and/or distributing illegal drugs into the United States. The scope of this commission will include the states of Arkansas, Mississippi, and Louisiana. FBI agents Clint Parker, Little Rock, Arkansas, and Amos Boudreau, New Orleans, Louisiana, have been attached to the commission. Any law enforcement officer in the tristate area possessing information or suspecting behavior connected with the activities stated above should contact one of our agents in Little Rock and/or New Orleans and report your suspicions to them.

Early in his teen years, Stan Murphy had wanted to be a police officer. While in high school, he had paid special attention to the stories covering the raid on Orville Carson's farm. The first stories covered the sensation of Orville blowing his head off in his home as an army of law enforcement people converged on his front door. However, the Little Rock paper continued to follow the story and revealed many of the details of how Carson had recruited workers and then held them virtual prisoners for decades. This type of slave labor had enabled Orville Carson to build one of the biggest dirt-farming empires in the South. This story had become the single most important motivation that made Stan Murphy committed to getting an education and pursuing law enforcement as his profession.

Clint Parker, at that time Sheriff Parker, was a prominent figure in that investigation. Since then Stan had always followed the activities of Parker and was aware of his moving to the FBI a number of years back. They had never met in person, but Stan felt as if he knew Parker and was very comfortable in approaching him with his story.

"Is agent Clint Parker available?" Stan Murphy collected his thoughts as he waited for Parker to come on the phone.

The polite voice responded, "Yes, may I tell him who's calling?"

"This is patrolman Stan Murphy with the Arkansas State Police. I have some information I'd like to share with him."

The thirty seconds it took for Clint Parker to come on the phone seemed longer to Stan. "Agent Parker here, how can I help you?"

"Yes, this is Stan Murphy. I'm a patrolman for the Arkansas Highway Patrol. I was just looking at an announcement regarding the creation of the new crime commission. I don't know whether it will amount to anything or not, but I had an experience yesterday, and I was just including it in my daily report when I saw the announcement regarding the commission. I decided I should pass this information on to you and you decide whether it's of use to you or not."

For the next few minutes, patrolman Murphy recited the details of his experience at Stuckey's truck stop the previous day.

Clint Parker chuckled when Stan Murphy covered the part involving his son Ricky's mistake while assembling his toy truck.

"Well, Stan, I really appreciate your thinking on this matter. It could be something important, and as you say, it might not be important at all. Why don't you check with your commander there and then send me a copy of your report? I'll run that information by the commission and my counterpart in New Orleans. We'll check out Latin Imports and see who they are and how long they've been around. We'll keep you and the state police informed if and when we have any results."

Stan Murphy had a proud grin on his face. "I really appreciate it, Mr. Parker. I've been a fan of yours for many years, and when I discussed this with my CO, he recommended that I take this action and pass along the information to the FBI. It would be very much appreciated if I were informed if anything develops from the information. I'll get a copy of my report off to you right away. Thanks again." Stan Murphy hung up his phone and gave himself a mental pat on the back.

* * *

Clint Parker stared at the phone after he hung up. He didn't know patrolman Murphy, but he thought he recognized a seriousness and conscientious motivation just from Murphy's voice. "He didn't sound like a young police officer trying to score points with the FBI," Clint Parker murmured to himself as he picked the phone back up and dialed the New Orleans office.

Amos Boudreau had a similar reaction after Clint relayed the conversation with Stan Murphy. "It sounds like a story that just might have legs!" Boudreau said after Clint had finished. "I'll do a check on Gulf Imports, poke the snake with a long stick, and see if it moves."

They ended the call, and for a while, Clint Parker stared at the phone while his brain sorted through his thoughts and filed them in order.

While his brain was still filtering through the ideas that had emerged, he reached back to the phone and dialed a Little Rock number. "Good morning. Arkansas Bureau of Investigation, how may I help you?"

Clint Parker put on his official voice. "This is Agent Parker with the FBI office here in Little Rock. Is Ken Kondraky available?"

Clint continued to assemble his thoughts, and then he heard the familiar voice. "Hey, Clint, it's good to hear from you again. How goes the battle in the big league?"

"Like you well know, Ken, it's kind of like the Chinese two-step, two steps forward and one step backward, but when I complain about it, my boss reminds me that I am making progress as long as the order doesn't reverse and I am taking two steps backward and one forward."

"Truer words were never spoken, Clint, but I sometimes think I'm having more days where it's two steps back and one forward. Anyway, how can a lowly little state employee help you today?"

"I was thinking that if you had time, I'd like to buy you lunch and catch up on old times and talk a little bit about current affairs."

Kondraky chuckled and said, "My mama taught me to never turn down a free meal unless I didn't like or trust the person paying the bill. I think she would approve if the cost of my lunch was going on Uncle Sam's expense account."

Clint replied, "I don't think Uncle Sam would disagree with your mother's philosophy. Is your diet okay with some genuine, down-home cooking?"

Kondraky responded, "To heck with my diet, I'll just worry about my bathroom scales. I've had that scale a long time, and I'm trying hard not to break it and have to buy a new one."

"If you're available today, how about meeting at the Real Southern Fried on East Wallace Street, say, one o'clock?"

CHAPTER 9

Clint Parker arrived at the restaurant at his usual five minutes early. This had become a habit over the years, and the longer he was in law enforcement, the more he understood how important that habit was. He was shown to a booth at the very back of the restaurant. He sat where he was facing the door and would spot Ken Kondraky's arrival, and when he saw him walk in at one o'clock sharp, Clint waved him back to the booth.

For the first ten minutes or so, the two men exchanged small talk, and of course, they had to talk about the Orville Carson case. Ken Kondraky gave Clint a current update on the aftermath of the sensational case. "As far as I could tell, it all boiled down to he said, she said, they said. The black boy, Sammy, who turned himself in and exposed all of the bad deeds, still got sent to prison for ten years, but he got out after five for good behavior. No proof was ever brought forward against Ham Turner, but I was pretty surprised when he joined the Arkansas Bureau of Investigation. I'm not sure who engineered that appointment, but I'm a lot more careful these days about whom I discuss things with and what I say."

Clint picked up on Kondraky's comments. "So you think somebody exercised some influence and pulled a string or two to get Turner into ABI?"

Ken Kondraky instinctively looked around the restaurant then spoke in a guarded manner. "It just didn't make sense to me at the time. We weren't short on staff, and there was no effort being made to hire new agents. We just showed up for staff meeting one Monday morning and there sat Ham Turner on the front row, and the boss introduced him as our newest agent. There's still no evidence that he has a specific set of duties assigned. I rank at least three or four in terms of seniority in the agency, and he rarely comes up on my radar. Three more years and I'll be eligible to have my ticket punched and then spend most my time trying to lower the bass population at Table Rock Lake. In the meantime, I'm trying to keep my nose clean and stay out of trouble."

The two men paused in their conversation and devoted an appropriate amount of time to consuming the fried chicken and grits with redeye gravy. Finally, Clint Parker looked up and asked, "Would it be too much trouble for you to get a look at his personnel file and see if it would tell you whom his sponsor might've been?"

Kondraky thought for a moment. "Probably not. The girl in charge of personnel has been there near as long as I have, and I've done her more than a couple favors through the years. I think she would get me the information."

Clint nodded and said, "If it's not too difficult for her to get copies, that would be a big favor and much appreciated."

As they finished lunch and a second cup of coffee, Clint sketched in the objectives of the commission, just in case anything interesting came across ABI's radar. Kondraky was a good cop and a team player. Having him in the loop couldn't hurt.

They finished lunch and walked out into the afternoon sun, shaking hands before they went to their respective cars.

Kondraky had estimated he would get back to Clint in a day or two with the documents. The conversation had not followed the path Clint had in mind, but he welcomed the opportunity to look closer at Mr. Turner. He had been a rogue law enforcement officer, performing tasks for Orville Carson that was, at best, unethical and, Clint suspected, illegal. He was positive that information on the sponsors of Ham Turner, who put him into the ABI, would be very welcomed by the commission and the FBI. It was a good lunch, and he felt sure good things were going to come out of it.

Clint was having a good drive back to his office—good country music was coming out of the radio—and he felt so good he was humming along with it. The traffic light up ahead turned red, and he came to a stop. The Cotton Belt Bank was just ahead in the next block, and Clint stopped humming when he saw a man and woman come out of the side door of the bank and walk into the parking lot. A second man was walking just behind them, and they all turned to shake hands and say good-bye.

Clint recognized Blake Stevens and his female companion, Gabrielle Fleming. He also recognized the man that was bidding them farewell in a most friendly manner: Ross Mathews, senior vice president of the bank.

There was nothing unusual about a customer being friendly with his banker, but what pushed Clint's curiosity button was, he'd never been aware of a connection between Cotton Belt Bank and Blake Stevens.

Clint Knew Blake had an account at Little Rock State Bank for the casino and hotel and that his partners worked with banks in Memphis and New Orleans. The connection was probably nothing, but he would just file this away for future reference.

If Clint had parked his car and observed the scene longer, he might have noticed a late-model tan Chevrolet parked across the street from the bank parking lot. The driver was looking directly at the two men outside the bank as he slowly raised a camera with a telephoto lens, and when he had the focus adjusted, he pressed the button and began recording the two men shaking hands and saying good-bye. Satisfied he had all he needed, the man laid the camera in the driver's seat, checked his watch, and made some notes on a pad and ended his surveillance. He was sure his employers would be pleased with his work this morning.

* * *

It was midmorning, and Mabel Thompson was supposed to be on coffee break; instead, she had brought a thermos from home and had carried it into the records vault from her desk. Most of the people from the surrounding desks were downstairs in the break room, affording Mabel an opportunity to pull Ham Turner's personnel file without explaining the activity to her superior, Ken Kondraky. Ken had treated her well since she joined the Arkansas Bureau of Investigation twelve years ago.

Ken was a dedicated professional and recognized Mabel's diligence and attention to detail. Ken was primarily responsible for her current job, personnel records librarian, and if he wanted information on Ham Turner, whom Mabel considered well below ABI's standards, what could it harm?

Mabel found the file and flipped through it until she came to the application and attending page of notes confirming his hiring. Turner had listed a Donald Simmons of New Orleans as a personal reference. A note on the attached page said "Simmons ++," and the initials next to the note was BC.

Must be Bruce Caldwell, Mabel thought to herself. *Wonder why Kondraky is interested and doesn't just talk to Caldwell instead of having me pilfer the file.* The *why* wasn't important since Ken Kondraky had always been someone Mabel could go to for advice and treat their exchanges confidential. She had learned that such a contact was very valuable in a law enforcement organization.

Mabel stepped to the copy machine and printed one copy of each page. She folded the copies and slid them inside her blouse and returned the file to its correct place in the four-drawer file cabinet and returned to her desk.

At 11:40 a.m., Mabel's phone buzzed. "Mabel, it's Ken Kondraky, and I thought if you didn't have plans, we might have lunch. Are you available?"

* * *

Carol's Garden was a nonpretentious restaurant featuring food like you might eat at home. The exceptions were its fresh-baked rolls and its private garden with tables scattered among its dwarfed trees and vine-covered lattice partitions. They both ordered the soup-and-sandwich special and iced tea. As Mabel placed her napkin, she retrieved the folded papers and slid them toward Kondraky.

Kondraky quickly scanned the sheets, stopping at the name and then the initials. "I really appreciate this, Mabel, and if this ever comes out, your name will not be connected in any way. You can trust me."

"I do trust you, Mr. Kondraky. I think you are one of the most trustworthy people at ABI, and I have no concern about giving you this information. I don't want to lose my job, but if I were to be concerned about someone, it would be the man, or men, in that paperwork."

"You're a good lady, Mabel. Now you just go on about your work and don't think about or worry about what just happened. I don't think it will be necessary, however, if I need any further assistance, I will call you."

CHAPTER 10

Glenn Wiggs had just walked into the conference room on the top floor of the federal building in New Orleans. He shook hands with Bill Gooding and Chester Abernathy and waved a hello to Clint Parker and Amos Boudreau, who were standing at the head of the conference table. He finished his greetings with the two members of the anticrime commission and walked forward to greet Parker and Boudreau.

Wiggs spoke to the two FBI agents. "It's a beautiful day in the Big Easy. You boys got a good meeting lined up for us?"

Clint Parker smiled as he shook hands with Wiggs. "We do have some new information, Glenn, and a couple of new faces to introduce to you."

Glenn turned as two young men in uniform walked in the door. The uniforms were different in color but similar in tailoring and features. The flat-brimmed hats identified both as state police. They removed their hats as they walked up to Parker and Boudreau, who introduced them to Glenn. "Gentleman, I want you to meet Mr. Glenn Wiggs, former governor of Arkansas and current chairman of our commission. Governor, this is Stan Murphy, Arkansas State Patrol, and Sonny Swofford, Mississippi State Police."

The men shook hands and greeted one another. Bill Gooding and Chester Abernathy joined the group and were introduced.

"Okay, gentlemen, I believe we all know one another and we have added two chairs to the conference table, so let's take our seats and get started. I think everyone knows I am Clint Parker, and this is my associate, Amos Boudreau. Amos is the resident agent in New Orleans for the bureau, and I am based in the Little Rock office.

"If you open the binders in front of you, we'll start with a review of information we have developed since our last meeting. I will welcome our two new members. Stan and Sonny each bring a record of exemplary service to their respective commands. We'll hear from each of them shortly. But I want to impress on all of us that these two men are going to be our eyes on the ground in the two states of Mississippi and Arkansas.

"On page 3 in your binder, you will see a few names that we have identified as persons of interest. The lawyers insist we don't call them suspects until we have more-specific information on them. The purpose of this commission is to determine the individuals and methods used to bring illegal drugs into the continental United States and distribute them for sale. Right now, I want Stan Murphy to tell us about an incident that he experienced just a few days ago on the highway between New Orleans and Memphis."

Stan Murphy stood from his seat and gave everyone a glimpse of what he looked like to a motorist he would pull over on one of the highways of Arkansas—six feet, one inch tall, 205 pounds of well-developed and toned muscles. His hair was dark brown and cut short, and his deep dark-brown eyes projected an ability to see right through an individual he might be addressing.

"Five days ago, I was on patrol just south of Little Rock, moving with the traffic. Two vehicles ahead of me, I saw a light truck with a short cargo box, and as we approached the Stuckey's truck stop, he began to slow and prepare to turn off the highway. It was then that I noticed his right signal was not working and only his left brake light was burning. I followed him off the exit and into the Stuckey's lot. When I questioned him, he said a dockworker in Memphis that morning had trouble loading a fork truck for him to haul back to New Orleans and had broken the light fixture. I followed normal procedure and proceeded to inspect the rest of the truck. When he pulled up the back door, I saw that he had one fork truck for his cargo. It was tied down properly, and everything looked pretty normal. He promised he would stop at the next exit and have a new light installed on his truck. I explained the dangers of operating a truck without proper lighting and let him proceed.

"I finished my tour and went home for dinner. My young son was playing with his tinker toys and Lincoln Logs, and he had built a truck. He had made a mistake initially on where to put the front wall of the cargo bed of the truck. To correct his mistake, he had simply put in a second wall ahead of the first one. As I explained the problem he had created for the truck, the image of the truck with the broken taillight came back in my head. As I thought about it, it was that discrepancy that bothered me for the rest of my patrol. When I had looked at the truck from the inside, I realized that it looked remarkably different from the outside because the two walls of the front of the box did not line up at the same place. A few days before, we had gotten a bulletin regarding trucks that might be used to transport illegal cargo. I called Clint Parker and reported the incident to him. Since that time, I was selected to work with this commission, and I must say, I am very happy to be doing so."

Amos Boudreau took over the meeting and reviewed the names on page 3 of the handout. "Frederick Sanchez is the registered owner of the Jolly Roger Bar and Grill in New Orleans. Deed records indicate he also owns a residence in St. Mary Parish, an area that is mostly bayous and fishing shacks. Sanchez has lived in New Orleans for the last five years. He has a record with the New Orleans Police Department consisting mostly of minor infractions around the operation of the bar and grill. One charge of rape, which was dropped, because the witness never came forward to testify."

Boudreau continued his report, "Orlando Perez emigrated from Mexico four years ago. He has a record with the NOPD that includes assault with a deadly weapon—seems he prefers a knife—possession with intent to sell cocaine, and is listed by the Jolly Roger as an employee but doesn't seem to be there very often. Carl Hoffman, the driver of the truck in Stan Murphy's report. Until a month ago, Hoffman worked as a deckhand on a Mississippi barge line. So far, we have been unable to establish an address for Hoffman. He served in the United States Army in Korea. Had some minor incidents on his record: disorderly conduct, a bar fight, and a general problem of not accepting authority. He drove a truck carrying supplies from airfields and ports to forward bases in South Korea. That's all I have so far. Clint?"

Clint Parker motioned toward Sonny Swofford, who stood to address the group. "I was appointed to this commission forty-eight hours ago and was told to come here to this meeting today. I have nothing of any substance to add except that a fellow patrolman responding to an alert that went out last week regarding Latin Imports trucks called me and reported that he did a courtesy stop on Friday last week on a truck pulled over to the side with a flat tire. The driver insisted he had everything under control and had a mobile tire repair truck on its way. The officer did not do an inspection or issue any citation, but he did note the driver's name from his license. The name the officer passed on to me was Samson Belou, and the name on the side of the truck was Latin Imports. If they're using the main federal highway from New Orleans to Memphis and repeatedly running the same trucks, we should get another shot at them soon."

Clint Parker spoke up, "If they're using the Latin Imports trucks to deliver from New Orleans to Memphis, we should have southbound sightings noted and reported but not stopped. Let's do the stops on the northbound traffic, where we are more likely to find what were looking for without causing any panic on their part. Amos and I will amend our alert to that effect."

Boudreau cut in, "One more item. FYI, our alerts will be limited to the people in this room, the commander of the state police in Mississippi, Arkansas, and Louisiana, and you are cautioned not to discuss the content of the alerts with anyone in other agencies. We must assume that the tentacles of this group may be larger and longer than we first thought."

The meeting ended, and everyone headed for home except Amos Boudreau, Clint Parker, and Glenn Wiggs.

Clint Parker said, "Glenn, what's the progress on Ham Turner? Have you gotten the information back from Kondraky?"

"He called me yesterday afternoon and said he had the information we were looking for. I met him earlier this morning, and he gave me copies of paperwork from Turner's personnel file." Glenn unfolded the papers he had removed from his jacket pocket. "You'll have to forgive the condition of the papers. The clerk who made the copies and brought them out of the ABI office was pretty concerned that no one would discover what she was doing."

Clint Parker shuffled through the three pages. "This looks pretty damned incriminating to me. The freaking idiot actually listed Donald Summers as a character reference, and this one is a letter from Summers attesting to Ham's good character. The character reference letter is made out to the ABI and marked to the attention of Bruce Caldwell, assistant director. That indicates they have no clue that anyone is suspicious or investigating their connections."

Amos Boudreau gestured as he spoke, "We have to assume, though, that they could become suspicious at any time. I think we need to move quickly on Ham Turner and see how cooperative he may decide to be. Clint, you're the obvious one to go after him."

Parker nodded. "I'll call him in the morning and see if we can have lunch. I want him totally relaxed before I punch him back on his heels."

Glenn Wiggs smiled as he looked at Clint Parker. "If you need any help with the slimeball, give me a call."

Each man left the federal building with a feeling that his work was about to pay off and some justice was about to be delivered.

At 8:30 a.m. the following day, Clint Parker placed a call to the ABI office and asked for Ham Turner. It took a couple of minutes before Turner answered the call, and Clint was suspicious that they had to rouse him out of the coffee break room. *That's probably where he spends most of his day,* Clint thought.

"This is Turner here."

"Ham, this is Clint Parker over at the bureau office. How's the world treating you?"

There was hesitation in Turner's voice as he replied, "Ugh . . . yeah, Clint, I'm . . . ugh, doing okay. What's up with you?"

Clint Parker raised the level of his voice and the speed. "Nothing very exciting. In fact, I'm looking at a pretty clean desk and a slow day and the thought just occurred to me that you and I haven't had chance to talk and compare notes since you joined ABI. I thought maybe if you had the time, we could meet over some fried chicken and bring each other up-to-date on our crime-fighting duties."

Turner, looking for the right words, responded, "Ugh . . . well, yeah, Clint, I reckon I could find time in my busy schedule. It's always good for professional lawmen like you and me to get together and compare notes. When did you have in mind?"

"Like I said, Ham, I got a pretty light schedule today, and I could spare a couple of hours for lunch. You familiar with Charlie's Chicken House on Twelfth?"

"Yeah, Clint, I've never eaten there, but I know where it is."

Clint Parker replied, "They do a good job of making the chicken edible. If we meet there about one o'clock, we'll avoid the crowd. Allow an hour and a half just to be safe, and I'll see you there."

"Right, Clint, see you there, and thanks for the call." Ham Turner hung up his phone and looked at it for a long time. His mind was asking the right question: why me? Clint Parker had never given him the time of day, and in fact, during the problems at Carson Farms, Parker had been downright hostile. "Maybe he's going to give me a little more respect now that I'm with ABI," Ham muttered as he continued to study the telephone. His own comment made him feel a little better, but he still couldn't shake the uncertain feeling awakened by the unexpected call. Anyway, he thought a fried chicken dinner with all the trimmings sure beat the hell out of the bologna sandwich he had brought from home.

Clint Parker had arrived at the restaurant early, and as a result of the phone call he had made to Charlie's manager after hanging up from his call to Ham Turner, a reserved placard had been placed on a booth at the rear of the U-shaped dining room. At straight-up 1:00 p.m., Turner entered through the glass door and looked around until he saw Clint's wave from a booth in the back of the dining area.

Most of the lunch-hour customers had finished or were in the process of finishing their lunch, leaving only about half of the tables and booths occupied. Clint Parker stood as Turner approached the booth, shook hands, and invited him to have a seat.

Turner was alert to the courteous manner that Parker was using toward him, and it convinced him that this was just one professional treating another professional with the respect he deserved.

They each ordered the chicken lunch special, and both men opted for the grits and redeye gravy and iced tea to drink. When the tea was brought to the table, Clint Parker raised his glass in a toast and said, "Here's to law enforcement and the people who make it work!"

"I'll drink to that," Turner said and took a long swig of his tea. "I have to tell you, Clint, I was a little surprised when you called and asked me to lunch today. Who would have predicted that after our first meeting during the debacle at Carson Farms, you would wind up with the FBI, I would become an agent with the ABI, and that we would be having lunch like this today?"

Clint nodded his head in agreement. "Right on, Ham. It's hard to predict what turns a man's life is going to take. I got a lot of attention after Orville blew his brains out, and shortly thereafter, the FBI was looking for additional agents in the southeastern region. I went in and took all their tests and their interviews and was really happy when they decided to hire me. What led you to joining the ABI?"

Ham was momentarily caught off guard. "Well, ugh . . . I . . . ugh . . . was without work for a while after Carson Farms. I picked up odd jobs here and there to make ends meet, and then I heard that ABI had an opening. They seem pretty glad to see me when I made my application, and then in practically no time, they hired me. They needed me, and I needed them, so it just went pretty smooth."

Clint finished chewing a mouthful of chicken and said, "That's kind of surprising! Who made the decision to give you the job? I know most of the people over there."

Turner sat up a little straighter in his chair and smilingly said, "It was a top-level decision. You may be acquainted with Bruce Caldwell. He's the number-two man at ABI, and he personally brought me into the agency."

Clint pushed his plate back and wiped his mouth with a napkin. "Usually, these government agencies have pretty strict requirements for references. With your former employer being dead, where did you go for references?"

Turner's gaze went vacant for a moment, then he replied, "I don't recall that references were ever an issue. I suppose they were satisfied with the interviews and information I had furnished on my application."

Clint leaned across the table and, in a lowered voice, asked, "Did it help for a Mr. Donald Simmons to personally recommend you?"

"What the hell is this?" Turner gasped as he started to stand up from his chair. "Is this some fucking trick by the FBI to try to make me look bad or spread false rumors about me? What the hell do you mean inviting me to lunch and then start throwing accusations around?"

Clint held up his hand and spoke softly, "Sit back down, Ham, and calm yourself. You need to know that you are a person of interest in an FBI investigation. So far, I'm willing to assume that the method used in getting you appointed to the ABI is legit, compared to the scope of everything we're looking at in our investigation. If you were to choose to cooperate with our investigation, it's possible for you to avoid some severe consequences when we're finished."

Turner's face was red, and a pulse was visible in both of his temples. "I have no idea what you're getting at or accusing me of. If you're out to destroy me and my reputation, my attorney will sue the hell out of the FBI!"

Clint's voice remained calm and steady. "Ham, you need to calm down before you have a heart attack. Don't give me any bullshit about your reputation or your career as an outstanding law enforcement officer. Neither idea has any basis in fact. I'm not about to disclose to you how much we already know, but I think the little amount of law enforcement experience you have tells you that we have a lot, or I wouldn't be having this lunch with you. If you cooperate with our investigation by answering some questions, it's possible I can protect you and minimize the legal consequences you are facing. If on the other hand you decide to play it differently, you should be aware that once your benefactor discovers you are under suspicion, I wouldn't want to issue any new life insurance policies on you."

Ham Turner sat quietly for a long time, trying to understand what had just happened to him and how he was going to deal with it. His services to the organization in New Orleans had not required him to commit any felonious acts. However, he knew that the FBI loved to include people at his level into the conspiracy to commit a felony, and then the most minor actions had major consequences. But he had to have time to think.

He spoke in an uncharacteristically thin voice. "I have to talk to my attorney."

"You can talk to anyone you like, Turner, but I warn you, talking to anyone besides me is risky business. I'd bet a dollar to a hole in a doughnut that whomever you know to talk to, the boys in New Orleans know the same people, and I'll let you figure out who would command the most loyalty. You know my number. You've got twenty-four hours to get back to me."

Clint raised his left arm and looked at his watch. "That's two p.m. tomorrow!"

Ham Turner left the table and hurriedly walked out of the restaurant. Outside, on the sidewalk, Turner looked both directions as if he expected the devil himself to be bearing down on him.

Clint Parker left a generous tip on the table and went to the register to pay the tab.

As Ham Turner rushed to his car, frantically looking about for anyone that appeared suspicious, he failed to notice the man slumped behind the wheel of the gray Chevrolet sedan parked two spaces behind him. The driver had pulled his hat down over his face and appeared to be napping. After Turner got in his car and started the engine, the man with the hat started his engine, waited for a car to get between him and Turner, and pulled into the afternoon traffic.

Clint Parker drove directly to his office and placed a conference call to Glenn Wiggs and Amos Boudreau and briefed them on the meeting with Turner and advised them that he had another agent following Turner.

Clint spoke as if thinking out loud, "We'll keep Turner under surveillance for the next twenty-four hours and see if he decides to cooperate with us or not. If he runs, I'll have to decide whether to bring him in or continue to follow him. I'll keep you posted, and in the meantime, let's see what our highway patrol boys are going to come up with!"

CHAPTER 11

The truck's engine, mounted below his seat, was sending out a monotonous whine that worked on his nerve endings like a bow on a badly tuned violin. The night was very still and very dark, helping the pavement swallow the twin beams of light projecting from the cab-over truck. On both sides of the interstate highway in this section of Mississippi were huge rice fields that stretched as far as the eye could see in the daylight. These lands were controlled by large corporate farms and were normally prone to periodic flooding. Growing rice on the land was a no-brainer, and building houses on it was out of the question, unless you wanted your home to be a swimming pool part of the year. When nightfall came, this area was as black as a bucket of used oil.

Pierre Gaudet shifted in the driver seat and leaned forward over the steering wheel in an attempt to stop the road hypnosis that was starting to set in. He was two hours out of New Orleans, making his first run taking spoiled fish to the fertilizer factory on the Mississippi River in the south end of Memphis. The special cargo was in the front compartment of his truck and would be off-loaded at the same location but would certainly not be used to make fertilizer.

This was Pierre's first opportunity to make an impression on the man in New Orleans. Impressing the boss in this organization was simple: deliver the cargo on time and don't get caught! The job was good, and he was lucky to have made the contact. It had only been sixty days since he walked out of Mississippi State Penitentiary, and here he was, back to work with a chance to make some serious money.

For the last five years, Pierre had been a guest of the state, and the only thing good about the facility in the Delta region of Mississippi was the day they opened the big door and let you out. The original facility had been built around 1900, and he was sure the state had deliberately selected the site because it was in the swamps, and he was sure the governor thought he and the mosquitoes would make good bed partners. The original old parts of the facility still stood and were still used, but over the years, they had built additional facilities to hold more prisoners. This was his second visit to the gray walls and barbed wire fenced-in acreage in Sunflower County. His first came from a blown truck hijacking, which got him six years and then out on good behavior. Unfortunately, the good behavior didn't last long after he got out. His ticket was punched a second time when he and an idiot helper had tried to hold up an all-night grocery. The idiot had brought the job to Pierre and assured him there were no alarm, lots of cash, and a single employee on site after midnight.

The night manager also had a helper. He was stocking shelves. The stock clerk heard the loud voices and, in a panic, dropped a box he was emptying onto the shelves. Pierre and the idiot had turned toward the noise, which gave the night manager an opportunity to push the little button next to the cash register. It was a silent alarm, and the police responded silently and was waiting for them in the parking lot.

That was strike two, and Pierre was on his way back to Sunflower County. He could still hear the judge's words as he pronounced the sentence, "Mr. Gaudet, I want you to understand that if you appear before me again, they will take the key to your cell and throw it away, and the state of Mississippi will be responsible for your life until you die!"

Since the age of sixteen, Pierre had been in and out of trouble with the law. He had started out with petty thievery and then connected with a pimp that hired him to loiter around on the street and keep a tally on his group of whores. How many times they got in a car or walked to the nearby motel with a John. If their revenue didn't match up with Pierre's tally, that prostitute would be using a lot of makeup to hide the new marks on her face.

The suspensions on the truck were very firm, causing the truck to transmit exaggerated signals to the steering wheel. The sensation snapped Pierre's attention back to the road. He immediately saw that he had wandered off onto the shoulder and the headlights had picked up a sign signaling a crossroad. He swerved back to the left and got the truck on smooth pavement just as he went past the country road that T-intersected with the interstate and went off to the east through the desolate farmland. The truck bounced back onto the pavement, leaving a cloud of dust behind. Pierre was scolding himself for the distraction when he glanced in his right-hand rearview mirror and saw the lights. The lights were red and blue, alternately flashing across the top of the car that carried them.

Pierre was immediately panicked. They were making this run at night because they believed there would be little, if any, police presence at this hour. He had found one dedicated Boy Scout cop out at this hour of night. To make it worse, he had gone off the road right in front of him. The red lights closed on the truck, and Pierre pulled over onto the shoulder, this time completely off.

"Hey, buddy, are you having a little trouble staying on the road tonight?" The patrolman was standing behind the window Pierre had started to roll down.

Pierre continued rolling the window down and replied, "Not really, Officer. I had just reached over to pull a cigarette out of the pack and didn't realize I was going on to the shoulder until I felt the bumps."

The patrolman pushed his hat back on his head as he glanced over his right shoulder toward the rear of the truck. "Let me see your driver's license and BOLs."

This was a lousy damn break, Pierre was thinking. He had thought it was pure luck when he'd met Carl in a bar a few nights ago and Carl said he might get him on to drive a small rig to Memphis once in a while.

He'd gone in to meet Perez, who'd quizzed him about his time as a guest of the state of Louisiana. Perez seemed to like him and, in just a few days, had put him in a truck for a test-drive. Some asshole was sick or hung over or just didn't show up. *Who cares,* Pierre thought, *why the stupid bastard didn't show? It was a sign of good luck!*

Luck or mojo didn't matter; it just mattered that he was making the bread, not some other guy. Now this fucking policeman was trying to make his luck go bad.

Pierre was jerked out of his thoughts by the insistent voice. "Hey, what's taking so long? Can't find your papers? You guys gotta learn that your papers are as important as your cargo. Did you come up from New Orleans?"

Pierre found the papers and looked in the outside mirror. The patrolman was looking at the truck's body behind the cab. Fear shot through Pierre's brain, and he felt a shiver go through his arms. He switched the papers to his left hand and held them out the window while reaching under the dash with his right hand. He felt the pistol grip slide into his hand, and after a firm tug, he heard a click and the full weight of the sawed-off twelve-gauge moved from its cradle.

The officer had taken the offered papers and was starting to scan the top page when he heard the sound of the truck door opening.

"Just stay in the truck till I—"

Then he saw the driver on the top step, holding the gun level, pointed at his head. "Hold on, mister. You got no call for that! I don't know what trouble you think you're looking at, but it's nothing compared to what will come from using that gun."

"Shut the fuck up!" Pierre said, his voice a couple of octaves higher than normal. "So you think there's something wrong with my load, do you? Just couldn't help snooping around, could you? You don't have any idea how much trouble I could have if you poked around the truck and found something that could lock me up forever. Well, I can't let you do anything like that, Mr. Lawman. I've done all the time locked up in an eight-by-eight cell I can handle."

The officer was holding both hands away from his body to appear in surrender. "If you'll just look at—"

He opened his left hand, and the papers fluttered in the night breeze, falling toward the ground.

For one second, Pierre's eyes focused on the falling papers then were snapped back to the motion of the trooper's hand drawing his .357 from its holster as his body dived toward the truck. Pierre squeezed the trigger and felt the shotgun buck in his hand and saw the patrolman's body change direction slightly as it fell under the truck. As the roaring sound of the Mossberg faded, he heard the cries of pain coming from the patrolman. There was a growing area of red wetness forming on the left side of the tan uniform blouse and the top of his pants. The service revolver was still in the wounded mans' hand, but there was no movement except involuntary jerks in his body.

"Goddamit," cried Pierre. "Look what you made me do!" Pierre walked toward the rear of the truck, holding his head with his left hand, the gun in his other hand pointed at the ground. "Sacre bleu, you stupid bastard, now what am I going to do? What a mess!" He walked back to the policeman, who was still making sounds but not moving. He reached to take the gun from the fallen man's hand and then felt a twinge of pain stab through his left arm. Looking down, he saw blood making a red line down his sleeve from just above his elbow, where the fabric was frayed. He tore the sleeve open and saw a furrow torn from the flesh two inches above his elbow and stopping about three inches long where the bullet had exited and continued in search of another target. He tore the remainder of the sleeve free and fashioned a bandage that he tied to prevent further bleeding.

Pierre used the patrolman's legs to pull him from under the truck. There were more involuntary quivers and jerks from the unconscious patrolman, but he did seem to be alive. Pierre knew he could not leave the man alive—too much danger if he would be found and recuperated enough to witness against him, Pierre thought.

He couldn't leave the patrol car on the highway. He needed to hide the car and give himself enough time to deliver the load and disappear. He'd call Carl when he got to Memphis.

Pierre went back and pulled the body back to the patrol car. He then realized that in all the excitement, he hadn't even noticed the lights were still flashing. He pulled the wounded patrolman into the car's backseat and closed the doors. He turned the patrol car around and drove back toward the gravel road. As Pierre turned off the highway, he could see by the headlights that the fields were rice paddies and nothing appeared to be growing out there now.

Pretty safe place to ditch the car, he thought. About a hundred yards off the highway, the road made a curve around a cluster of three cypress trees. Pierre made a sharp turn as he passed the trees and stopped the car. He picked up the shotgun from the passenger seat and turned to the backseat. He'd never killed a man in cold blood, and this poor bastard was helpless, but it had to be done. *Him or me,* he thought. He opened the back door of the police car and fired the second shell into the form on the seat. There was no sound except the loud clap of the twelve-gauge.

Pierre closed the door and began the walk back to the truck. Thirty minutes had elapsed since he saw the flashing lights pulling him over.

It took about ten minutes to get back to the truck. Pierre's nerves were a mess, and he hurriedly climbed up the cab and pulled back onto the highway toward Memphis.

All things considered, he thought everything was turning out pretty good. A lot better for him than the cop. A smile creased his face as he watched the white stripes on the black pavement disappear under the speeding truck.

CHAPTER 12

Clint Parker and Glenn Wiggs were just winding down a phone call in which they had summarized the progress that each felt they were making with the commission.

Glenn was just finishing his evaluation of the meeting when Clint raised his right hand. "Hold on, Glenn, I'm being told that I have an urgent call from Amos Boudreau. Can I call you back?"

"Sure thing, Clint. Maybe I'll just hold on. I'm curious about what has Amos in a dither."

One of the traits that made Amos Boudreau an ideal agent for the FBI was his rock-solid temperament, which kept him cool in the midst of crisis. However, as he started to speak, Clint could tell that Amos was excited and concerned.

Amos Boudreau came on the line and hurriedly began his report. "Clint, I thought I better give you a quick update and let you know that we may have a problem in Mississippi. Last night, actually in the early hours of this morning, a Mississippi highway patrol officer called in and reported he was pulling a commercial truck over. The truck had veered off the road as it had passed a rural road where the officer was sitting, monitoring traffic. That time of night, there's hardly any traffic to monitor, and when he saw the truck moving erratically, he decided to check it out. He said the name was printed on the side of the truck, but it was in very small lettering and the only word he made out as the truck went by him was *Imports*. For some reason, he didn't report the license plate number before he approached the driver. Bottom line is, he never confirmed the stop, and dispatch has been unable to raise him. He did report the area he was in and the location of the stop. Dispatch has ordered a nearby car to go to that area and see what they find. Sonny Swofford called to alert me and will check back with me as soon as he finds out the status of the patrolman."

By the time Amos had finished his report, Clint was inserting this piece of troubling information into the puzzle then made a decision. "All right, Amos, you stay in the information loop from Mississippi. If it's something Swofford can handle, then you may not need to do anything. If the news is bad, you may have to go to Mississippi and make sure that no details are left uncovered. It's a damn shame that the officer didn't get the full name on the truck before he called, and you say he didn't even get a partial license plate?"

Amos, "No, he said the license plate was bent and he would call back when he had the number. Said he thought it appeared to be a Louisiana plate, but he couldn't be sure."

Clint Parker was silent for a few seconds then said, "You'll know what to do once the information is clear. I have a couple guys following Ham Turner, and I thought this call might be them. I thought Turner would fold up before this and call me back to negotiate a deal. I need to stay on that, but I'm eager to know what happened in Mississippi. Call me when you get some information. I have a bad feeling on this." Clint Parker punched buttons on his phone and went back to Glenn Wiggs, who'd been waiting.

Clint related what little information he had to Glenn, who agreed they couldn't accomplish anything further in this conversation, and they said good-bye and hung up.

His phone buzzed, and Clint saw the blinking light and punched the button, and the voice on the other end identified himself as the agent following Turner.

The tone of his voice revealed the frustration the caller was feeling. "I went to his house this morning, Clint, right on schedule, 5:30 a.m. Turner didn't come out of the house until 6:00 a.m. to pick up the newspaper lying near the front steps and went back in the house. It was 7:30 a.m. when his garage door opened. He backed his car out and headed toward downtown. I thought he was going to work because he parked in a lot just a block from his office. He went in a little café next to the parking lot. I parked on the street where I could see his car and the front door of the café and waited. About twenty minutes passed, and when he didn't come back out, I walked into the café, sat down at the counter, and ordered coffee and a doughnut. While I waited for my order, I glanced around at the tables and did not see Turner anywhere, so I got up and went to the men's room. It was empty. I went in the kitchen and spotted a back door. The man at the grill confirmed that a man matching Turner's description had exited that door about a half an hour ago. I'm really sorry, Clint. I haven't had that old trick pulled on me a long time."

Clint told the agent, "Don't feel too bad, Charlie. I would have probably done the very same thing you did. There was no reason to believe he would rabbit on you, because there was no reason to believe he knew he was being followed. This guy is scared, and my bet is he naturally took evasive action just in case we or one of the bad guys was keeping an eye on him. He's probably much more afraid of them than he is of us."

After Clint hung up from the young FBI agent, he decided to call Ken Kondraky at ABI. Kondraky said he wasn't aware of Turner being absent from work. "We don't work on the same floor, and I might not see him for days. Let me check with my friend Emma. She'll know if he's here or not."

A couple of minutes later, Ken was back. "Nope. Emma says he called in sick just after 8:00 a.m. Wonder what illness he's come down with," Ken asked and chuckled mischievously.

It was twelve noon when Clint pulled into the parking lot of the Dew Drop Inn, a redneck country tavern where the same clientele went to on the same nights each week, sat on the same stools, and told one another and the waitstaff their troubles and lied about their exploits. Connie Sandusky had listened to most of them, never judging or complaining, because she learned quickly that the more she listened and sympathized, the bigger the tip.

Clint's information was that Ham Turner was a regular at the DDI. After numerous exchanges between drink orders, Connie and Ham had drawn together in the recognition that they were both a little sharper than the other knives in the drawer.

Connie and Ham had each survived two efforts at marriage, and while neither had totally figured out why it hadn't worked, both knew they needed the occasional company of the opposite sex, and after trying it out together a few times, each concluded there was reassurance and release each gave the other. They also liked each other's presence and thoughts, often without outside interference or debate. Over the last couple of years, Ham and Connie had developed an irregular but steady relationship. Didn't make much sense to anyone but them, and as Ham liked to say, "It is what it is."

Connie came to Clint's table. "What's it gonna be, Mr. Parker?" Clint was not a regular, but they had become acquainted when an old boyfriend of Connie's was caught in a stolen car operation. He was a driver who took the selected cars to Gulfport, Mississippi, and loaded them on a rust bucket freighter headed to South America, where they were parted and sold back to repair shops across the United States.

"I'll just have one of your barbecue pork sandwiches and a Coke, maybe a few country fries on the side. How have you been, Connie?"

Connie assured him she was as fine as forty-eight years and twenty-five extra pounds would allow and went off to the kitchen with his order. Clint surveyed the bar to see if he recognized anyone that he had known or thought, by his or her posture and uncomfortable squirming, he might meet in the future. There were no suspects or prospects that stood out, so he unrolled the paper napkin holding the knife and fork as Connie came back with the sandwich and a Coke.

"Seen Ham much recently, Connie?"

"I see him when I see him, Clint. You know how it is."

"I had lunch with him couple of days ago. Wondered if you'd seen him since then."

Connie's eyebrows raised. "You two had lunch? Didn't know you boys ran in the same circles." Connie's eyes began to dart from side to side.

Clint picked up the sandwich and paused. "He was going to check on some information and get back to me, and I haven't heard from him. Thought you might know where I'd find him."

"You mean the FBI wants me to find people for them? Thought that was your specialty, Clint!" Connie stood with both hands on her ample hips and a smile that looked like she was having fun with Clint.

"You may have the wrong idea about me and Ham, Connie. We're both in the law enforcement business, and even though we may not go to church together on Sunday morning, don't mean we don't watch each other's back the rest of the week." Clint bit off a mouthful of pork.

"Is that why you want to find Ham, to watch his back?" Connie's smile faded and her bottom lip quivered.

"You may find this hard to believe, Connie, but Ham's safety and well-being is my main interest right now."

Connie's eyes narrowed. "I don't know what the two of you are up to, but all I can tell you is, Ham is a creature of habit. I think you know a little bit about Ham's past. It might be helpful to look in that direction."

Clint took the last home fry, wiped his mouth with the paper napkin, and laid a ten-dollar bill on the check and stood to leave. "The pork was very good, Connie, and the service was better than most places. You have yourself a good day now, ya hear?"

Connie's eyes followed the tall lawman as he put on the western hat and went out the door.

* * *

When Clint arrived back at his office after lunch, he saw the bad news before he heard it. The girl at the front desk had a new stress furrow over her brow and a sad look in her hazel eyes. "Well, did the world go to hell in a handbasket while I was having lunch?"

Tears came out of each eye and rolled down her cheeks before she could reply, "They found the missing trooper in Mississippi. Amos wants you to call him right away."

Amos answered the phone instantly. "Yeah, Clint, it's as bad as we had hoped it wouldn't be. They found the trooper in the backseat of his car, hidden behind some trees about one hundred yards off the main highway on a dirt road. No official confirmation of the identity until the medical examiner takes a look. They are pretty sure it's the missing Trooper.

"It's pretty bad, Clint. Looks like both barrels of a shotgun, the last one making his face almost unrecognizable. I'm gonna leave here as soon as we finish and drive up there to see if we can get the bloodhounds on the trucker quickly."

Clint sat down in his chair, numbed. This was not his first time to get a report on a dead law enforcement officer, but it didn't get any easier no matter how many times. "Did you get some basic data on the scene?"

Amos picked up the page of handwritten notes. "The bloodstains on the pavement indicated that the truck was northbound. The killer drove the squad car behind the trees after the shooting and then appears to have walked back to his truck. Officers on the scene say the evidence indicates the patrolman was shot the first time as he stood by the truck. Looks like he was then dragged back to his patrol car and put into the backseat. This is based on scuff marks along the edge of the blacktop. The officer who found them has twenty years on the job, and he thinks the second shot was done after the car was moved. The officer's .357 was found lying beside the road, and tire tracks indicate it was under the truck while it was stopped. It may not have been obvious until the truck was driven away. One spent cartridge was found in the cylinder, and they're looking for a bullet, but it would be a miracle if they found one. No way to tell if it hit something first or how far it traveled from where the shot was fired. They've collected blood samples, and everything is going to the crime lab in New Orleans. Whatever they can't do in New Orleans, I suppose we'll send it to DC for further tests."

"That's a damn bad report, Amos, but very well done, and I'm impressed with how much they have already found at the crime scene." Clint drummed his fingers on his desk and then made a decision. "You go ahead and follow up with the shooting. I'm going to stay here and follow a hunch. I had an interesting lunch today, and the lady who served my lunch gave me some thoughts to chew on. And unless I'm totally out in left field, I may know where to find Ham Turner. I'm going to drive over to the old deserted town of Carsonville. The lady serving my lunch today thinks he just might be out there. If I find him and can persuade him to come back and put himself into our custody, that should put me back into Little Rock by tonight. We don't have a good safe house in this area to keep him, so if you have any thoughts on that, you can tell me when I call you at home tonight. Things are getting a little sticky out there, so keep those eyes in the back of your head opened."

"I'll do that, Clint, and you take care to do the same."

They said their good-byes and hung up their phones. Clint went down to the parking garage and began the drive over to Carsonville.

CHAPTER 13

Blake Stevens walked to the oak railing that lined the edge of the balcony overlooking the main floor of Blake's Place. The scores of empty chairs surrounding each of the tables, their tops polished to a high shine, accentuated the lack of people and made the grand room appear to be larger than it actually was. Blake had driven over from Hot Springs yesterday afternoon after dropping Gabby at the small airport just outside the city. The charter plane had been waiting for her, and as soon as she was on board, it lifted off and headed toward Kansas City. Today, Gabby would be in meetings all day with her investment advisers, reviewing the progress and alibiing for the shortcomings of her portfolio.

Everyone at Blake's Place was happy to see him. There was still, as there had been in the beginning, a special feeling of closeness between Blake and the people who operated the roadhouse for him. The area around the roadhouse had grown and prospered, and the prosperity in the community had prompted Blake's Place to make incremental improvements to keep up with the clientele. The front porch had been extended outward and enclosed, creating a foyer that hosted a coat-and-hat check counter on one side and leather upholstered seating on the other with a maître d' station at the main entrance to the dining room and bar.

Blake looked down at the shiny tabletops and the padded seats in the low-back chairs and remembered what it was like many years ago, when he had walked in with everything he owned over his shoulder, except for the horse, which was tied to a bush out front. Then, he had been full of optimism and confidence that he was going to change his circumstances and make a fantastic life for himself. The day he bought the roadhouse for a few hundred dollars was the biggest event of his life to that point. He realized now that Jess had been a major anchor to his life in those early days. She gave him someone to attach himself to, and that stabilized all his ambitions and made him feel there was nothing he couldn't do. Success had been sweet. And when the man from Memphis approached him with their proposal, he felt that a dozen doors to his future had just opened.

But the day to top all days was the day he went to the Spa in Hot Springs and saw the beautiful Gabrielle Fleming standing behind the hot pool of mineral water, her nakedness presenting her beauty to him like a gift from the gods.

All that was more years earlier than he liked to admit, and during those years, he had experienced some setbacks and some disappointments. But all things considered, he didn't know how he could've done any better. The most significant cloud over all his success was his partnership with the men from Memphis, New Orleans, Little Rock, and other places he continued to discover as he learned more about the organization he had become part of. But standing here this morning, he did not resist the feeling of power and potential that swelled inside him. This was still the place he could go to and feel totally in control. He walked down the long staircase, almost bouncing from step to step.

"Good morning, stranger. Great to see you again! Do you just get better looking with every birthday, or is it that I'm just that lonesome?" Bobbi's eyes twinkled, and her soft giggle was a welcome home he looked forward to every time he went to Blake's Place.

"Save that flattering crap, you horny toad, for the cash customers. I'm just a freeloader around this place. Didn't you know?"

"Honey, you can freeload off me any day of the week! Can I get you something?" Bobbi stepped around from behind the bar and went to him and pulled him against her in a full-body hug. The only kind she ever did.

Blake pushed her back and looked her up and down. "I'm not kidding. You girls seem to look better every time I'm over here. Is it true or just the imagination of a middle-aged man?"

Bobbi brought two cups of coffee, and they sat at a nearby table. She still had the mischievous smile as she said, "Its hard work and clean living that does it. You should try it sometimes."

"Is everybody else in as good a mood as you seem to be? How's Shirley?"

"Wait till you see her, Blake. She just had some new surgical touch-up work done in Kansas City, and she is downright beautiful. You won't believe it when you see her!"

For the next fifteen minutes, Bobbi filled Blake in on everybody. Jess had a new suitor. A fifty-year-old farmer whose wife had died four years previously. "I hope it doesn't bother you, Blake. He is so good to her and good for her. We are all very happy for her, and she is on cloud nine. Shirley is a different story. Every man that sees her wants to marry her and run away, but when Shirley went through the incident at the motel, a part of her went behind a very high wall with no door. She can make herself available for one or two hours at a time, nothing more. The plastic surgeons have performed miracles on her outside, but so far, nobody's figured out how to fix the inside. She and Jess will be over in a couple minutes. Can I get you some breakfast?"

Blake had just finished the last bite of his breakfast and Bobbi had carried the dishes off to the kitchen when Jess and Shirley came through the front door. Shirley ran to Blake and threw herself at him, her arms locked tight around his neck until he thought he couldn't breathe. When she finally loosened her grip and leaned back, Blake saw the tears running down both her cheeks. He held both her shoulders and looked her up and down. He was stunned at the transformation of her appearance. "Whatever the doctor charged, it was worth every penny," Blake said with sincerity not lost on anyone in the group.

Then he turned to Jess, who also looked different. She looked like she was at peace with the world. As she stepped into his tender embrace, he thought, *Not with the world, idiot. She's at peace with herself!* He gazed into her eyes for what seemed an embarrassingly long time before he pulled her close and whispered, "Congratulations!"

Jess leaned back and smiled, letting him see that she knew he had seen the change. For a moment she seemed reluctant to turn him loose but finally stepped back and looked him in the eye. "Thank you, and I don't have to ask you how you're doing, Mr. Stevens. Your eyes tell it all. You're one happy son of a bitch, aren't you?"

The girls all laughed, and Blake held on to Jess's hands and said, "It's a good life, babe. I recommend it to everybody." The laughter became shrieks of joy, and everybody hugged and danced and shared their genuine love for one another. Finally, they all sat down around the table and began to tell the stories that had occurred since their last meeting. The noise level was comparable to a medium-size crowd on Saturday night until the front door opened and a familiar figure stepped inside.

"Well, I'll be damned if it ain't Clint Parker! Is this old home week or what?" Blake said as he rose from the table and walked toward the door.

Clint Parker shook hands with Blake, who looked sincerely pleased to see him. "This is a pleasant surprise, Blake. I left Little Rock this morning and was starting to feel a little hungry, and I thought I remembered this being a pretty good place to take care of that feeling. Didn't expect to see you here, though."

"Well, I didn't expect to see you either, Clint, but you are sincerely welcomed and you tell the girls what you'd like to have and they'll see that the kitchen puts it together. I just finished a small steak, fried eggs, and hash browns, and I can highly recommend that!"

Bobbi took Clint's order and headed for the kitchen. The other girls drifted off, finding things to do, and left Clint and Blake to themselves. It was mostly small talk between the two men; each guarded that they not say the wrong thing to each other.

Bobbi brought more coffee as Clint finished the last of his breakfast and Bobbi cleared the plates. Clint looked up at Blake and asked, "How are you doing, Blake? Really happy, it appears."

Blake's expression sobered, and he looked straight across at Clint and said, "Nobody deserves to be as happy as I am, Clint. I've been very successful in business, but more importantly, I have a most-beautiful lady who adores me and fills my days with joy from sunup to midnight. I tell you, sure, no farm boy from the Dakotas ever dreamed of the life I live."

Clint looked steadily at Blake. "You know, Blake, I'm pretty good at reading people, and I can see that what you just said is true, at least 90 percent of it. But I do see a little shadow hanging back in the background that says from time to time there's trouble in paradise. I don't mean to throw cold water on your enthusiasm. Everybody in life has those little shadows, but I assure you I am very pleased to hear you are so happy. I wish I could stay longer and visit. I remember a number of years ago when I came by here and you and I would talk, and I always felt that you were fundamentally a good and honest man. It's really good to run into you again."

Blake looked back at Clint. "It suddenly occurred to me. Clint, what brings you out into this part of the country on a day like this? I heard that after you quit being sheriff, you joined the FBI, and I hope the FBI didn't send you to my place of business!" Blake put on a smile and chuckled.

Clint stood to prepare to leave. "Nothing like that, Blake. I'm just on my way over to the Carson Farms and remembered that the food used to be good here, and I'm happy to say it still is."

"What interest could the FBI have in Carson Farms? I thought the law had done about all the damage to that place that there was to do."

"Nothing major, just following up on some old business. You know how the government is. Nothing is ever done until the paperwork is finished."

Blake laughed as he shook hands with Clint. "As an owner of a couple of businesses, I can agree with that statement 100 percent."

Clint paused. "Yeah, I forgot to ask you, how's the casino doing in Hot Springs? I've never made it over there, but I hear it's an impressive operation."

"If you like to deal with gamblers and drunks, it's a dream job. But seriously, it's done really well for us, and I have good help that's experienced in that business, so my main job is just to keep an eye on the help. Hey, again, it's really good to see you, Clint. And thanks for stopping by. If you ever get over that way, ask for me, and I'll see you get the VIP treatment."

Blake watched through the front glass as Clint drove away in the dark-blue Ford. He didn't buy Clint's downplaying the reason for his visit to Carson Farms, but he could not think of any reason that would tie the FBI back to Carson Farms. Most people connected to Carson had been tried and sentenced to prison or exonerated and turned loose. Maybe there was something going on that Blake didn't know about. His attention was brought back to his own business when Jess walked up and laid the company books for the last month in front of him. "There's something that ought to keep you busy until lunchtime," she said and laughed as she walked away.

CHAPTER 14

Amos Boudreau checked the odometer on the dash of the Ford LTD and saw he had ten miles to go to reach Jackson, Mississippi. Shortly after he had gotten on the road, he heard a few serious inquiries from officers who had just started their patrol shift. They all looked for reassurance following the death of a fellow officer. Somehow they had missed the order to avoid discussing that issue on the air, but five minutes later, all chatter about a state policeman being shot stopped.

The body of the slain officer had been taken to a morgue in Jackson, and Amos was losing what little patience he had when he started the trip three hours ago. He had maintained his speed at ninety miles per hour except for areas of more traffic, where he had adjusted his speed in the interest of public safety.

The investigation being conducted by the crime commission had made significant progress. They were pretty sure that the dead officer had been well identified, and the officers assigned to the investigation were preparing dossiers that would be reviewed at the next meeting of the commission in New Orleans.

Amos manipulated the LTD through the city traffic as he came into the city limits. Thankfully, the state officials had the foresight to locate the headquarters of the state police on the edge of town right off the main highway and not in the state office building downtown. The morgue was in the basement, and that was the button Amos pushed on the elevator from the lobby of the building. Quick introductions were followed by Amos being escorted to the examination room the medical examiner used to probe the remains of the dead in an attempt to determine the cause of death.

It didn't take exceptional talent to reach a conclusion in the death of the state policeman, whose body was still lying on an examination table.

The shotgun had done major damage to the man's left side and upper hip. Then the second blast of the shotgun had torn away enough tissue and bone, leaving his face virtually unrecognizable. The examiner directed his attention to a plastic cup half-filled with spheres of dark-gray lead.

"Three or four of these would be enough to kill a man," the examiner commented. "As you can see, he got hit with enough shot to disintegrate part of him. There's no question about the cause of death, and there's no way to do an open casket at his funeral. His wife and kids are upstairs, being consoled and informed by a couple of female officers. You may want to say a word to them before you leave."

Amos got a copy of the report from the examiner, put it in his briefcase, and took the elevator back to the first floor. He spotted through a window of an interrogation room the family and the two female officers seated around a small table right off the lobby. He was starting toward the door to the small room when he heard his name called. He turned and saw Sonny Swofford going in his direction.

"Amos, sorry I wasn't here when you arrived. Have you been downstairs? Did you get everything you needed from the examiner?"

They shook hands as Amos replied, "I think so, Sonny. The situation downstairs is pretty simple. It was a pretty savage attack. In my opinion, the odds are pretty strong that the one shot fired from Allen's .357 wounded the shooter. No way to tell how badly, and I assume it wasn't too bad, as he was able to drag the body to the car and drive it off the road. Let me go in and say a few words to the widow and the kids, then you and I can go to a conference room here and call Clint. We'll have to decide what moves to make next. A quick arrest would be a morale booster to the law enforcement community, but we have to consider whether that would be in the best interest of the overall investigation."

Ann Allen was an attractive woman in her early thirties. The two kids looked to be preschool-aged, a boy and a girl. Amos had dealt with this scene previously in the ten years he had served the FBI.

"Mrs. Allen, I'm Agent Amos Boudreau with the FBI based in New Orleans. I drove up here this morning as soon as I got the news, and I can't tell you how sorry I am over the loss of Bob. I have some sense of how devastating this is to you and your children, but I'm sure that neither I nor anyone else can truly appreciate your pain unless they have been where you are themselves. I want you to know that the investigation Bob was working on with the bureau and the crime commission was extremely important and will ultimately be successful in making all of the people of this area safer. It will take time for you to deal with your grief, but I think it's important that you understand the community, the state police, and the FBI are available to help you in any way you need."

Ann Allen's slight build was made to appear even smaller by the sudden realization of what had happened to her husband and what could happen to her and her children.

She straightened herself in her chair and looked up at Amos. "Thank you, Agent Boudreau. When Bob decided to be a police officer, we both talked about the possibility of what has happened. He believed so strong in what he was doing, and even though we both agreed that the risk involved in his job was justified until it happens, it's just so many words. Now it has happened, but it seems unreal, except for the fact that he's not here. I know that I will find a way to adjust to my loss and to fill my children's life with information about what a fine man their father was and would have been. I do hope you will be successful in finding whoever did this and bringing them to justice for this terrible deed. Thank you again!"

When Amos got to the conference room, he found Sonny Swofford on the phone with Clint Parker. Amos picked up an extension phone and joined the conversation.

Clint said, "Well, gentlemen, I think it's safe to say we got our stop of a northbound truck, and I'd bet a week's pay that it was a Gulf Imports truck. It's a damn shame that the stop went down the way it did and we lost a good man. As we discussed a few days ago, we would prefer to be able to follow the truck to its destination rather than pulling it over. Unfortunately, Patrolman Allen wasn't in the loop on our thinking. I've been on the phone with the commander of the state police, and he has agreed that special instructions should go out to all his officers that they are to observe and report any sightings of Latin Imports trucks but not to apprehend without assistance from the bureau or a crime commission–assigned officer. I'm in a phone booth in front of a gas station just down the road from Carson Farms. As soon as we finish, I'm going to drive into the old Carsonville and see if Ham Turner is hanging around there."

Amos Boudreau said, "Good luck, Clint. I'm going to head back to New Orleans as soon as I make sure everything is okay here. Two agents from the bureau in St. Louis are flying into New Orleans to observe activities at the two addresses we have identified for Latin Imports, the Jolly Roger Bar and Grill on Water Street and the warehouse at 320 Gulf Street.

"They are new faces that are not apt to be recognized by anyone, and at this point, we aren't in a position to trust all of the local law with this kind of investigation. I think it's safe to say the people we're after throw a pretty wide loop, and we need to be cautious about whom we share information with. Sonny will stay here in Jackson and give us up-to-the-minute reports on anything the state police develop on the shooting. Let me know how it goes in Carsonville."

CHAPTER 15

A low-hanging cloud of dust arose from the gravel road and followed Clint Parker's car as he drove into Carsonville. What had promised to be a monument to the man who built it had turned out to be a ghost town that testified to the folly of men who callously played with and abused the lives of their fellow man for self-enrichment.

The dust trail ceased as Clint slowed the car to a crawl, his eyes scanning each building for a telltale sign of recent activity. The closed shops stared back at him with disinterest, signs in the doors of each informing of their closing, hung at odd angles. He turned the corner at the drugstore/café and approached the front of the jail/police department. There was no sign on the door advising that it was closed or posted as private property.

He's here, Clint thought as he turned at the next corner, past the building housing the jail and offices. He turned again and went up to the backside of the jail building. There was an overhead door leading to a one-car, garage. Clint got out and walked toward the door while his eyes scanned the ground. The tracks were pretty clear leading up to and disappearing inside the garage.

Clint walked over to a door just left of the garage door and gripped the doorknob. He was able to rotate it to the right, and the door opened. Ham's car was parked just inside the overhead door, and just ahead was a flight of stairs leading to the quarters upstairs.

Clint reached inside his jacket and pulled his Browning 9mm free from its holster. He held the gun close to his right leg, pointing at the floor, and began to climb the stairs. Halfway up the stairs, he sensed movement above and behind him. He turned toward the movement, raising the pistol as he turned, and saw Ham Turner peering over the banister. He was holding a long-barreled Colt 45 in his right hand, and Clint could detect the tremor.

Ham's voice was strained. "Jesus, Clint, what the hell are you doing here?"

Clint held the gun trained on Ham and answered, "I think you know what I'm doing here, Ham! There's no place to run to, and there's too many people looking for you. You need to man up and start looking for solutions to your problems. When you do that, I might be able to offer you some help. I already know quite a bit about you, and I can guess the rest to make a scenario that tells me you're in some pretty hot water. You can't jump out of the water, but I might be able to help you turn the heat down. Don't you think that makes some sense?"

The tension seemed to go out of Ham's body, and he drew the gun back over the rail and let it drop to his side. "I don't know, Clint. I didn't plan all of this. It just seemed that one thing led to another, and before I could change directions, here I was."

Clint walked to the top of the stairs and around the railing. "Just let the gun fall to the floor and let's go where we can sit down and talk."

Ham Turner obeyed Clint's instructions and headed back into the meager living quarters above the jail. Clint picked up the heavy revolver and followed.

For the next hour, Ham Turner attempted to bear his soul. At times he broke down in tears, but in the end, he had described what happens to a man who abandons his principles in the quest for money and power.

He could identify the man in Little Rock and the others in New Orleans as well as a mysterious character in Miami, Florida. He had never met the man in Florida, but he had heard him referred to enough times that he was sure he existed.

Clint made a decision. "I have to get you out of here, Ham. Gather your personal things and take them to my car. Leave your car here. No one will think to look for it in this forsaken place. I'll talk to some people and figure out the best place for you to stay for a while. In the meantime, I will sit you down with a court reporter and put everything you know where it can be used."

Ham Turner's complexion turned a little yellow. "Clint, you know what kind of jeopardy I'm putting myself in. The trouble I have right now with you is nothing compared to the trouble I'll invite once I talk to you and tell you in a sworn affidavit what I know and what I suspect. I've got to have some immunity and some protection."

"I think I can give you everything you want, Ham, but you're going to have to trust me, because right now, the most important thing is to get you in a place where the wrong people can't find you. We've got a lot of powerful people behind this investigation, and I'm sure they will give us what you need to protect yourself if they get what they need to eliminate this nest of scumbags."

The two men went down the stairs. Ham tossed his bag into the trunk of Clint's car, and they left Carsonville in a cloud of dust along the gravel road.

They came out of Carsonville and turned onto the highway headed toward Little Rock. A couple of miles down the road, they passed a direction sign with arrows pointing to the right and read, "Jonesboro, Arkansas—22 Miles" and "Kennett Missouri—64 Miles."

Clint slowed the car and turned right when they came to the intersection. "Where are you headed?"

"To the home of a good friend," Clint replied and regained his speed.

The route Clint followed was a series of turns that took him east and north. Soon they were driving closer to a high ridge of land referred to as Crowley's Ridge. They continued to skirt the ridge until they came to a dirt road that turned off to the east and wound through a grove of walnut trees, stopping at a homestead sitting on the banks of the Current River.

The Current River originates in Missouri, and at its origin is a mere trickle of water until it reaches the community of Van Buren, Missouri. Then, an amazing geologic phenomena happens to the river. A boiling torrent of water, known simply as Big Spring, comes gushing out of the ground and flows into the Current River, increasing the river's volume by four or five times. Geologists had traced the source of the huge body of water across the plains northward into and across Canada, where, for centuries, the glacial runoff has found its way into an underground aquifer that does not find its way back to the surface of the earth until it reaches the southern edge of Missouri. Then the bigger, colder waters surge out of the bowls of the earth to join the timid Current River and flow out of Southeast Missouri into Arkansas with an ample supply of trout, catfish, and other species for the avid sport fishermen that crowds its banks when the fishing season opens. One of those fishermen made his home here along the banks of the Current River.

Cam Wilson had been the county sheriff prior to Clint Parker and had talked Clint into running for the office when Cam decided to retire. Cam had mentored Clint for a few years and finally decided that Clint knew as much about law enforcement, maybe more, than Cam. From that time on, Cam was satisfied to sit on his porch and watch the river flow by, dropping a hook in the water as often as he needed for his entertainment and food supply. Every now and then, Clint would drop by and join him at the fishing dock and hold a pole for an hour or two and tell him about something that had Clint stalled. Cam would give his thoughts, and pretty soon, Clint would lay down his pole and drive off back to wherever he needed to be. The grove of walnut trees added a subsidy to his retirement and Social Security. It was a good life.

Cam heard the sound of it before he saw the car. He was sitting on the fishing dock in a lawn chair, and he turned in it as he heard the doors slam. Two men walked toward the dock, one man he recognized as Clint, and while the other looked familiar, Cam could not put a name to him.

"Howdy, Cam," Clint called out. "The fish biting today?"

"They bite every day, just not always on the stuff I have on my hook. Pull up a couple of more chairs and join me!"

"Cameron Wilson, I want you to meet Ham Turner. Ham, say hello to Cam."

Cam reached into a nearby ice chest and pulled out two Budweiser cans and offered them to his guests. "What brings you boys out to God's country today?"

Clint pulled the tab on his beer and settled in the chair. "It's a long story, Cam, but the short version is, Ham has worked around the edges of law enforcement for a few years and has recently gotten involved with some characters that are usually on the opposite side of things from the law. He's decided that it's in his best interest to act against these individuals and cooperate with the law, and that is going to make him a very unpopular man in certain circles."

Cam adjusted his fishing pole. "So what you're telling me is, he needs to, like, disappear into thin air until an appropriate time for him to reappear."

Clint set his beer can down and mused, "Yep, I never could put anything past you, Cam. You're just too damn smart for me, and I thought a smart man like you might know someone that could help us with this situation."

Cam smiled and sparks flickered from his eyes. "Believe it or not, that's exactly why I built two bedrooms onto this house. Not that it makes any difference, but how long do you figure you'll need a place?"

"Maybe a spell, Cam. Can you help?"

Cam reached for his pole, which was jerking up and down. "You don't have to ask twice, Clint. If Ham can put up with me, I'll figure a way to tolerate him." Cam turned the handle of the reel until a nice-sized trout broke the surface of the swiftly moving waters and landed on the dock next to Cam's chair. Cam reached down and gently removed the hook from the pulsating fish and tossed it back into the river. "Got enough in the house for dinner tonight. I just like to say hello to the beautiful bastards. You'll stay for dinner, Clint?"

"Can't do it, Cam. Too much happening back in civilization. We may be getting warm on this bunch, and I don't want to miss an opportunity for the kill. These are a well-organized and brutal bunch. Killed a Mississippi State trooper yesterday. It was messy!

"If you notice anything odd around here, you'll know what to do. Don't give them any quarter and don't expect any. I don't think we'll be very long wrapping this up. I'll call you every day or so and keep you posted."

Cam and Ham watched Clint's car disappear in a cloud of dust as it headed back to *civilization*. Cam muttered, "I'm sure glad I got out of civilization when I did. Seems like it gets more uncivilized every year! Come on, Ham, let's go up to the house and I'll show you where to put your stuff."

They walked toward the house, still hearing the soft noises made by the river as it sped along the way to the Mississippi then on to New Orleans, delivering its bounty to the Gulf of Mexico.

* * *

A few miles further south, Glenn Wiggs sat on his porch, watching the mighty river make its way toward the gulf. The murder of the state policeman in Mississippi had added emphasis to Glenn and the other members of his commission. This morning, he had called Lorna Summers and filled her in on the killing, and she said she would talk to the commander of the Arkansas State Police and raise the alert level. "I don't want any of my people to be surprised. Funerals for dead cops are not a function I'm eager to attend."

Movement on the river caught Glenn's attention, and for the next half-hour, he watched the big barge train come around the bend going downstream then hanging off to the right side, leaving room for another set of barges that were heading north. The captain of each boat maneuvered their craft to accomplish the complex process of gauging their angle of moving through the changing currents against the heavily loaded barges filled with precious cargo that powered the economy of numerous states.

When the two barges had completed the task and disappeared into the distance, Glenn reminded himself to finish packing his overnight bag and begin the drive down to New Orleans.

As he walked down the hall toward the master bedroom, Glenn heard the phone ring in the kitchen. He walked into the bedroom and picked up the extension phone on the nightstand by the bed. He heard Clint Parker's voice and immediately thought he heard a concerned tone.

"Glenn, we've got some late developments in our investigation that I thought you should know about. I played a hunch and went out to Carsonville yesterday. I found Ham Turner hiding out there in the old jail facilities. It took a little persuading, but after some real straight talk, Ham decided it was in his best interest to come clean and cooperate with us in our investigation. He doesn't know everything, but I think he knows enough to give us a big jump in our mission. I'm confident we can fill in the holes of his story, and I decided to take him into an official protective custody. I've got him stashed out at Cameron Wilson's place on Current River. Over the next day or two, Cam will lead the conversation to bleed as much information as Ham possesses about our target. I think he's going to be pretty valuable to us. He won't know all the specific occurrences and/or people, but I believe he can give us supporting evidence on both and help us focus the investigation. I've gotta finish my report and get it off to St. Louis and DC, so I'm not sure if I will get down to New Orleans today or wait and drive down early in the morning. Why don't you go ahead and start the meeting tomorrow? And I'll join you as soon as I get down there. Sorry I'm going to miss dinner tonight with you guys. Had my mouth all ready for some good Cajun cooking, but another time, as they say."

* * *

"Hot Springs!" A buzzing sound resembling that of a bumblebee's resonated through the suite. A call on his private line—an unlisted number—always made Blake fearful that something might be wrong. Only three or four people knew the number, and they rarely used it except to report a problem or to ask him to perform a task he was not eager for.

"Blake here!"

The voice on the line was not of a regular caller. In fact, Blake had never heard this voice before.

"Chadwick here. Are you alone?"

Blake looked around instinctively to be sure. "Yes. My wife will be back from shopping shortly, but I am alone."

"Listen very carefully," the voice said without emotion. "I am very troubled by a death in our family. It is important to me to know if this was a stupid, unavoidable accident or a lapse in our organization. I will get reports from other relatives, but I want one from you. From what I know about you, I can trust you not to be influenced by emotion or personal relationships. I want the background of the person who carried the disease and what his or her relationship is to our family. I have heard that individual is not a blood relation and was just visiting one of the cousins. I want to know all about him, including where he is. You should be able to get the report to me by this time tomorrow." The voice recited a ten-digit phone number, which Blake scribbled on a message pad, and the line went dead.

For what seemed like a long time, Blake sat looking at the telephone. He ran the words through his mind over and over, trying to understand the significance of the call. He was sure he had never heard the voice before, but he had heard offhand comments about "the man in Miami" always mentioned with a tone of respect, or maybe fear, on the part of the speaker. It had been a few years ago, but Blake recalled a man and woman attending the grand opening of the casino. Many VIPs had come to the opening, and he suspected many wanted to be seen by the VIPs or to have a chance to ingratiate themselves for future favors. This particular man had been stuck in Blake's memory because at the time, he was puzzled why the number-two man in the Arkansas Bureau of Investigation would come to his party.

Blake remembered noticing the man being in clusters of people that often included Blake's partner from Little Rock. The idea flashed in Blake's mind that he might get the report his anonymous caller had requested directly from the ABI. There was risk involved in going too such a man and being curious about a murder of a state policeman in Mississippi. If he was wrong about the man, he could bring suspicion on himself. He would have to have a plan on how to approach Mr.—Mr. King, yes that was his name. Alvin King!

The plan on how to approach Mr. King developed quickly in Blake's mind. He reached for his casino extension phone and asked the operator to get him Mr. Alvin King at the Arkansas Bureau of investigation in Little Rock.

* * *

It was about four thirty that afternoon when Alvin King walked into the Razorback lounge, a few blocks from the capitol building. Blake saw the straw hat with the red band around it King said he would be wearing and waved him back to the booth.

"It's very good of you to take the time to meet with me, Mr. King. I remember you attending our opening over in Hot Springs, and I'm sorry I didn't get to spend more time with you. Have you had a chance to come back to our establishment?"

"I'm sorry to say, Mr. Stevens, I haven't, but let me say I was very impressed with the grandeur of the place. I'm not much of a gambler, but my wife and I have talked about coming to Hot Springs just for the baths. When we do that, I'd like to stop in and say hello to you and maybe see if my luck came with me."

They ordered their drinks—a martini for Blake and a Manhattan for Mr. King. While they waited for their drinks, King leaned back in the booth. "I was surprised when you called me and asked if we could have a drink together. Is there anything in particular I can do for you?"

"As a matter of fact, I could use your input regarding a new reporting form that the state is going to require from us. It has to do with revenue, and I am unsure whether we include the food and beverage revenue from the restaurant and the room income from the hotel. I thought, since I was going to be in town this afternoon, you might be able to advise me so that I do the form correctly."

Mr. King replied in a very official-sounding voice, "I would have to check it out to be sure, but that form is from the gaming commission that was formed to oversee your operation and any others like it. I'm pretty certain that their only interest is in revenue from gambling."

"Is that something your agency would be responsible for auditing?"

"I don't think so. The gaming commission has their own investigators to probe into compliance issues. We don't usually get involved until we're certain that a crime has been committed."

"So I would gather your work is much more dangerous than the commission," Blake said and noticed a slight swelling of King's chest as he heard the words.

"That pretty well sums it up, I suppose. The danger is part of the job, and sometimes, it's what attracts a man to our work."

Blake saw that his plan was working perfectly. "I was just reading in the paper yesterday about the state patrolman being killed in Mississippi. Do you know if they've made any progress on finding out who did that? From what the paper said, it must've been a pretty grisly scene!"

"Yes, I read a copy of the report from the investigating officer, and it appears it was an extremely vicious shooting. His conclusion is that two shotgun blasts caused the officer's death, and the second shot was pretty close up—face, head, neck were torn up, making recognition very difficult. When a killing of a cop occurs, the entire force gets pretty mobilized and will work harder in the next weeks to find that killer than most of them have done all year long."

Blake's eyes opened wide as he said, "I just remembered that I met a fellow when he came into my country bar a few years back, and I think I've heard that he's with the ABI now. Do you know him, Mr. Ham Turner?"

King coughed and cleared his throat. "As a matter of fact, I think I have met Mr. Turner at a staff meeting once or twice. I think he used to be a marshal of sorts for the little town called Carsonville. Seemed like a pretty nice fellow."

"Hey, it's a small world. If you happen to run into him, say hello for me."

"It's possible that Mr. Turner may be ill. Someone asked me about him this morning. Apparently hasn't been to work for the last few days, and I guess he didn't call in sick. But if I run into him, I will tell him you said hello."

The two men continued the small talk through a second round of drinks. Blake noticed toward the end of the second drink that King was developing a slight slur in his speech, and Blake concluded the man had a low tolerance for alcohol or he had gotten a head start today.

After King left the lounge, Blake went back to a pay phone near the restrooms and dialed the number in Miami, Florida. He told the voice on the phone what he had found and what he suspected. When he mentioned that Turner had not been to work for two or three days, he thought he heard the man swear under his breath. When they finished, the man uncharacteristically complimented Blake. "You did good work, Stevens. I'm impressed with how much you found out in such a short time. You're a real competent guy. Maybe we'll meet in person one of these days."

Before he left town, Blake drove to the Cotton Belt State Bank, where he handed Ross Mathews $10,000 in cash to be the final deposit into the special accounts Mathews had established for Blake and Gabby. Feeling like, all things considered, it had been a pretty successful day, he began the drive back to Hot Springs. When he pulled into his parking slot in the back of the casino, he noticed the lights were on in the executive suite. He rushed upstairs with anticipation surging in him.

When he opened the door to the suite, the first thing he saw was Gabby standing at the bar, wearing a lace-trimmed gown that clung to her body in all the right places. She turned to the opening door, holding a martini in each hand. "Hi, handsome, would you care to share these with me?"

"Lady, I want to share everything with you. I have missed you painfully for the last three days."

She went into his arms, holding the drinks in her outstretched hands, and welcomed his long deep kiss.

While they enjoyed the perfectly concocted martinis, Gabby filled Blake in on the meetings she had in Kansas City with her financial managers. She then went back to the bar and made two more drinks and listened attentively while Blake filled her in on his phone call and trip to Little Rock.

Gabby's face turned serious, and she inquired, "Darling, you would tell me if you had serious fears about our business partners, wouldn't you?"

Blake didn't hesitate in his reply. "Babe, I don't keep anything from you, that I know for sure. However, I don't like to worry you with things that I only suspect and don't know. I don't mind telling you that I spend a little part of each day speculating on different scenarios of how we might separate ourselves from our partners and live to enjoy it. I haven't figured that out yet, but I feel it in my bones that the solution is getting closer. I just want you to know that keeping you safe is my number-one priority."

Gabby got up from her chair and walked over to Blake and slid slowly into his lap. With her mouth close to Blake's ear, Gabby whispered, "Let's go in the bedroom, you handsome devil, and I will demonstrate what my number-one priority is!"

CHAPTER 16

It was well past 9:00 p.m. when Clint Parker pulled into his driveway. It had been a long day, but he thought it had been especially productive. If he could keep Ham Turner more frightened of the people in New Orleans, Little Rock, Memphis, and God knew how many other places there might be than he was afraid of the FBI and the assorted law enforcement agencies in the Southeastern United States, there would be a real opportunity to deal damaging blows to the drug cartel.

His wife, Jean, had heard the car pull into the garage and was in the kitchen, heating up his dinner. "Hey, there, mister, I had started to think you have forgotten your way home."

Clint set down his briefcase, hung his coat on the back of a stool, and spotted the glass of red wine sitting on the island. He picked up the glass and took a sip of the rich red liquid and swallowed. Setting the glass back on the island, Clint smacked his approval as Jean moved across the kitchen to give him a welcome kiss.

"Did I ever tell you that you know how to welcome a man home better than any other woman in the world?"

Jean pulled back from the kiss and looked at him with a scolding on her face. "Now, how would you know about other women and how they welcome a man home?"

Clint flashed a smug smile and said, "Because, my dear lady, I am with the FBI, the world's foremost investigating agency, and after using all the investigative techniques, the conclusion is that no one gives you any competition. I just have to feel sorry for all the other husbands in the world. But don't worry, I'm not going to brag so much about it that they begin to give me competition."

Jean turned away from him and went back to the dinner on the stove. "This is going to take another five minutes. Should give you enough time to return Glenn Wiggs's phone call. His message is on the pad next to the phone in the living room."

Clint took his wine out to the living room and slid into the overstuffed La-Z-Boy and placed a call to Glenn. The soft leather was cool and comforting as it began to take away the stress of the long day.

Glenn Wiggs answered on the second ring. "Clint, I gather you've had a pretty long day. I hope it was as productive as it was long."

"It was a very productive day, Governor. It seems that I have persuaded Mr. Turner that his best interests for his future safety are solidly with the FBI and the commission." Clint went on to fill the governor in on the events of the day and ended his brief report, disclosing the whereabouts of Ham Turner.

"Excellent judgment, Clint. I can't imagine anyone figuring out that Cam's house on the river would be where the FBI would hide a witness. Have you heard anything further on the shooting in Mississippi?"

"Not today, Governor. Amos is handling things on that end, and I'll know more after I talk to him in the morning. If we keep chipping away, I predict things will start to move faster as the bad guys begin to feel the pinch. We'll all be back together next week in New Orleans. In the meantime, you and your commission members should be giving some thought to proposed legislation, federal and state, that will put some teeth behind our efforts. I hate to think so that our actions are going to be out in front of the legislators. We mustn't forget that we already have laws against smuggling illegal drugs into the United States as well as the other activities including murder and assaulting an officer of the law. I'm gonna eat some dinner and try to get a good night's sleep. We'll probably be talking again tomorrow morning after I visit Amos. Give Mary my love, and thanks for all your help."

Clint carried his empty glass back to the kitchen, where Jean gave him a prompt refill and sat with him while he ate the warmed-over pork chop, mashed potatoes, and green beans. Jean talked to him while he ate. They took an hour in front of the TV set while Clint digested his dinner and then went up to bed. Before Clint dropped off to sleep, his mind went back to Carsonville. Finding Ham hiding in the strange town reminded him of how Orville Carson tried to use the town as a hiding place for his inhuman deeds of using slave labor to develop and work in Carson Farms. The thought of the horrifying executions of those poor souls that tried to escape sent an involuntary shudder through Clint.

Maybe Orville had thought that building the town would give him the protection from the cries of anguish and the demands for justice that were eventually heaped on his head. *Oh well,* he thought, *that's why society needs people like me, to expose brutality and bring justice to people like Orville Carson.* That thought comforted him as he drifted off to sleep.

CHAPTER 17

New Orleans

Carl Hoffman resisted the urge to slam the door behind him and began to descend the stairs at the Jolly Roger Bar. Frederick Sanchez had just chewed his ass raw, and his pride was pushing him hard for a violent reaction.

From the beginning, Carl had detected in Frederick a quiet but lethal temper that he didn't want unleashed at him. At the same time, Carl saw no harm in bringing Pierre Gaudet into the warehouse and introducing him to Orlando. Orlando and Pierre had hit it off right away, and the pressure was on to get another truck off to Memphis. At that time, Carl was suffering a bout of the Asian flu and couldn't stay out of the bathroom, either throwing up or shitting himself, long enough to make a truck run to Memphis.

Pierre's background seemed to qualify him for the work, and in his haste, Orlando made a bad mistake. Orlando did not check with Frederick and get his approval on the new man. It was highly probable that Frederick would have approved the hiring of Pierre just as Orlando had. The difference was Orlando made the decision without the authority of Frederick, so Frederick had a scapegoat to blame for the shooting of the state policeman in Mississippi. Carl speculated that Orlando had already had his ass chewed out before the session that just ended. Nevertheless, during Carl's ass-chewing session, Orlando made no move to defend him.

Carl stopped at the bar downstairs and ordered a Comfort maker. He carried the whiskey and stein of beer over to a table and sat, feeling very sorry for himself. Carl had met Pierre through Alice. From time to time, he had been Alice's source in getting to get the recreational drugs she used. Alice had not heard from Pierre since the shooting. He probably figured he was in deep shit with Orlando and assumed that someone would be watching Alice's pad in case he showed up there. Frederick was very angry that two fuckups like Carl and Pierre could jeopardize his entire enterprise over a cop killing. Frederick didn't kill cops; it was much cheaper and more effective to buy them.

Carl had told Orlando and Frederick that he had not heard from Pierre since the shooting. He had heard about the shooting from Alice, who had seen it on TV news. Frederick had slammed on his desk and told both men that he didn't give a damn how we got it done, but he wanted Pierre to be taken out. He had gotten the information since the shooting that Pierre was a two-time loser and the prospects facing him from a pull-over by Mississippi State Police was spending the rest of his life in prison. If that motivated him enough to kill a cop, it could encourage him to rat out the operation in New Orleans to avoid life behind bars.

Carl remembered that the man who had just chewed his ass out was still upstairs and decided the Jolly Roger was no place for him to get drunk. He took the last swallow of the whiskey, drained the stein of beer, and went out on the street to flag a cab.

He was still hanging out at Alice's apartment, so he gave the cabbie the address and leaned back in the seat to focus on what he was going to do. He hadn't been in New Orleans long enough to know where to look for people. He'd try to get Alice's help, but he knew she'd be slow to give up a drug source. When the cab stopped in front of Alice's apartment, Carl handed over a handful of bills and went up the steps. Alice gave him a friendly hello and went over to rub herself against him.

"Knock that shit off. I'm not in the mood! If you want to do something useful, pour me a stiff shot and open a beer. What the hell's going on around here anyway?"

"Well, Mr. Asshole, I got a nice dinner waiting for you and here you show up sore as a boil and mean as a wild pig. Maybe I should just throw the stuff out. Would that make you happy?"

"Since when did you go domestic and start fixing dinner? The only thing I've ever seen you do to fix dinner is make a rum and tonic and decide where to go out to eat."

Alice plopped herself down on the sofa. "Well, tonight I thought it would be nice, so I went down to the barbecue place and bought some pulled pork and all the trimmings. Whenever you decide you're hungry, we'll eat dinner."

Carl sat on the other end of the couch and drank from the tumbler of bourbon, setting it on the coffee table and holding on to the can of beer.

They sat in silence for a while until Alice spoke, "I heard from Pierre today. You were asking me if he had called, and I hadn't heard from him until this afternoon."

Carl straightened up and looked at Alice. "Where was he? Is he coming over here tonight? Where is he staying?"

"Take it easy, Carl. He's not coming over here. In fact, he's still in Memphis. Said he's not sure he's coming back to New Orleans. He sounded real weird, wanted to know if the cops had been by here, looking for him. I told him, 'Hell no, and if they did, I'd say, he don't live with me.' Why would the cops come here looking for him anyway?"

"Did he say where he was staying in Memphis or give you a phone number on how to reach him?" Carl was back on his feet, pacing across the room and into the kitchen.

"He didn't have a place when he called. Said he was gonna have to lie low for a few days and that he would call me to find out what was happening here in New Orleans. What's going on with you two? Is he in some kind of trouble? What am I asking? He's always in some kind of trouble. What's going on, Carl?"

Carl went back out of the kitchen and stood in front of Alice. "I'll tell you what's going on. Your friend Pierre is a crazy son of a bitch, and he's got me in hot water with Frederick and Orlando."

"How could Pierre get you in trouble with Frederick? I've never introduced them, and I don't think they even know each other."

"I'll tell you how he got me in trouble, you dumb bitch! The other day, when I came down with the flu and was so damn sick, I was supposed to make a run to Memphis. You'd introduced me to Pierre, and he said any time we needed some help, he needed work. I took him down to the warehouse and introduced him to Orlando. I told Orlando I was too sick to go but Pierre could take my place. I told Orlando he was the kind of guy that didn't ask questions, he had experience driving a truck, and they wouldn't have to worry about him."

Alice scowled. "I don't get it. How did your introducing Pierre get you in trouble with Frederick? Did he wreck the truck or steal it?"

"He didn't steal anything. He got to the delivery point in Memphis and told them he couldn't bring the truck back to New Orleans. He said he had to drop off the radar for a few days. One of the guys in Memphis had to drive the truck back."

"Is that what Frederick got mad about, someone in Memphis having to bring the truck back? Seems like a pretty small thing to make a federal case about. What does Frederick want you to do about it?"

Carl was pacing across the apartment. "It wasn't a simple thing that riled Frederick. He thinks Pierre killed a cop! Frederick knows that when you kill a cop, all the rest of the cops come down on your head. The FBI will probably get after Pierre, and that's something Frederick does not want to happen. Frederick's organization is running smooth, and the last thing he wants is a bunch of nosy feds sniffing around his operation. He wants me to go to Memphis and find Pierre. Do you know any connections he has there? I need someplace to start."

Alice thought hard for a minute before she spoke. "I remember him saying that he worked a job in South Memphis. I think he said he lived down that way, had an apartment or room next to the industrial district along the river. Oh yeah, I remember. He said he stayed in an apartment with a buddy—a cellmate—when he was in Joliet. That's all I can remember. Pierre didn't talk much about his past."

Carl stopped his pacing. "I have to go to Memphis and find Pierre. Frederick said that right now, it's a small problem. If I clean it up while it's small, Frederick will forget all about this. If he has to clean it up because it got bigger, he will take care of the problem, and I'm afraid that includes me."

* * *

Three hours later, the sun settled behind the low hills in the west, and darkness was closing fast. A city bus stopped in front of the French Courtyard, and a man stepped to the pavement and began walking along the line of parked cars. The two valets were swamped, and the cars were beginning to back up in line. The man stood in the shadows across the street from the restaurant and watched as another car pulled to the back of the line, and two couples got out of the car and walked to the front door. The door opened as they approached, and the maître d' inside welcomed them as regular customers. The restaurant was known for its authentic French cuisine, and the man in the shadows calculated two to three hours for dinner. The valet station was empty. While both men shuttled cars to the parking lot in the next block, the figure in the shadows moved quickly across the street to the burgundy Cadillac. One look inside told him what he figured: the keys were in the ignition. The big V-8 engine responded to the signal from the key, and in less than twelve seconds, the car made a

U-turn and then a right at the next light and disappeared into the blackness of the night.

Once he was satisfied that no one had observed him taking the car and the rearview mirror confirmed there was no pursuit, Carl adjusted the seat and the rearview mirror. Ten minutes later, he was on the interstate highway, northbound to Memphis. By the time the owner finished his after-dinner drink, Carl would be driving into South Memphis.

CHAPTER 18

It was eleven fifteen that evening when Carl walked in to the River Rat. He had checked into a Motel 6 a little farther from the bar than the one he normally stayed in. He knew the motel a block away from the River Rat had connections with Frederick and his organization and on this trip. He wasn't anxious for Frederick or Orlando to know where was staying.

Cindy Murphy was busy setting drinks on a table full of boisterous drinkers. Their clothes indicated they were part of a bowling league and were celebrating a victory that evening.

Carl pulled the chair out from a small table just behind Cindy, and he waited. When she had finished with the demands of the bowlers, she turned to go back to the bar and saw Carl.

"Well, damn! Look what the cat dragged in while I wasn't looking. It's been a while, Carl, and I was beginning to think you didn't like the service here anymore."

Carl smiled. "You mean the best service in Memphis? How could a man not like that? When you're headed back this way, bring me a Southern Comfort on the rocks and a glass of beer. I just got off the road, and I need to take the kinks out."

For the next two hours, it remained pretty busy in the bar, but as the crowd dwindled down to a handful of serious drinkers, Cindy went over to join him. As she slid into the chair next to him, her firm breasts brushed over his shoulder. "I really have thought about you, Carl. Are you here for long?"

"I don't know yet," Carl answered as he took a swallow from his drink. "I have some errands to run, and it may take a day or two. You doing anything after work tonight?"

It was near 2:00 a.m. when Cindy finally went out of the bar and joined Carl in the parking lot. She looked at the Cadillac he was standing next to and asked, "Is this your wheels just for tonight, or did you trade the fish truck for the Cadillac? I'd say you are moving up in the world."

Cindy slid in his arms, pressing her body against him, telling him in no uncertain terms how much she had missed him. The Sedan DeVille had bench seats that allowed her to slide snugly against him, and they spent a few minutes reacquainting each other with the pleasure that was promised.

Carl finally pulled free of her and started the car, driving carefully onto the street and to Motel 6.

"So you decided the motel by the bar wasn't good enough for you anymore?" Cindy inquired as she continued to nuzzle him on the ear.

"I didn't call ahead and make a reservation, so I thought they would be full. And the Motel 6 had a vacancy sign out, so I just stopped there. I don't think it's any nicer, but come on in and see what you think."

The room was standard Motel 6. There was a small refrigerator, and the ice tray was adequate for two drinks. Cindy dropped the ice cubes into the glasses and poured them half-full of Southern Comfort. Carl sat in one of the two plastic-covered chairs and slipped his shoes off. Cindy slid into his lap and offered him his drink. She took a long pull from her drink and set it on the small table by the chair. As she turned to face him, her lips brushed across his once then again. Her breath felt warm against his cheek, and he reached for her. It only took about two minutes of stroking and groping before they began pulling each other's clothes off. Carl set down his drink and stood from the chair, holding Cindy like a baby. He sat her down on the bed, and she finished pulling off her few remaining clothes. Together they pulled the covers from the bed and lay down on the fresh sheets as if they were one body. They finished with Cindy on top of him, and for a while, she just let herself lay there while her lungs resupplied her body with the oxygen it craved.

When she finally rolled off Carl, she lay facing him and looked as if she expected some new revelation. "You're a man full of surprises! The first time I met you, you were driving a truck and staying in one motel. The next time you're driving a Cadillac and staying in a different motel. It's kind of exciting. I've never known one before, but I think I like a man who surprises me."

Carl's mind went back to what his important mission was tonight. "I'm sure you must know a lot a guys. Are you sure none of the others haven't surprised you?"

"You may have the wrong idea about me, Carl. A lot of guys do flirt with me in the bar and some have tried to go further than flirting, but I'm pretty careful about keeping the relationship between customer and us as barmaid. We get some pretty strange guys coming into the River Rat, and I'm still a small-town, country girl. I don't want you to get the wrong opinion of me. It's just different with you. I don't feel threatened when I'm with you."

Carl reached for her and pulled her closer. "You say you meet strange guys in the bar. What makes a guy strange to you? Is it the way he looks or the way he talks? What exactly makes you feel strange?"

"I don't know if I can describe it. I don't like guys with an accent, and sometimes, if their eyes are too close together and small, that kind of thing can give me a queasy feeling."

Carl brushed her hair back with his right hand and let it slide onto her shoulders and down her arm. "Do you get many guys with accents in the bar? Like, maybe, French-sounding or something like that? I know a guy that fits that description, and I think he's here in Memphis. I think if I were a girl, I wouldn't trust him. I've met quite a few men like him in New Orleans. Down there, they call them French Creole. They got a lot of different blood mixed together. French, Indian, black! It makes him look funny, and they talk even funnier."

A scowl formed across Cindy's face. "That's really funny that you would mention someone like that. A guy came in the bar maybe two days ago that looked and talked like you just described. It was early in the evening, and I had just started my shift. I was helping the boss tend the bar because there was nobody at the tables yet. He came in and acted a little shy. Well, I thought it was shyness. He kept looking around the place like he thought he may see someone he knew. I guess he didn't because he finally came to the bar and sat at a stool nearest the door. I had to walk from where I was working down to him to take his order. Kind of pissed me off, but I walked down to where the inconsiderate bastard was sitting and took his order. He had a real accent! I didn't know what it was then, but now that you mention French, I think that's what it was."

Carl loosened his hold and asked, "Did he tell you his name?"

Cindy concentrated. "I don't think so, but I didn't talk to him much. After I poured his drink, the boss came back and I asked him to take the guy his drink. They talked a little bit, but I couldn't hear what they were saying. I was glad to be rid of the guy, and then business started picking up and I was busy and didn't think any more about him until now."

"Do you think your boss would remember if you heard his name?"

At Carl's urging, Cindy was persuaded to call her boss at home. Despite it being in the middle of the night, 3:00 a.m. to be exact, he scolded her for bothering him and then recalled the man at the bar saying his name as being Pierre. He remembered it because it was so unusual.

He said, "You don't run into a Pierre in a third-rate bar very often." Cindy thanked him and hung up the phone.

Carl was sitting up in the bed as Cindy went back and pulled the sheet up over both of them. She was sure it had been just two nights ago.

Carl's thinking was that it must have been the night after he dropped the truck and disappeared from the warehouse. The warehouse wasn't very far from the River Rat bar, so it made sense that he must be hanging around in this neighborhood. He had no idea how to find an address for Pierre, but he had a good feeling that he was on the right track. Cindy was squirming against him, and when she reached between his legs and began to massage him so carefully, he decided that tomorrow would be soon enough to worry about finding Pierre. It was after 4:00 a.m. before the two of them surrendered to sleep, pleasingly exhausted.

* * *

It was about noon when Carl and Cindy left the motel room. She directed him to a nearby restaurant that served breakfast all day long. After they ate, Carl asked Cindy what she was doing the rest of the day. She said she'd planned to do some light shopping, drugstore stuff, but she didn't have to do that today. Carl said he'd be glad to drive her to the drugstore, and she responded with a quick kiss and skipped to the Cadillac. She obviously didn't feel strange with Carl, he thought.

At the drugstore, Carl told her he would just wait in the car while she did her shopping.

The drugstore was an old-fashioned pharmacy that had added enough sundries and minor grocery items to keep the shop opened. Across the street, Carl noticed a combination of businesses on the first floor and what appeared to be apartments or sleeping rooms upstairs. This was the kind of commonsense development that many cities allowed and encouraged in the early 1900s. An alley cut between the buildings in the middle of the block and was probably the access to off-street parking for the people who lived on the block. Carl used the tuning knob to adjust the radio, as all the presets had been to stations in New Orleans. The sounds of blues began to come through the radio, and as Carl struggled to fine-tune the selector knob, movement caught his eye and drew his attention to the alley across the street. He had to look twice before he believed what he was seeing. Pierre Gaudet walked out of the alley and onto the sidewalk, stopping to look in both directions and removing his cap to scratch his head. He looked like he might have just gotten out of bed and was thinking about something to eat.

As Pierre turned and started to walk north, Carl got out of the Cadillac and began to follow on the opposite side of the street and half a block behind. Pierre walked a slow, steady pace, keeping against the front of the buildings. He was obviously trying to stay as inconspicuous as possible. In the middle of the third block, he paused in front of a sign that simply read Groceries. He paused and slowly looked in all three directions. Carl turned and looked in the window of a store on his left. Through the reflection in the glass window, Carl saw Pierre, obviously convinced he was not being followed, turn and walk into the grocery store.

Carl returned to the parking lot of the drugstore and found Cindy anxiously waiting. "Where did you go? When you weren't here, I thought you might have gone into the drugstore to look for me. I was just about to go back in there to see if I could find you. Did you have to get something? You don't have a bag. What was it you needed?"

Carl pushed the remote to unlock the car. "I didn't need anything. I just got out to stretch my legs and walked farther than I meant to. Did you get everything you needed?"

Carl drove Cindy to her apartment, not far from the bar where she worked. She asked him if he wanted to come in, but he made an excuse that she needed to get ready for work soon and he would go back to the bar later tonight. She agreed, saying that she needed to get a nap. "It's Saturday night," she said. "It'll be a long night, but if you came in late, we could leave together." She blushed and giggled as she turned toward the apartment.

Carl drove back to the drugstore and parked in its parking lot.

During his time in New Orleans, Carl had met various acquaintances of Alice. One of the youngest in her circle of friends was a man they all referred to as the Duke. The Duke was a flashy dresser and a fast-talker. He tried to befriend Carl, and as they got to know each other pretty well, he remarked, "My man, you're new to the Big Easy, and there's something you should know. This is the most fun town you will ever find, and at the same time, it is the most dangerous streets you will ever walk and live to talk about. What makes it easier to be sure you're going to live to talk about it is if you have a gun in your pocket. For a very modest price, I can help you acquire the protection Alice would want you to have."

Carl had given the Duke the money, and in a few days, Duke delivered a very nice Smith & Wesson .38 with a snub nose that made concealed carrying simple.

CHAPTER 19

As Carl prepared to leave the car in the drugstore parking lot, he reached to the glove compartment, unlocking the door and retrieving the little Smith & Wesson and dropping it in his jacket pocket. He walked across the street and down the alley until he came upon an entrance door that led to a small foyer. A small sign next to the door read Rooms for Rent, and across the bottom were the words No Vacancy!

Carl carefully stepped inside the foyer. A small nest of mailboxes were built into the wall to his right. Two wooden doors, painted brown to match the rest of the wall, opened onto the small area. Above, one door was the number 1 and the other, number 2.

Carl looked at the mailboxes and saw there were five, so he assumed the other three doors were up the flight of stairs to his left. Four of the mailboxes had names written on little slips of paper and inserted in the metal slots provided. The number 5 mailbox had no identification name. That was where he would find Pierre, he thought. The man who does not want any attention will not put his name on his mailbox. He went up the stairs quietly and turned back down a short hall to the door marked 5.

The door was equipped with a lock in the handle and a deadbolt lock above. He tried the door handle, and it turned freely, but the door remained closed. *Pierre must be relying on the deadbolt for his security,* he thought.

Carl went back down the stairs and returned to the Cadillac. He waited about half an hour before he saw Pierre coming back down the sidewalk, carrying a medium-sized shopping bag. Pierre turned down the alley and entered the rooming house's door. Carl did not want to leave the parking lot and risk Pierre leaving his room and heading for a destination unknown, so he waited, the blues station sending out the melodious notes and sympathetic lyrics through the surround sound of the Cadillac's radio system.

As the sun settled over the western skyline of the city, darkness began to settle. Carl was relieved to see a mercury-vapor streetlight illuminate on the corner of the building next to the alley. It was about 7:00 p.m. when Pierre came out of the alley onto the sidewalk. He looked about as if he couldn't decide which direction to take. "Getting a little bored, are we, Pierre? It gets a little nerve-racking when you don't know who to trust and you're not sure what the guy that may be coming to you looks like," Carl muttered to himself.

Pierre made a decision and turned left, proceeding south on the block. Carl watched from the car until he thought it was safe to go on the street and follow at a very slow pace. The Cadillac moved quietly, maintaining a safe distance behind Pierre.

The surveillance extended for five blocks before Pierre approached a group of three men standing on the corner. The conversation went on, at times animated, and then Pierre pulled something from his pocket and handed it to one of the men. A few more words and Pierre resumed his walk southward. At the next corner, a man stepped out of the shadows and Pierre turned to him. After a brief exchange, the man pulled something from his pocket and handed it to Pierre. Carl knew that he had just witnessed a pretty common drug buy.

Pierre turned and started back in the direction of the rooming house. Carl had the Cadillac parked on the street with the lights off and watched in his rearview mirror until Pierre was a block and a half away. Carl turned the Cadillac in a *U* and followed at a very slow speed. Back at the drugstore, Pierre turned down the alley and reentered the rooming house's foyer. Carl watched the second floor of the building until he saw the light come on in room number 5. That time was now 8:00 p.m.

After two hours of blues music and consuming half of the Southern Comfort still in the bottle he had brought along, Carl decided it was time. He figured Pierre would be very much under the influence of whatever drug he had bought. He didn't have a definite plan; he just knew that Pierre had to go for Carl's own protection.

Carl went soundlessly up the stairs and tried the door handle again. "Getting pretty careless, Pierre!" he muttered half to himself as the door began to open. As he was preparing to walk through the door, a small squeak came from one of the hinges. Pierre heard the sound, and though his reactions were slow, he turned to look at the door.

Pierre recognized Carl, but his senses were moving slow in processing the picture he saw. Carl saw the look of recognition cross Pierre's eyes. There were about two paces for Pierre to reach the kitchen cabinet and about six for Carl to go from the door to the table. Pierre won that race.

And when he turned around, he was holding a kitchen knife with a five-inch blade. Carl was holding the .38, but it was still in his pocket. The cocaine Pierre had purchased on the street was on the table, in neatly arranged rows, a single-edge razor blade lying nearby.

"What the hell are you doing here? I know you, you son of a bitch. What are you doing in my room?"

Pierre's speech was jerky as he struggled to put the right words in order to be understood and for his own understanding.

Carl made a quick decision and sat down at the table in a chair across from where Pierre had been. "Pierre, old buddy! I'm Carl, your friend from Big Easy. What's new? I haven't seen you for days, and Alice is concerned about you. We thought maybe you'd been hurt in a car wreck or something!"

Pierre's eyes blinked rapidly, but his brain was moving ever so slowly, like a man trying to walk fast in wet cement.

Carl continued the talking. "Looks like some fine stuff you got here on the table, Pierre. You planning to use all of this for yourself, or do you want to share some of it with your friend?"

Pierre loosened his grip on the knife and let the point migrate toward the floor.

"Come on, old buddy, I do favors for you. Now you can share with me. What do you say, friend?"

A shudder went through Pierre's upper body as he laid the knife on the table. "Carl, right? Your name is Carl? You got me the job, driving the truck. I remember. Bad job, driving the truck. Stupid fucking cop saw me veer off the road and just decided to pull me over. He was nosy, looking at places in the truck that he shouldn't have been looking at.

"Not going to send me back to prison. I couldn't let him do that to me. You showed me the shotgun, remember? That's why you showed it to me, so I could stop him from sending me back to prison. Have you ever been to prison?" Carl shook his head. "It's bad."

Carl let Pierre ramble on; it seemed to be taking his mind off the knife, but the knife was exactly what Carl was concentrating on. He pulled the bottle of Southern Comfort from his jacket and set it on the table.

Pierre shifted his gaze. "What's that you got? That's good stuff, isn't it? You're all right, friend. You brought Pierre some good whiskey."

Carl stood from his chair. "Let me get you a glass, Pierre, and I'll pour you a drink. A real good drink!" Carl took a glass from the counter and turned back to the table. He walked up on Pierre's right side, placing himself between Pierre and the knife. He set the glass down directly in front of Pierre and reached around him to pour the golden liquid into the glass. Pierre watched his every move and, as soon as he stopped pouring, picked up the glass and raised it to his mouth. Carl set the bottle back on the table and, in a continuing motion, picked up the knife. Carl's left hand went around Pierre's neck and held him tight as his right hand plunged the knife into Pierre's side. Pierre's hands clawed to find the knife and stop the pain sensation. Carl withdrew the knife and, while holding Pierre still tight against his own body, drove the knife between two left ribs again. He felt Pierre's body begin to relax as he eased him to the floor. The second thrust of the knife must have hit Pierre's heart. Blood was streaming from the two wounds, and in just seconds, Pierre appeared to have died.

Carl was breathing hard. He had never killed a man before, and the realization of what he had done was leaving him numb and slightly disoriented. He looked about the grisly scene, trying to decide what he should do. He took a towel from a hanger in the kitchen and began to wipe the bottle of Southern Comfort.

Fingerprints, he had to get rid of fingerprints! His brain was screaming for him to leave. He wanted to run away from the bloodstain that was getting bigger on Pierre's shirt. Then he remembered the knife. He hastily wiped the handle of the knife with the towel and looked about the grisly scene and was satisfied there was nothing left there that the police could trace to him. He didn't even seem to have any bloodstains on his own clothing. Amazing! He went to the door and let himself out. As he backed through the door, he took one last look at the cocaine spread on the table and the kitchen knife sticking out of his friend's chest. He pulled the door close and hurriedly went down the stairs to the Cadillac.

It was eleven thirty that night when Carl arrived at the River Rat. Cindy saw him and directed him to a small table. The place was crowded and noisy, and Cindy leaned close to say, "You're late. I thought maybe you weren't coming. What are you drinking?"

"SC on the rocks and a coke," Carl snapped. "I fell asleep watching TV and just woke up."

She brought the drink and noticed his hand shaking slightly as he raised the glass to his mouth. "Looks like you didn't get enough sleep. Hands a little shaky."

"Nothing wrong with my hands," he snapped. "Don't you have some tables to wait on?"

Cindy's eyes showed hurt as she turned and walked through the other tables, looking for empty glasses she could fill. "Asshole! He should be thanking me, not talking hateful!" she said to no one but herself.

By 1:30 a.m., there were only three tables with diehards still trying to tell the biggest lie or get the drunkest. Cindy called for last drinks, and one by one, they navigated to the front door and left.

After Cindy finished cleaning the tables, she walked out to the parking lot, where Carl waited in the Cadillac, motor running. She got in and sat for a few seconds, stared out the windshield, then turned to Carl and said, "I assume you wanted me to get in the car. Did you or didn't you?"

"I'm sitting here, ain't I?" Carl started the Cadillac, slammed it in gear, and peeled out of the parking lot.

"You want some Memphis cop to pull your ass over and haul you off to jail? You better get used to this big Cadillac before you run over and kill somebody!" Cindy had just finished critiquing Carl's driving and didn't see the back of his hand coming from the steering wheel and catching her across the mouth and nose.

Her head snapped back, and she felt the warm sensation moving down her upper lip. She reached her hand to her mouth and looked down; she had blood dripping onto her waitress dress. "You son of a bitch, you busted my nose and my lip. What the hell's wrong with you?"

"Wrong with me? I'll tell you what's wrong! You've given me a bunch of smart mouth, talking about the cops gonna get me. Well, let me tell you something, little cotton-picking, dumb-ass girl from the hicks and sticks! You don't know nothing about what's going on! All you got to do is wait your ass around for another guy and then drop your drawers and another customer will hop right in bed with you and screw your lights out."

Cindy was bent over, holding her arm against her nose to stanch the flow. "You mean the way you couldn't wait to get in bed with me? I got in bed with you because I thought I liked you. I thought you were just an ordinary guy driving a truck, working for a living, and you seemed to like me. Then you show up driving a big fancy Cadillac and act like an asshole! You probably stole the damn car, Mr. Phony!"

Carl's arm repeated the arch, but before it connected, Cindy turned and ducked to the right. Carl's knuckles slammed against her left ear and the side of her head. Pain shot through her as she fell against the door. Her hands fumbled and found the door handle and pulled. The door opened, and as she felt another blow from Carl on her shoulder and back, she rolled out of the car into the parking lot.

Carl was halfway across the front seat, glaring at her with an intense fury coming from his eyes. She thought he was going to come out the door onto her, but then he quickly grabbed the door handle and pulled it shut. The Cadillac motor roared to life, and the car squealed out of the parking lot onto the streets, headed toward Motel 6.

Cindy managed to get to her feet and walked unsteadily back to the door of the River Rat. Inside, her boss had just finished shutting down the bar and was turning out the lights. "Hey, Cindy, you're back already! Did your boyfriend—holy shit, girl, what happened to you?" Her boss went around the bar and grabbed a nearby chair from the table. "Sit down here and let me look at you!"

When the man reached toward Cindy's bloody nose, she winced and pulled back away from him. "Don't touch me. I'll be okay. Just give me some ice and a bar towel."

"I think I better call an ambulance, Cindy. You could have a broken nose." Not waiting for her to argue, he turned and went behind the bar and picked up the phone.

The fire department was only a few blocks down the street, and two of their emergency technicians showed up in about ten minutes. A Memphis PD car arrived two minutes later. Two officers stood and watched while the EMTs finished repairs on Cindy's nose, mouth, and ear. When they were finished, they asked Sandy if she would be willing to go to a hospital. She said no.

In the opinion of the emergency crew, Cindy had no broken bones and would heal in a few days. As they returned their tools and supplies to their bag, one of the policemen stepped forward. "Miss, would you mind telling us how this happened and who did this to you?"

The bartender spoke with emotion and anger. "Her boyfriend beat her up out in the parking lot, and she came staggering in here. I heard tires squealing just before she came back to the door, and so I guess he took off!"

The cop turned to the bartender and said, "Let's just let the lady tell it in her own words what happened, then you'll have your chance." The cop turned to Cindy and said, "Ma'am, did you know the man who did this to you?"

Cindy raised her head up and tried to look as normal as possible. "Sure, I knew him. We've dated a little for the last month or so, and he's never laid a hand on me until tonight. I don't know what got into him. We were together earlier today, and he seemed to be in a good mood. We had planned for him to come here before closing and go out for a while after. When he got here, he had a couple drinks and went back out in the parking lot to wait for me. When I got to the car, he seemed to be in a bad mood, and when I gave him a bad time about his Cadillac car and said he might have stolen it, that's when he hit me, the first time. It really pissed me off, and it hurt, so I got in his face about his attitude and he hit me again. I don't understand. He's never been like this before."

The cop had gotten out a small notebook and scribbled in it with a lead pencil. "What made you suggest that he might have stolen the Cadillac, miss?"

"I don't know. Nothing in particular. It was just a dumb remark. When we first met, he was driving a truck, and this time a Cadillac. It was just a dumb, smart-mouthed remark."

The officer finished scribbling and looked at Cindy. "You said he was driving a truck. What kind of truck, and whom for? Did it have a company name on it?"

"I didn't see much of the truck. It was parked in the motel parking lot, a block down the street. He just told me that's what he did. I think it was fish—yeah, he said he hauled fish! I asked him about it, and I think he said they made fertilizer out of them. I don't remember him saying anything about the name of the company, and I didn't see the truck good enough to remember any name."

The two cops looked at each other and shrugged. The one who'd been asking the questions said, "Well, miss, if you don't want to press charges against the man, there's nothing more we can do. We'll write a report and put it on file. If you have any more trouble with him, though, you should file a complaint and let us pull a guy like that off the street. You got off pretty lucky tonight, but a big, strong truck driver with a hair-trigger temper can hurt a girl your size seriously and quickly. Oh, one more thing. You said you didn't see the truck well enough to remember the name, but maybe you could give us a good description of the Cadillac. Just for future reference, in case anything else comes up."

After the cop finished his notes on the Cadillac, the two went back to their car and on patrol.

The bartender helped Cindy to her feet and said, "Come on, kid, let me get you home so you can start sleeping this off."

* * *

After Carl had sped away, leaving Cindy in the parking lot of the bar, his temper cooled and he began to feel remorse for what he had done. He thought about turning back to the bar and trying to make up with her. His next thought was, that would be pretty stupid. The bartender would stand up for her and might want to kick his ass. Cindy's remark about the Cadillac being stolen touched a real nerve that Carl hadn't realized until now was beginning to twitch without any comments from Cindy. He had told himself earlier that there were real possibilities the Cadillac was getting warm. It was not improbable that the want for the Cadillac would have made it from the metro police in New Orleans to the state radios and possibly an APB through the FBI. Cindy had just struck a nerve that was already twitching. He needed to get rid of the car.

Preoccupied with his thoughts about Cindy and the car, he didn't see the police car until he had turned into the motel parking lot. No red lights flashing, it was parked near the motel office, with headlights on and motor running. Carl saw a uniformed cop in the office talking to the night clerk.

Carl's mind raced. *How had they known to come to this motel? Had Cindy called about the scene at the bar?*

Panic grabbed Carl, and the fight-or-flight impulse took control. He stepped on the Cadillac's brake, the tires squeaking in protest, and threw the car in reverse. He knew he'd pushed the gas pedal too hard when he heard the tires squeal again.

The cop turned from the front desk and looked toward the Cadillac surging backward onto the street, and he moved toward his patrol car as Carl shifted forward and the tires squealed for a third time.

There was virtually no traffic on the streets. Carl pushed the car then slammed on the brakes as he turned right down one street then accelerated three blocks, watching his rearview mirror. He continued this erratic pattern until there had been no sign of pursuit for ten minutes.

Now Carl began to talk himself down. He had to get out of Memphis, and the Caddy was the fastest mode of transportation available. In his panicked thinking, speed was the most important element to his survival. He realized that driving a truck full of drugs or stealing a car was not his biggest threat; no, he had killed a man this night. That could put him in prison for twenty or thirty years or in the electric chair.

He made a decision. He must get out of Memphis, and if he went north or east, he'd still be in Tennessee, where the cops would be cooperating with Memphis.

Carl began to weave his way west, trying to avoid the main streets, until he came to an on-ramp to I-55, which would take him to the bridge, south, over the Mississippi River into Arkansas.

The APB had gone out to the Owl Patrol in Memphis, and the joint agreement between the MPD and WMPD (West Memphis, Arkansas), assured that the night shift on the Arkansas side of the river would be included in the alert. Trooper Donald Carter, just finishing his rookie year with the Arkansas State Police, heard the APB on his local PD radio and turned his patrol car at the first ramp up to I-55, at the west end of the bridge. As he came into the approach lane, he spotted the Cadillac traveling at a high speed in the far left lane. Donny turned on the lights and siren and radioed his pursuit.

As Donny was approaching seventy miles per hour, a Memphis cop flew past him, continuing the chase from the east side of the bridge. Donny was doing a flat one hundred miles per hour when he slowly caught up with the Memphis cop, and the Cadillac was a hundred feet in front, bobbing up and down like a boat in heavy seas.

Carl knew there was not enough speed in the Cadillac to outrun the Arkansas patrol car. He swung the wheel right and began cutting across the freeway. The state car backed off slightly, but Carl was watching him for his next move. Now the Memphis cop had pulled into the lane to his left, and the state car was on his bumper. Carl was starting to push the gas pedal the remaining distance to the floor when he sensed a new movement just ahead.

CHAPTER 20

Sonny Dawson had been driving big trucks since shortly after high school. He'd gotten on with Dixie Gas and Oil three years ago and had been driving one of their dual hookup rigs for the last six months, doing store deliveries to Dixie Gas service centers all across Northwest Arkansas. He'd just filled the underground tanks at their all-night eight-pump station just off I-55 and had enough on board in the rear tanker to do their truck stop at the west edge of town. The traffic was nothing this time of night, and that was what made this shift kinda fun. All this pavement to himself, he thought.

Sonny pushed the Peterbilt tractor for more speed as he climbed the ramp up and onto I-55. He was having fun with the powerful truck and had not checked his side mirror, which was framing three sets of headlights and two sets of flashing red lights. When his eye caught the lights, he was past fifty-five miles per hour and gaining speed. He had his left signal on, but the approaching lead car was not changing lanes to pass him. Sonny stomped the brake pedal, and he knew instantly it was the wrong move. The layout at the next station made it easier to pump from the rear tank, so he had emptied the front tank first. The sudden brake caused the heavy rear tank to push against the empty one in front, and in seconds, Sonny felt the control of his rig slip away. The lighter tank moved its rear end to the right, while the heavier tank began to skid to the left across three lanes of highway.

Carl saw the gyrations of the tanker truck just ahead and, for a brief moment, was captured by the graceful dance happening in front of him. One cop was close behind and the other, almost beside him. He stood on the brakes, and the heavy car complained as its momentum refused to be stopped. It did stop as the hood went under the middle of the tanker, and the large lettering Dixie Gas was the last thing Carl saw. The last thing

Carl heard was the thundering explosion as 1,200 gallons of gasoline became a towering, billowing explosion of fire.

The two police cars in pursuit had been able to avoid the fiery collision by veering hard to the left. Donny Carter recovered and put out the call for fire department and ambulance response. The tractor had disconnected from the lead tanker, and Sonny Dawson had brought it to a stop a couple hundred feet from the burning wreckage.

Chapter 21

Arkansas State Police
Little Rock

Clint Parker arrived at his office at 7:30 a.m., which was normal for him. He loved his work and was readying for the day's agenda when his staff arrived an hour later. The morning papers, Memphis and Little Rock, were beside the front door. He unlocked the door and scooped up the papers and headed for the kitchenette and punched the On button on the coffeemaker, which the girl always prepared with coffee and water the night before. Turning on the lights and tossing the papers on his desk before going to the large window behind his high-back chair, he pulled open the drapes and surveyed the still-peaceful city that was just starting to drive to work and face the challenges of the day. As he turned to go for the first cup of coffee, his eyes swept across the headlines of the Memphis paper:

FIERY TRUCK CRASH—ONE DEAD!

Clint picked up the paper and read as he walked to the kitchen and poured the coffee. The article identified the driver of a late-model Cadillac as the deceased. The story was he had lost control of the car while being pursued by Memphis and Arkansas State Police. The body of the driver

113

had been badly burned, and his identity had not been determined, although the car had a New Orleans sticker on the rear window.

Clint's phone started ringing, so he reluctantly laid down the paper and picked up the receiver. "Good morning, the FBI."

"Good morning, Clint. This is Glenn. Have you gotten any information on the car-truck crash last night?"

"Matter of fact, Glenn, I was reading about it in the Memphis paper when you called. Sounds like it might have been pretty gruesome, what with all the fire and explosion. I haven't read far enough to know what happened to the trucker, and it seems strange that a Memphis car and an Arkansas State car were in pursuit. 'Course it's not unheard of. The chase must have started in Tennessee and the Arkansas officer joined in as they crossed over. It's not something the FBI gets into, but it is interesting. What's prompting your interest?"

Glenn replied, "A friend of mine who works in the crime lab in Memphis just called and said the crime commission might want to get in the loop on this one. Preliminary information suggests the Cadillac was stolen in New Orleans a couple of nights ago. A couple on their way to dinner left it in a concierge parking in front of the restaurant, and it was gone when he and his wife finished dinner. They don't know for sure, but he thought we might piece it together faster than three different jurisdictions acting on their own timelines."

Clint was not eager to be the helper to MPD and ASP, but if there was a connection between New Orleans and Memphis, one could not ignore the possible connection. "Glenn, can you run over to MPD and see if they have anything we would want, while I work on ASP here in Little Rock? Don't want to invest much time, but it's worth a quick, early feeler. Be sure you get assurance from command that they keep us in the loop twice a day with anything that rings bells."

"I'll get started. I should be calling you by noon with an update."

By noon, Clint had talked to Amos Boudreau twice and with the ASP for thirty minutes and was anxiously awaiting Glenn's call with updated info from Memphis.

So far, ASP was waiting for NOPD to confirm the data on the burned Cadillac matched the one stolen from the concierge in New Orleans.

The ringer stirred Clint from his mental filing system on his phone. "Hello, this is Parker."

"Glenn here, Clint. Let me update you on what I know. I've talked to Memphis and West Memphis. MPD officers have interviewed a Ms. Cindy Murphy. She's a waitress at the River Rat bar in South Memphis who was beaten up last night by her boyfriend, who kicked her out of his

Cadillac after smacking her around. She said he was a truck driver from New Orleans, but this week, he showed up in a near-new Caddy, and when she made a joke about him stealing it, he backhanded her in the face."

"What name did she give you?"

"Carl, Carl Hoffman was the name she knew him by. Said he never acted strange or unfriendly before yesterday afternoon, when they were out shopping. She said Carl had taken her to a drugstore and waited in the car while she shopped. When she came back to the car, he wasn't there. She said she was about to go look in the store for him when he came walking up to the car. She said, when she asked him where he had been, he said he'd just been stretching his legs."

Clint thought about Glenn's report for half a minute then said, "Well, Glenn, that sounds like a reasonable explanation. Just two lovebirds having a lover's quarrel."

Glenn doubted Clint's thinking, pausing a moment, then continued, "She said he seemed excited when he came back to the car in the afternoon. Later, he volunteered to take her to work and said he'd be back about ten, but he didn't get back to the River Rat until eleven thirty. She said he seemed nervous, had one drink, and left, saying he would wait in the car till she got off work. Normally, she said he would keep drinking till she closed. Said he could drink more than any other man she'd ever known. You're the policeman, but I've got a feeling we're onto something here. You know, a connection."

Clint considered Glenn's thinking. This man had been governor two terms and had pushed investigations that resulted in one man's suicide and others going to jail. Clint knew the man's instincts were good and should not be ignored. "Okay, Glenn. Tomorrow, I want you and I to go to Memphis. You take me to the drugstore, and we'll walk the neighborhood and talk to a few people and see if anything grabs us."

CHAPTER 22

It was 6:30 p.m. when Clint hung up the phone after nearly an hour with Amos Boudreau. They had brought each other current on developments in the killing of the state trooper in Mississippi and the possible connections of the death to the crash of a late-model Cadillac and a fuel truck in West Memphis, Arkansas. Amos was very supportive of Clint going to Memphis and checking any connection of the dead man to the investigation in New Orleans.

Earlier in the afternoon, Clint had called Ken Kondraky at ABI. The investigator had agreed to a loose surveillance and monitoring of the activities of Alvin King. It was an uncomfortable assignment for Kondraky since he was, technically, Ken's boss. If other personnel in the bureau found out about the monitoring, it could cost Ken his job.

Kondraky's report indicated there had been a significant change in King's schedule. King seemed to be staying in his office more recently and had canceled three outside meetings with civic groups, where he often gave luncheon speeches about fighting crime in the state of Arkansas. Clint had obtained a federal court warrant to put a tap on Ham Turner's phone and, that monitoring, had discovered two unanswered calls from the ABI office and one from King's home. King was not one of Turner's direct supervisors, and it was suspicious that the phone call to Turner's residence from King's residence at 9:30 p.m. would have anything to do with normal ABI operations. This information seemed to warrant continued monitoring, in Clint's thinking.

When he had finished the conversation with Kondraky, Clint called Cameron Wilson to get a report on Turner. Wilson reported that Turner was very glad to be at Wilson's cabin on the river. The anonymity of the location was causing Turner to think less about the threat to his own safety and more about the next fish he was going to catch from the dock.

Satisfied that he had covered all the bases he could for today, Clint turned out the lights and headed down to his car, looking forward to a relaxed evening at home and an early start to West Memphis tomorrow morning.

* * *

At seven the next morning, Clint had the government-issued Ford sedan on the freeway, headed northwest toward Memphis. As he entered the city, he turned off the freeway and headed toward West Memphis PD. The sergeant at the front desk said he thought the officer that responded to the crash site of the Cadillac and the gasoline truck was back in the squad room, finishing his reports.

Five minutes passed before patrolman Alvin Cross went into the front office and shook hands with Clint. Cross led Clint into a small interrogation room, and they sat at the little square table in the middle.

Cross began the meeting. "I don't know that I can add much to what you probably already know. The pursuit of the Cadillac began on the Tennessee side of the river, and by the time I picked up the chase on this side, the gas truck came into the picture, and the collision happened very quickly afterward. I directed the fire department to the site. The MPD officer briefed me on the origin of the chase, and I'm sure you'll get a copy of his reports this morning, which should give you some additional details."

Clint requested the WMPD forward a copy of the report as soon as it was available. When he went back out to the front desk, Glenn Wiggs was waiting.

Clint and Glenn shook hands, and Clint quickly summarized his visit with patrolman Cross. "There's not much here that we're interested in, and I think we should just go on over to Memphis and catch that patrolman before he gets back out on the streets. He can give us the info on where we can find the girl. You can leave your car here and ride with me."

They crossed the bridge into Memphis and drove straight to the MPD headquarters. The front desk sergeant there invited them to have a seat and he'd get patrolman Carter. The Sergeant came back and directed them to interrogation room number 3.

Clint Parker and Glenn Wiggs walked down a narrow hallway and found patrolman Donald Carter hunched over a typewriter. They waited a couple of minutes until the officer struck a final key and nodded his head with satisfaction. He looked like he had had a pretty rough night and needed a shave. He stood and shook hands with Clint and Glenn and offered coffee. The two visitors asked for half a cup of black coffee each and pulled two chairs up to the desk with a typewriter.

Clint started off by explaining to the officer what they had already learned from MPD and ASP.

Donald Carter handed each of his visitors a copy of his report and gave them a minute to glance over it then started his verbal summary of the report. "I got the call about 1:40 a.m. and drove to the River Rat bar. I found Ms. Cindy Murphy inside, where the bartender was patching her up. Her upper lip, right side, was cut and swelling and started in the corner of her mouth. The piece of skin was missing on the left side of her nose, and her left eye started to show swelling and bruising. She said her boyfriend, Carl Hoffman, had spent much of the day with her, taking her to a drugstore in the afternoon to do some shopping. Then, when it was time for her to go to work, he drove her to the River Rat bar. She said he then wanted to go back to his motel and grab a nap, promising to be back about ten o'clock and have some drinks while he waited for her to get off work. He didn't show up there until sometime between 11:30 p.m. and twelve midnight. She said she had begun to worry that he might not show up. When he did arrive, he seemed nervous and distracted. He ordered double shots of Southern Comfort with a beer chaser. He drank the first two quickly. She said that seemed to settle him down, but he was still not normal. He snapped at her over nothing and, about one a.m., said he was going outside to wait in the car. When her shift ended, he was waiting in the parking lot with the motor running. The Cadillac he was driving was new to her, as he had always before been driving a truck. They had a bit of an argument, and she said something about the car being stolen. He became furious and hit her with the back of his hand twice. Her nose was bleeding, and she thought her lip was as well. He was yelling at her and told her to just get out of the car. He reached across her to open the door and then shoved her, causing her to tumble out of the car and fall to the pavement."

Clint held up his hand to interrupt the policeman's thorough account of the statement the girl had given him. "Did I hear something about the trip to the drugstore? Something about him not being at the car when she came back out?"

The MPD officer referred to his notes. "Yeah, I must've skipped over that. She did say that when she came out to the car from the drugstore, it was locked and he was nowhere in sight. She thought about going back into the drugstore to see if he was in there, looking for her, but before she acted on that thought, she saw him coming down the street."

"Did she say anything about his behavior when he got back to the car?" Clint asked the question while he scribbled notes on a pad.

The officer again referred to his notes and replied, "She said she asked him where he had been, and he answered that he was just stretching his legs and to mind her own business. I think it's pretty obvious that they had a sexual relationship going, and for the first time, according to her, he was not the attentive, sexy partner she had known in the early days of their acquaintance."

There was silence in the room while Clint tried to conjure up the scene at the drugstore. There was something tugging at him, telling him there was more here. More questions to be asked. He asked, "I know you guys keep an incident log for each day. Could I see a copy of that log from the day before yesterday? It might be interesting to see if anything else of significance happened in that neighborhood on that date."

The officer went to fetch the log while Clint and Glenn waited in the small room. He returned in about five minutes with a smile on his face and a knowing look in his eyes. "I'll be damned. I never thought to check, but here it is. A man was found dead in an apartment on the second floor of the building directly across from the drugstore. The landlord went there because he had not received the rent. When no one answered his knock on the door, he tried the handle and found it unlocked. He opened the door and looked inside. Saw the tenant slumped over a table, not moving. He called it in, and a detective from homicide went to the scene and called for a medical examiner. The victim was pronounced dead at the scene, and his report notes that traces of cocaine were found on the table, and additional drugs were found in a dresser drawer in the bedroom. The detective has been treating it as a quarrel between the deceased and an unknown assailant, probably over drugs."

Clint was now leaning forward in his chair when he asked, "Have you established an identity of the victim yet?"

"He gave the name Paul Good on his rental application, with no previous address. There was no trace of any Paul Good, so we have assumed that to be false. We took a set of prints from the body and have run that through the NCIC, and the detective is now waiting for the results. We also got some prints from Motel 6, which we will compare. The detective said he would join us shortly as soon as he finishes a phone call. In the meantime, here's a folder with pictures of the crime scene."

Clint and Glenn scanned the photographs, not recognizing the facial shot of the deceased man. After viewing a photograph, Clint passed it over to Glenn. The last photograph was taken from behind the chair in which the victim was seated. The body was slumped forward, with the head resting on the table. As he started to hand over the picture, his eye's caught a small inscription on the dead man's neck, two inches below his left ear. He picked up a magnifying glass from the table and held it above the photo. At first it looked like a human face. Clint raised the magnifying glass and recognized it as a skull but with eyes still in the sockets. Clint reached for the phone hanging on the wall behind him.

* * *

In New Orleans, Amos Boudreau was clearing off his desk, preparing to go to lunch. "Good morning, this is Boudreau. How can I help you?"

"Good morning, Amos, this is Clint, and I'm calling from the Memphis PD. I'm looking at a photograph of a man who was found dead yesterday. He has what appears to be a small tattoo on his neck just below his left ear. The tattoo artist did a great job of putting eyes with dilated pupils instead of the empty sockets that you normally see on a skull. You ever run across anything like that, Amos?"

Amos Boudreau reached into the right-hand drawer of his desk, and in the file marked Voodoo, he pulled a single sheet of paper. The title of the document was Tattoo Symbols Commonly Used in the Cajun Community, and in the very top row was the figure of a skull with eyes drawn into the sockets. Under the skull where the words "Used by voodoo priests to ward off evil spirits, commonly used by Cajuns in the Louisiana and Mississippi bayous."

Amos picked the phone up from his desk and spoke to Clint. "Offhand, Clint, it looks like you may have a guy that was involved in the art of voodoo. Sounds like the same symbol I'm looking at on this list of common identification marks. The symbol is supposed to protect the person from evil spirits. From what you say, I guess it didn't work very well."

Clint scratched his head. "It didn't work very good for him, but it may help us tie the dead man back to New Orleans, and it may be connected to the crash of the Cadillac and fuel truck night before last in West Memphis. Any further sightings of Gulf Imports trucks from Mississippi, Louisiana, or Arkansas patrols?"

"One or two, but they were both southbound, on the return trip to New Orleans. Those were not stopped since we do not want to raise the alarm level until there are pretty good odds of catching them with the goods in the truck."

Clint nodded. "Yeah, that's our strategy, and I just hope we're right. Glenn Wiggs met me this morning, and I need to drop him back at the WMPD. By the time I get back to Little Rock, we should have a fingerprint report on both the deceased. They couldn't get much from the guy that crashed into the gas truck. Most of the fingers were burned too badly to give any kind of print pattern. They did get two that they think the FBI can possibly make an ID from. I'll forward it to you as soon as it comes to my office."

CHAPTER 23

At three o'clock that afternoon, Clint was working on the last paper in the stack that awaited him on his return from Memphis. The girl from the front desk stopped and handed him a transmission that had just come over the wire. It was the fingerprint report from Memphis, and it reported that the Memphis police had confirmed matches between prints taken in the dead man's apartment and Motel 6. They still had some work to do to prove the identity of the driver of the Cadillac. The statement from the waitress identified him as Carl Hoffman. Hoffman had already shown up in their files, and even though they didn't have direct confirmation by photograph, Clint was sure that Hoffman and the dead man in the caddy were the same. He dictated a short report to this effect and had the girl put it on the Teletype to New Orleans. He'd give Amos a day to digest everything before calling him on the phone and getting his thoughts on the next step to take. For some reason, Ham Turner was on his mind as he reached for the telephone.

* * *

One hour earlier . . .

The tan Ford coupe moved patiently down the dirt road. The weather had been dry, and the driver was trying to be cautious about causing any dust trail. He was very confident in accomplishing his mission, but there was no point in giving anyone an early warning that he was coming. He pulled the photograph from his jacket pocket and took one more look. He was satisfied that he had the image memorized and would recognize the individual at first sight. He had been doing this for many years and had honed his skills into a virtual art form.

The Ford crossed a couple of chuckholes in the road and gently bobbed up and down, and then the shocks recovered the balance and the car proceeded steadily down the road. The driver glanced at the passenger seat and confirmed that the 9mm target pistol with a ten-inch barrel had not moved from the position he placed it in when he began his trip. He had received the picture by mail two days ago, and this morning he had received a phone call on which an anonymous voice confirmed that the fishing was good on the Current River.

It was good terrain for an ambush, but the subsequent escape was problematic. The cabin sat at the far end of a dead-end road. The good thing about the terrain was that no one else appeared to live within hearing distance. Regardless, *caution* was always the operative word.

He calculated he was about fifty yards from the cabin when he spotted a level, cleared area in the trees. He drove past the opening and then backed the car into the space. Reaching into his jacket pocket, he withdrew a silencer about four inches long, which had a threaded end, that he began to screw into the barrel of the pistol. Stepping out of the car, he opened the back door and removed his sport coat and exchanged it for a camouflage hunting jacket lying in the backseat. There was a custom pocket sewn on the inside of the jacket that accommodated the target pistol, including the silencer. He needed to keep both hands free while navigating through the woods, just in case he had to use his hands to balance himself as he navigated the rough terrain.

No accidental discharge of the gun while trying to avoid falling on my ass, he thought.

The man slowly proceeded through the wooded area until he was above and behind the cabin and the river. He chose a position about 120 feet from the dock, where he had a clearer view of the two men sitting in folding chairs, attending to their fishing poles. As he moved himself into a comfortable shooting position, one of the men on the dock stood up and began to walk toward the cabin. "Dammit!" he swore to himself. He had been thrilled at the sight of the two men sitting beside each other. It would have been so easy to shoot them both and then make his departure without fear of being pursued. The man remaining on the dock leaned forward and picked up his fishing rod and began to reel in his hook to check the bait. Satisfied, he cast the bait back into the river, secured the pole, and sat back in the folding chair. In the process of checking his bait, the man had given the observer a full view of his face and confirmed that he was the target for this mission. He decided that he would shoot from a prone position, and he proceeded to get himself prepared.

* * *

Cam Wilson had made the adjustment from living alone, doing exactly what he pleased when it pleased him, to finding pleasure in coordinating the day's activities with another person. He and Ham Turner shared a lot of common traits in their personalities. Neither man was given to excess in his conversation, and while he had learned that Ham was not as developed intellectually as he thought himself to be, the two men shared similar opinions about how to do things, especially when it came to fishing. They had enjoyed some good action for the last hour and had a pretty good string of trout hanging from the dock in the cold water of the Current River, keeping them fresh for tonight's dinner.

"What you think, Ham? Isn't it about *Ham's time* on the Current River?" Both men knew that Cam was referring to Ham's beer and was playing on words from the musical commercial that ran frequently on the television set.

Ham kept his eye on the red-and-white floater and replied, "Yes, Sir Cam. I would say your timing is just about perfect. Want me to get it?"

"No, I'll get it. My legs could use the exercise anyway, and I'll put a couple potatoes in the oven and get them started baking. I'll be right back!" Cam walked off the dock and began walking toward the cabin.

Inside the cabin, he opened the refrigerator and took two of the blue-and-white cans filled with the golden liquid and set them on the counter. He took two baking potatoes from the bag and brushed them with cooking oil. He set the oven to 350 degrees and laid the potatoes on one of the racks and closed the door. He retrieved the beers and had just opened the door to go back down to the dock when he heard a sound.

After a tour in Europe with the army in WWII and twenty-five years as sheriff, his sensitive ears could still detect the sound of a silenced gun. He reached back inside the door, pulling open a cabinet drawer, retrieving his Smith & Wesson .38 police special. He jammed the pistol into his belt and picked up the twelve-gauge shotgun leaning next to the door. From the corner of his vision, he saw Ham stiffen and fall sideways from the chair, still holding the fishing rod in his hand.

Cam ran to the corner of the cabin and cautiously peered around the corner, immediately jerking his head back as a second shot splintered wood from the corner of the house, just above his head. He ran six strides and dived behind a rack of firewood as another shot struck a piece of the wood just behind his butt. He peered through the cracks between the pieces of firewood and saw what he thought was the shooter lying prone under a low-hanging limb. He pulled the 9mm from his belt and squeezed off a shot, allowing some elevation for distance, and heard a squawk of pain and a stream of cursing. He ran to a nearby row of bushes near the edge of the road approaching the cabin. He looked back at the site he had last seen the shooter; the man was no longer there.

Cam went to the southern end of the shrubs and calculated the risk of trying to cross the road. He decided to take the risk. But before he could start, he saw the limping man come from behind a tree on the other side of the road. His left hand was pressed against hip, and his right hand was hanging straight down but still holding the target pistol. Cam calculated they were about fifty feet apart. He pushed the pistol back into his pocket and raised the twelve-gauge as he stepped from behind the shrubs. "Drop the gun or I'll blow your fucking head off!"

The man stopped in his tracks, and from that moment forward, his movements seemed to be in slow motion. His feet seemed to be frozen to the ground where he stood; his upper body turned to the left and made his legs appear to be the beginnings of a pretzel as he raised the pistol toward the voice he had heard.

Cam squeezed the trigger on the Remington semiautomatic. The big gun exploded, kicking backward violently against Cam's shoulder. The pistol barked twice in rapid succession, its barrel still pointed downward at a thirty-degree angle, causing the bullets to go harmlessly into the ground twenty feet in front of the falling man. The pistol slipped from the dying shooter's hand and tumbled to one side. The body of the shooter fell on top of the gun.

Cam walked rapidly to the fallen body, kneeling beside it and feeling for a pulse in the throat. There was none. Satisfied, Cam turned and began to run back toward the cabin. He ran past the corner and, as he passed, noticed the fresh notch by the angry bullet that had come close to Cam's head.

Ham's body was lying at the edge of the dock, his right arm dangling in the water. A large red stain on his shirt started at the shoulder and wicked its way down his back. He heard a low sound coming from the wounded man. Thank God he was still alive! To prevent him falling into the river if he should try to struggle, Cam moved the body gently away from the edge of the dock. Satisfied that he could leave him alone, Cam turned and hurried to the cabin.

* * *

Clint was just reaching to make a call when the girl out front told him he had a call on line 1. He spoke his name into the receiver and instantly heard the urgency in the caller's voice.

"Clint, this is Cam! We've had a shooting here at the cabin. Ham is down but still alive. The shooter is down, and he's not getting up by himself. Ham was hit in the right shoulder, near his neck. I didn't try a detailed exam, but my best guess is it's a through and through shot. One inch further left and we would need the coroner. What we do need is a hospital as quick as possible. Thought you would be able to arrange that faster than I."

Clint's mind was moving fast. Baptist Hospital had a medevac helicopter, and if it was available, that would be the fastest transportation. Second choice would be Memphis Memorial, but he hoped he would not have to make two calls.

He began to instruct Cam. "You get back to your patient and do whatever first aid you think will help. I'll get a helicopter on its way to you, and if they'll wait for me, I'll be on board. I can be at the hospital in five minutes. Any indication the shooter had help?"

Cam answered quickly, "If he had, I probably wouldn't be making this call! I'll see you in a few minutes."

Clint made record time to Baptist Hospital, headlights flashing and horns blowing all the way. The tires screeched as he skidded the car into the hospital parking lot and stopped near the waiting helicopter, its big blades slowly turning.

Twenty minutes later, the pilot was setting the big bird down in Cam's backyard, near the dock. Five minutes later, the medic was satisfied that the wounded man was ready for the flight. They fitted the stretcher into the back area of the copter and headed back to Baptist Memorial Hospital, where a United States marshal was standing, ready to protect the wounded man against any further assault.

Clint followed Cam across the road to the place where the assailant had fallen. The man's face struck a familiar chord in Clint, but he could not be sure of an identity. He had grabbed a camera on the way out of his office and now proceeded to photograph the body and all the points of interest involved in the shooting. Satisfied that a proper record was established inside the camera, the two men lifted the dead man and carried him across the road to Cam's Jeep waiting in the driveway. They folded the backseat down, thus making a pretty good hearse out of the sturdy vehicle, and deposited the body.

During the drive to Little Rock, the two men discussed the developments, and Clint finally made a decision and said, "I want to keep this very quiet as long as we can. I don't want the newspapers, TV, and radio informing whomever hired this guy that they need to go to plan B. I'll take the body to the morgue in Little Rock, and I'm sure the medical examiner will work with us by keeping his mouth shut. Thank God you were watching over him and had the ability to stop the attack before it became successful. Thank you!"

In Little Rock, the Jeep Cherokee, having no official marks on it, drew no one's attention as it turned down the alley that led to the back door of the morgue. They unloaded the body and carried it into the examining room. The medical examiner advised Clint he would need three hours before he could give him a thorough report. It was 4:00 p.m., and the examiner agreed to stay until he finished. Clint told them they would be back at 6:30 p.m. and thanked him for his assistance. Cam drove Clint to the hospital to pick up his car and declined the invitation to spend the night at Clint's house, saying he best be getting back home before the fish started missing him.

Clint decided to drive to his house before he needed to return to the ME's office. Jean would have dinner ready and would not worry so much if she had some idea what he was involved in and why he would be out later this evening.

Clint pulled into his garage and, out of habit, closed the garage door with the remote in the car, always mindful that not everyone in the world loved him and appreciated his work. So just in case one of those few were lurking about in his yard, he always pushed that button on his visor as soon as he was inside the garage. He got out of the car and walked into the kitchen, immediately sensing the aromas coming from the stove. Jean turned from the sink, where she was washing her hands, and turned to him, looping the towel around his neck and kissing him a loving hello.

"I opened a bottle of wine, and it's sitting on the buffet in the dining room," Jean said as she reached for two glasses.

"Sorry, honey, you'll have to drink both glasses tonight. I have to eat and go back to work," Clint said as he went to the cabinet and retrieved two plates.

While they ate a quick meal at the breakfast bar, Clint gave Jean a brief summary of the day's events. He had learned over the years of their marriage that she was a trusted partner. She did not need to know details and did not try to influence his decisions, but her knowledge of the events that shaped his days and kept him awake some nights comforted and assured her that her husband could be trusted to bring himself home uninjured and untroubled by any distress she might feel.

At 8:00 p.m., Clint was in his office, talking to Amos Boudreau and filling him in on the events at Cam's cabin. "From everything you told me, we're just lucky that our witness is still breathing," Amos said after Clint finished.

Clint corrected Amos, "It wasn't just luck, Amos! We selected a man who was experienced and capable of doing the right thing in the event of an attack. When you have the help of an old-timer like Cam, you just need a tiny bit of luck, and his good judgment will take care of the rest. Any late developments from New Orleans?"

Amos referred to a prepared list he had typed this afternoon. "The phone taps on Donald Simmons are starting to pay off. He received a suspicious call night before last, but we couldn't make sense of it. The caller referred to a package that had been misplaced and they would advise him as soon as it was located. The people monitoring the phone tap assumed that the package was referring to a shipment from New Orleans to Memphis. Then yesterday, Simmons made a call to Kansas City. He talked about a friend that had tipped him on a great fishing hole on the Current River. He gave the man a phone number in Little Rock to call for directions on how to get to the location. Today, we were able to track the number. It's a rollover number that's not published, and it's located at the Arkansas Bureau of Investigation. I was getting ready to call you when you called and reported the shooting. It's pretty strong circumstantial evidence that the man in Kansas City was the shooter and somebody at ABI helped set up the target."

Clint was rapidly making notes on his pad and finally said, "I have a pretty good idea who that somebody is at ABI. We need some harder evidence for a grand jury, but I think things are starting to break open. It's been a long day, but I think, all things considered, we came out of it in pretty good shape. These phone calls are a sign of panic on the part of some people that would normally not be directly involved in the communication channels. Let's tighten up the surveillance on the Jolly Roger and Latin Imports. We need to catch somebody with his hands in the cookie jar!"

Clint gathered his notes, putting everything back in his briefcase, and went out to his car parked on the street. Ten minutes later, he was walking into the ME's office, where John Skinner had been the medical examiner for ten years. When he started, the job didn't pay much and forensic science was not advanced enough to make the work very valuable. The last two or three years, however, had brought big changes in his ability to help law enforcement and others more quickly understand evidence gathered from crime scenes and develop theories and suspects before the crime became cold.

As Clint drove home with the ME's report in his briefcase, a satisfied feeling settled in, assuring him that progress was being made and he could feel the conclusion coming nearer. Tomorrow morning, he was sure, his associates in Kansas City would fill in the blanks on the Current River assassin.

CHAPTER 24

Blake Stevens was just finishing the last of the eggs Benedict the restaurant had sent up to the suite. He had only ordered one breakfast because he had risen up so early that he was positive Gabrielle would not join him for another hour.

He stared at the phone and struggled against the impulse to pick it up and dial the number on the slip of paper he held in his hand. The man in the casino had slipped the piece of paper to him as he said good-night and went up to his room.

He was a new face to Blake, and Blake always took an interest in new faces. The man had invited Blake to his table and engaged him in conversation about the casino and the hotel. He had ordered dinner, one of the best on the menu, and had seemed to thoroughly enjoy himself as he consumed the sumptuous meal and a bottle of fine wine. As the comedian had started his routine, the man ordered one of their most-expensive cognacs and coffee. He seemed to enjoy the routine performed by the comedian, but when the artist took his break, the man had called for his check. Blake had gone to his table to make sure everything was okay. The man had told Blake everything was perfect. He paid his bill, and as he started to leave, he shook hands with Blake and thanked him for a memorable evening. While they shook hands, the man reached in his inside pocket with his left hand and withdrew a small slip of paper. He offered the paper to Blake and, in a soft voice, said, "Please call this number in the next two days and ask for Antonio."

It was now two days later, and Blake was sure he had looked at the slip of paper one hundred times. He was sure he had the number memorized, and the name Antonio echoed in his ears. The urge to dial the number became stronger, and he reached for the phone. A female voice on the other end of the line repeated the number he had just dialed. "May I help you?"

"Antonio, please." Blake's voice sounded hollow and distant to his own ears. He waited for what seemed like an eternity until a male voice spoke, "This is Antonio. How may I help you?"

Blake wasn't sure how to start the conversation, so he just said, "This is Blake Stevens."

The voice was calm and came through the phone line with a rhythmic pattern. "Mr. Stevens, how good of you to call. I was hoping to hear from you today, and here you are! It seems that I know so much about you and your businesses in Arkansas that there's little need for me to ask you questions. However, I'm sure there are many questions you will want to ask me. Questions that would be best not discussed on the phone, so the one question I need to ask you is how soon would it be possible for you to make a trip to Kansas City?"

Blake's mind was whirling, trying to fathom who this man could be and why he could be proposing a trip to Kansas City. Blake knew he had to be careful with unexpected phone calls. It could be law enforcement officials or his partners; either of whom were capable of propositions that, if acted on, would be detrimental to his own interest, if not his freedom.

"I don't have any trips planned to Kansas City, but if there were good reasons, I could drive up there later this week. Can you give me some good reason why I would go to Kansas City?"

The voice on the other end of the line continued as if Clint's question had been anticipated, "There will be many good reasons, Mr. Blake, and, as I stated, none appropriate for telephone conversations. Shall we plan on your trip occurring on Friday of this week? There will be a reservation in your name at the Hotel Muehlebach, and I hope Ms. Fleming will accompany you. Her participation in our meeting will be critical and time-saving. I will call you as soon as you have checked in, and please plan on joining me for dinner that evening at the City Club. Until then, have a good week and safe driving."

Blake hung up the phone and only then realized his heart was beating much faster than normal. He called the catering office and asked them to pick up his tray from breakfast, poured himself another cup of coffee, and scribbled the notes pertaining to the phone conversation.

He moved his second coffee out to the balcony and surveyed the hills of the Ozark Mountains as the morning sun highlighted the changing colors of the oaks and elms that painted the hills and valleys to the west.

He had finished his coffee when he heard stirrings in the kitchen. He turned in time to see the lovely Gabrielle carrying a cup and saucer in one hand and a coffeepot in the other, her full-length gown flowing behind her. Would he ever get tired of just looking at her beauty? he wondered.

She smiled as she approached the table and began pouring him another cup of coffee. "Good morning, handsome! I just had the most awful things happen to me."

Blake stood and kissed her on the cheek. "And what terrible event did I just miss, you beautiful thing?"

"I woke up in a cold bed, and I was all alone. I searched and searched, but there was no man there to warm my shivering body! I finally had to get out of bed and search for coffee and a man that could warm me." She giggled as she sat in the chair close to Blake.

The smile did not soon leave Blake's face as he continued to look at her. "The man that usually takes care of your heating needs was having an early breakfast and making an interesting phone call." Gabrielle leaned toward him, her eyes wide with anticipation and excitement. He related the conversation precisely, and when he had finished, her expression had turned to one of puzzlement and she leaned back into the chair.

"I don't know anyone in Kansas City named Antonio. Do you?"

Blake looked at Gabrielle seriously and said, "No, darling, I don't know anyone named Antonio, and I'm not even convinced that was the man's name. The whole thing is a mystery to me, except for one thing. You and I have been talking, privately, for a long time about how we might go about removing ourselves from our business interests in Arkansas without endangering our lives. A few nights ago, a very unusual man came into the casino and, after enjoying one of our finest meals and a floor show, expressed to me how memorable his evening had been and gave me the slip of paper containing the phone number I called this morning. He indicated that he knows many things about you and me and our business, and if we come to Kansas City, he will answer questions that we may have of him."

Gabrielle sipped her coffee and studied her cup as if it would produce answers. "And you want to go and meet this man? When would we leave?"

The rest of that day and all day Wednesday, Blake reviewed every detail of the operation with the responsible staffers and then on Thursday, drove to Blake's Place. When he pulled up in front of the country roadhouse, he still got the nostalgic feelings that this unusual operation had always given him. This was the incubator that had prepared him for and propelled him down the road that he had traveled, lessons learned here and judgments developed that had served him well over the years. A hell of a journey, he thought, from a one-horse cow farm in the Dakotas. Oh well, as his mother used to say, "all good things must end when their time is finished." He stepped into the saloon and saw Shirley behind the bar, setting up for today's clientele.

Some things never changed.

Shirley went around the bar and gave him a full-body hug. He enjoyed the gesture but soon pushed her back so he could look at her. "My goodness, woman, you do get better looking all the time. I sure hope we paid those doctors in Kansas City enough money for the magic they performed! What am I saying? There isn't enough money for what they did."

"We do have to consider the excellent material they had to work with, but I see something else that I don't think they had anything to do with. It's in your eyes—your beautiful blue eyes show happiness that I haven't seen for a long time."

Shirley turned and poured a cup of coffee and set it on the bar in front of Blake. "I never could put anything past you, Blake Stevens. You could always read me like a book. No, more like the front page of the newspaper." She tucked her chin down, looking at the floor and then back up to Blake's inquiring stare. "I'm going to get married, Blake! I'm going to marry a farmer from Blytheville. His wife died two years ago, and he began coming in here for his meals, especially dinner. At first he was just another customer, but he was very nice to me, treating me with respect and courtesy unlike any other man that came into this bar. After a time, he began to ask for my table, and it just became a regular thing for me to serve him his dinner. As time went on, he began to stay after dinner, and when I had time, I would sit and talk to him.

He and his wife were married for twenty years and never had children. He told me everything about them, the good times and the bad, but even in the bad times, he loved her very much, and when she came down with cancer three years ago, he stayed by her side and comforted her until she died. He didn't want to live the rest of his life alone, but until we met, he couldn't imagine replacing her with anyone else. I just told the other girls a few days ago, and I've been waiting for you to come over here so I could tell you. I hope you will be as happy for me as I am for myself!"

Blake reached across the bar and took both of Shirley's hands. He looked into her beautiful large eyes and told her sincerely, "Babe, you are one of the most special women I have ever known. When I met Gabrielle, I knew she was the woman I wanted to spend the rest of my life with, and the only regret that I might have had was that I would not spend it with you. The fact that you are so happy and have met a guy that you think will be good to you and make you a great husband and a good provider is the best news I could have gotten on this trip. You tell me when the big event is going to be, and I will foot the bill for the best wedding this guy ever dreamed of."

Blake stepped around the bar and took Shirley in his arms and held her for a long time, until a voice behind them said, "Well, hell, I didn't think I would be breaking anything up this early in the morning. Should I go back upstairs and give you two an hour and then come back?" Bobbi's big, boisterous bark was full of mischief as she came across from the stairs and grabbed them both in a three-way hug. She looked at Shirley and said, "Did you tell him the good news?"

Shirley's smile answered the question, and Bobbi turned to Blake and asked, "What do you think, Dad? Do you think she's old enough?"

Blake put on a stern look and replied, "Probably, but we may need to put her on curfew for a while. Maybe home by eleven. Call in every couple of hours so we can be sure she's okay? I'd be okay with that." The three were still laughing when Jess came over from the motel. She had seen Blake's car pull in, and she was eager to see him.

Blake and Jess walked back over to the motel office, where she shared her reports and presented him with a briefcase with a combination lock. For two years now, he had Jess keeping one set of books for the partners' eyes and another set for Blake. The contents of the briefcase represented the difference in the two sets.

Blake made a call to Little Rock to Ross Mathews at, Cotton Belt State Bank. Mathews agreed to meet Blake for lunch and transact their business outside the bank's walls.

All the girls gathered 'round Blake before he left, each one eager to tell him about the latest adventures they'd had. There was a special bond he had with each of these girls. Whatever had occurred between them individually, each of them had come through that experience, and today their relationship was all about mutual respect and loyalty. As Blake drove to Little Rock, he thought about his relationship with the people back at the roadhouse and promised himself he would not betray that loyalty whatever developed in Kansas City.

When he finished lunch with Ross Matthews and handed over the briefcase, he repeated his instructions to take 10 percent of the contents for his handling fee and transmit the balance to the numbered account in the Cayman Islands. This had been their arrangement for ten years, and the account had grown quite large by this time. About $3 million was the current balance, and Gabrielle had an account in the same bank that was three times as large. They had decided that even though her income from the trust in Kansas City was all legitimate and untouchable, the ability to have anonymity to a portion of her estate was a no-brainer. Yes, Blake thought on the drive back to Hot Springs, the financial security he had built for himself and Gabrielle was pretty well done for a country boy from South Dakota.

Tomorrow morning he and Gabrielle would travel to Kansas City and see what new adventure might be awaiting them. He felt a tingle that varied from pleasant to nauseous, causing him momentary fear that he might throw up. *Just nerves, old boy,* he thought, *just nerves.*

CHAPTER 25

Friday morning, Blake and Gabrielle left Hot Springs, northbound to Kansas City, before the sun cleared the low elevations of the Ozarks. It was a beautiful time of the day to be driving through Southwest Missouri, and they both enjoyed the show. As they traveled up Highway 71, they noticed the valleys were dotted with small family farms, the fields creating cross patterns of lines and colors from the different crops then yielding to the massive mix of colors from the ridges populated by a wide variety of trees and shrubs. He had the top down on the new convertible, and Gabrielle was letting the wind blow her beautiful reddish-blond locks backward into a surprisingly stylish arrangement. The woman was just too damn beautiful to be made ugly by the wind, he thought.

Gabrielle had ordered the staff to prepare a picnic basket for them, and at some point, they followed the signs to a small state park, where they unloaded the basket and enjoyed the delicacies the kitchen staff had prepared. They also enjoyed the bottle of white wine the staff had slipped in unexpectedly. They fetched a blanket from the car and carried it to the edge of a small lake. It was part of the park. Completely satisfied with the food and the wine, they lay on the blanket, facing each other, and let the fall sun warm them until they fell asleep.

Blake awoke with a start and jerked his arm up to look at his watch. They had been asleep for an hour. He kissed Gabrielle until she woke and began to pull him to her. "Not now, beautiful, we're going to be late, and as tempting as it is to not care, we better get back on the road. Save that thought for tonight in the hotel."

It was about six o'clock when they pulled in front of the Muehlebach Hotel. One valet took the convertible to the garage, while another carried their luggage into the lobby. The Muehlebach Hotel was getting old, but it had been the shining crown of Kansas City's hotel industry for many years, and it was still struggling to put forth the elegance and class that it was famous for. The room clerk recognized Blake's name as soon as he supplied it to the man. He retrieved a registration form already filled in and asked Blake to affix his signature. He handed them two magnetic stripe card keys that, he informed Blake, would give them access to the penthouse suite on the top floor. He further informed them that there would be a small fruit plate and chilled wine that were compliments of the house, and he wished them a pleasant evening. Gabrielle looked at Blake and rolled her eyes as they turned toward the elevators and began their ascent to the penthouse.

The suite was everything one could dream of. A full living room including a grand piano and a built-in bar along one wall, and next to that were a small table and four chairs. The drapes were pulled open, the view of the Kansas City lights leading to the Country Club Plaza with its dazzling array of white lights outlining the towers and balconies of every building in the ten-square block shopping wonderland.

The tower in the southeast corner of Nordstrom was built to a scale replica of the tower of Seville, Spain.

Gabrielle walked directly to the huge window that offered the phenomenal view. She turned to Blake and said, "In all my years of living in Kansas City, I was never in this suite, and I had never seen this view from this vantage point. And now that I have, all I can say is I am glad I waited to see it with you!" Blake went to her and took her in his arms and held her tighter than he had ever held her before, and together, they turned to look out at the breathtaking view.

Finally, Blake said, "Surely, this must call for champagne!" He pulled from her embrace and walked to the bar, where a bottle of champagne sat on ice. With a little persuasion, the cork popped, and he poured the bubbling liquid into the two fluted glasses that stood by the bucket of ice. She joined him, and they raised the glasses in a confident toast to their future together. "If I'm dreaming, don't let anyone pinch me and wake me up!" Blake said, and Gabrielle laughed heartily and kissed him.

On the desk, Blake found an embossed envelope with his name printed on the front. Inside was an engraved invitation to the City Club for dinner for two at seven. They freshened themselves up and dressed for dinner. Blake had brought a tux, and Gabrielle donned an elegant champagne satin dress that fit her figure, leaving little to the imagination. Downstairs, the valet whistled for a cab and instructed the driver to take them to the City Club. Gabrielle explained to Blake as the cab navigated the few blocks that the City Club was one of Kansas City's most exclusive private retreats for the very wealthy.

The cab stopped after only a few blocks at the front entrance of a rather ordinary-looking ten-story brick building with a recessed entry managed by two heavy aluminum-framed glass doors. They went into a lobby that was tastefully trimmed and a directory that pointed them to the City Club on the tenth floor. When they got off the elevator, they entered a rather small foyer and, straight ahead, saw the arched entry to the club. The maître d' stood behind an ornate dark wood station that had a small fluorescent light fixture, which was the brightest source of light in the softly lit room, illuminating a book that contained the reservations for that evening.

When Blake gave his name, there was an instant smile and bow from the maître d', who asked that he and Gabrielle follow him. The pencil-thin man turned to walk through another open doorway down a long hallway and stopped at a closed door. His tuxedo almost matched the one Blake was wearing, except for the long tails on his coat. A smile flickered across Blake's face as he tried to imagine himself in a tux jacket with long tails.

The maître d' knocked once on the closed door and then turned the handle and entered. The room was small but elegantly appointed. A large Persian rug covered 80 percent of the floor, leaving its perimeter to show off the rich gloss of the hardwood floors. The walls to the left and right were covered with a deep-red flocked wallpaper accented by columns of gold swirls running from ceiling to floor, repeating every eighteen inches. Crowning the rich texture of the paper was a four-inch border trimmed with a gold band at the top and bottom, sandwiching the same crimson red.

Two men were in the room, awaiting their arrival. They were both standing at a small bar, and when Blake and Gabby entered, one turned to walk toward them.

Blake looked the man over carefully as he approached. He appeared to be in his forties, over six feet tall, approximately two-hundred-plus pounds, and his general build in the way he carried himself suggested a daily visit was made to the workout room. His olive complexion supported his jet-black hair, parted in the middle and combed straight back. A natural curl defied the mission of the gel and produced a wavering pattern to his hairdo. As the man approached his guests, he flashed a broad smile that exposed even white teeth that almost sparkled and illuminated the remarkable eyes. They were so black they appeared to have no physical substance, just two empty black holes that consumed all energy that came near.

"Mr. Blake Stevens, I am so pleased to see you, and I assume this beautiful lady on your arm must be Gabrielle Fleming. I am Armando Genelli, and I am honored to have you as my guests this evening." Genelli stopped shaking Blake's hand and turned to take Gabby's hand and lift it to his lips, all the while never taking his eyes off her.

Genelli pointed Blake and Gabby to the table, and they all sat down, except the man whom Blake had thought was going to join them. Instead, the man remained across the room, his back stiff against the wall and his hands hanging loosely at his sides.

Blake took a moment to look carefully and saw the man was much larger than he thought. Not tall, only about five feet, ten inches, but wide and thick through the upper body. The size of his sleeves suggested his arms were enormous, and his neck was short and seemed to merge into his head with almost no variation in dimension. The man's hair was as black as Armando's but now had liberal portions of white mixed in with the remaining black to signal the years and, Blake suspected, the experiences that went with what he again speculated was his profession. *Bodyguard and general security,* Blake thought.

A waiter entered the room and took their drink order then turned and stepped to the small bar and prepared the sumptuous drinks. When he brought the drinks and placed them in front of each, Armando instructed him to give them twenty minutes to get acquainted then begin to serve the meal.

Turning to his two guests, Armando said, "I have taken the liberty of ordering dinner for the three of us. The chef here has a special recipe for preparing prime rib, and he needed the order earlier today to give him time for the preparation. I hope that meets with your satisfaction."

Blake quickly responded, "It sounds delicious, especially if it lives up to all I have heard about Kansas City beef. We are happy to be your guests this evening, and from what I have heard about the City Club, I'm sure the meal will be prepared to perfection."

"Have you not dined here before at City Club?" Armando inquired as he adjusted his drink glass closer to him.

"This is my first time, but Ms. Fleming has been here on many occasions when her husband was living. I must say I am most impressed with the atmosphere, and the precision exhibited by the waitstaff is remarkable. If only my staff in Hot Springs were half as professional, I would be very pleased."

The small talk continued between the three of them, and it seemed to Blake the large man at the wall had not moved one inch since they had arrived.

In precisely twenty minutes, the door opened, and two men entered the room, one pushing a cart with a stainless steel dome over the top hinged along one side. One man opened the dome cover, exposing the rib roast, which looked perfectly done. The other man confirmed its appearance with a large fork and carving knife. He expertly carved three generous servings and placed them on plates. The second waiter opened the doors on the lower portion of the cart and withdrew three baked potatoes, which were distributed to accompany the beef, and lastly, a stainless steel serving dish heaped with steamed asparagus tips, which the man placed on each of the dishes. One of the waiters placed each of the dishes in front of the three guests while the other went to the bar and returned with a large bottle of red wine.

As soon as the portions were set on the table, the two waiters disappeared back into the hall, closing the door softly behind them.

The conversations over dinner were mixed with exclamations, generous praising of the meal, and a pleasant exchange between Armando and Gabrielle expressing their knowledge and appreciation of many items about Kansas City. When they had finished the meal and over half the bottle of wine, the waiters magically appeared and cleared the table. Small stainless steel ice cream dishes replaced the empty plates, each with a healthy scoop of the Italian ice cream crafted to cleanse the palate without removing the memorable taste of the fine dinner they had just enjoyed.

Armando refreshed their wineglasses and, setting the bottle aside, raised his glass in a toast. "I propose a toast to new friendships and prosperity between them!"

They each sipped their wine in the toast. Then Gabby and Blake set their glasses back on the table while Armando held his in his hand and began to speak to his two guests. "It has been a delight to become acquainted with the two of you, and I must say, I am as impressed as I thought I would be. I am very familiar with your business interest in Arkansas, and you should know that my business interests in Kansas City and beyond are varied in scope and locations. My group and I have recently expanded into Florida, primarily the Miami area. At this point in our development, we are interested in expanding our operations into most of the southeastern states. Your operations in Arkansas include many of the activities found in our businesses."

Noticing Gabrielle leaning forward with a questioning look on her face, Armando paused. "Yes, Ms. Fleming?"

Gabrielle asked, "I am very familiar with most businesses in Kansas City. Would I recognize any of your establishments by their name?"

Armando, clearing his throat, replied, "Indeed you would, Ms. Fleming. Many of the businesses along Broadway, in the blocks midway between downtown and the Country Club Plaza, are operations that we own. They range from apartment buildings, hotels, cocktail lounges, and even the famous Patio Pancake Place that is renowned for having the finest pancakes and waffles in the city."

Blake was beginning to see the connection and where this conversation might be going. "My question for you, Armando, cutting to the chase as they say, is, are the similarities between our business and some of your business the reason we are here for dinner tonight?"

Armando smiled and took another sip of his wine. "Indeed, Mr. Stevens. Aside from the fact that I have decided I like you two, the nature of your businesses and their similarity to my own are precisely why I asked you to come here this evening. I appreciate your cutting to the chase and bringing us to the proposal that I want to present to you this evening. My associates and I want to buy your interest in the casino and hotel in Hot Springs and the roadhouse called Blake's Place near Camp Chaffee. We are aware that you have partners in those two enterprises, and I'm sure you, as well as we, recognize the difficulty you may have in terminating that partnership."

Blake glanced at Gabrielle, recognizing the look that expressed both hope and fear. He turned back to Armando and saw a look that was completely calm and reassuring. "I don't suppose it would serve any purpose for me to inquire further about your knowledge of our partners and how you think you could negotiate a dissolution of that partnership better than I."

Armando smiled as he said, "It would serve no purpose, Mr. Stevens. From what I know, you have used good judgment up to this point, dealing with your partners. I would hate to see you stop using that good judgment."

Blake and Gabrielle looked at each other again, and Armando continued, "I think it would help if I finished the proposal we are making. When you tell me you are ready to proceed with our agreement, I will deposit in whatever account you designate $1 million each. You will then allow me one month to negotiate a settlement with your partners, at which time I will deposit an additional $1 million each to that same account or any other account you designate. There will be no further obligations on your part to me, nor mine to you. If you have concern for your employees, I assure you that we know all of your employees, and the ones that mean the most to you will be offered an opportunity to stay with our organization for a minimum term of three years or longer if they choose."

For a moment, Blake was speechless, and glancing at Gabby's slightly open mouth and saying nothing, he knew she was experiencing the same condition.

The thoughts whirling through his brain finally settled into an orderly grouping. He said, "Obviously, it will take a month or more for arrangements to be made for us to relocate in a manner that would provide us security from anyone who would be unhappy about our business transaction. This decision is not totally new to us, but until now, we had not thought through the details of the steps we would need to take. If I could have a few days to process those details and think some things through, it would be very helpful. At this point, I can just say we are very willing to make an effort for your proposal to be accepted. Your offer is generous, and I suspect you are in a position to follow through on the assurances you seem to be making."

Armando reached under the table and pressed a button. One of the waiters reentered the room and went to his side. "I think my guest and I would like to have some of the brandy I ordered this afternoon, and coffee." He looked at Blake and Gabby, who nodded in agreement. The waiter turned and left the room.

Armando retrieved a small notepad from his jacket pocket and scribbled some numbers on the top sheet; tearing it off, he handed it to Blake.

Blake looked at the ten digits written together without spacing and looked back at Armando.

Armando smiled at Blake and Gabby then said, "It has been one of the better business dinners I have ever had. You two are refreshing people to talk to and deal with. Those ten numbers will ring a phone that only I will answer. If you call, we will not use names, but I will know your voice and you will know mine. You will say that you are looking forward to seeing me at my ski lodge in one month. After that, I will tell you that I will make the travel arrangements, and my personal travel agent will be calling you with the flights and times. The next day, an attorney will call on you at the casino with appropriate papers for you to sign. The deposit will be made the following day. When you have completed all you need to do, you will call that number again and say that you are ready to get on the plane and you will see me in Snow Country. The second deposit will be made the following day. Do you have any questions?"

Neither Blake nor Gabby made a sound.

"Very well. As I said before, it's been a delightful evening. My driver is downstairs with my car, and he will take you back to the hotel. Enjoy the rest of the evening and have a safe trip back home."

Downstairs, Armando's driver was standing by the back door of the Lincoln Town Car. He opened the door as he approached, and they slid into the backseat. It was quiet in downtown Kansas City; the few people who used downtown for social and entertainment purposes were still tucked into their closed-door environment, giving the Town Car virtual exclusive use of the streets.

The Country Club Plaza had become the place to be in the evening. It offered an endless choice of top restaurants sprinkled among the top brand-name shops that stayed open into the evening for the convenience of their discriminating patrons. At Blake's suggestion, the driver agreed to drive down Broadway, past the varied business places Armando had enumerated, and cruised the streets of the Plaza. They were encircled by the endless array of tiny white lights that outlined every building and storefront. The sidewalks were full of people moving among the elegant shops and supper clubs.

The Lincoln completed the tour and drove back north to downtown, stopping in front of the Muehlebach. The driver declined any offer of a tip for his services, but the valet had no similar hesitations as he opened the front door for them. The elevator delivered them back to their suite. Only after closing the door did they let their guard down, looking at each other until Gabby threw herself into Blake's arms, and they both began to laugh. Finally, the tension was released, and Blake went to the small refrigerator at the bar and selected two small bottles of scotch, a tray of ice, and two glasses. He poured the two drinks, adding a short burst of seltzer from the gas-powered dispenser on top of the refrigerator, and walked over to Gabby, who was leaning back on a chaise lounge. Blake handed Gabby one of the glasses and, clinking hers against the other, said, "To my lovely soul mate, a toast to a very interesting and, I think, successful evening!"

Gabby took a sip of the Chivas and seltzer and expressed her approval of the taste. "Mr. Stevens, my sincere admiration for how you conducted yourself this evening. I have always known you have an innate talent for judging other people and an instinct for making timely, strategic moves when it comes to business. I was so proud of you tonight and was reminded while we were having dinner that I truly do love you with all my heart!"

Blake hung his head and limply waved his hand toward Gabby and said, "Oh, go on, ma'am. Next thing you know, you'll be asking me to marry you and stuff like that."

Gabby bent over and howled with laughter. She staggered to one side and fell on the bed. Clint followed her and sat down to recover from breaking himself up. Eventually, Gabby controlled her laughter and looked up at Clint. "I'm starting to think that would not be a bad idea. I don't ever want to be apart from you, but it seems that you are a little mixed up on who does the asking."

Clint reached for her and, for a long time, just held her. Finally, he put his mouth close to her ear and said softly, "The right time in the right place, sweet woman. I just want to make sure that when I ask the question, you're in no position to say no."

They pulled the drapes open and sat in the two chairs, looking out at the beautiful skyline. Forty blocks to the south, the outline of the Spanish architecture of the buildings on the Country Club Plaza formed a mosaic that was hypnotic to them both. Each balcony, tower, arcaded porches, and arched corridors were precisely outlined with endless rows of small white lights. They sipped their drinks while never taking their eyes off the magical scene. It was the perfect way to end what had been a magical evening. Gabrielle imagined what the conclusion of their time in Arkansas might look like.

Chapter 26

"I can't believe it. You've got it made, Mr. Stevens! How can you even think about walking away? You've put your whole adult life into this business. I'm sure it has made you a rich man already, but from here on, you can just keep getting richer. I can understand that you and Gabby could be happy somewhere without all the headaches that go with this business, but I've got this operation under control. And you have good people, professional people taking most of the load in Hot Springs. I guess if you're getting a lot of money for it, maybe you're smart to take the money and run!" Jess stopped talking and just sat, shaking her head side to side.

Blake reached across the table and put his hand across hers. "I know it's hard for you to understand, Jess. I have confided in you more about my business than anyone else except Gabby. As I said in the beginning, the new buyers will make it very easy for all of you to stay with the business, if you want to.

"If you find that you're unable to work for them, they will not try to keep you from leaving. Gabby and I have decided that we will move away from Arkansas and, for the first year or two, not be available for phone calls. However, I will call you every month on the same date of our departure and inquire as to how you're doing. If you tell me the old pain has come back in your legs, I will make calls and either remove the problem or secure approval for you and any of the girls to leave. I think you're going to be happy with the new owners. Keep your heads down and don't overreact to any rumors or incidents. You may be asked to add some activities to your job description. Probably nothing that you will object to, but if you do, just let me know."

He stood to leave and just stepped close to put her arms around her holding him tight. Eventually, he pulled himself free and kissed her on the forehead. He held her out at arm's length and said, "You're a good woman,

Jess, and you deserve to be happy and successful. If I didn't think you would be both, I would not recommend you to stay. Don't say anything to the girls until the first of the month. You'll get a phone call advising you of the new ownership and setting up a meeting for the staff to meet the new manager from Kansas City. You should then meet with the girls and tell them the news and give them each their envelope I am leaving with you. Your envelope has a piece of paper as well as the cash bonus. The piece of paper has a phone number that you must memorize and then burn the paper. You should not share that number with anyone."

Jess nodded, leaning up to him and kissing him one last time. "Take care of yourself, Mr. Stevens. It's been a real experience!"

Blake backed the car away from the roadhouse, took one last look, and headed toward Little Rock. He was ready to make the final arrangements with the banker for the trip to the Caribbean.

CHAPTER 27

The doors to the jury room opened, and the US marshal stepped to one side and allowed the people inside to leave. It was lunchtime, and the members of the federal grand jury were going into a room down the hall to have their lunche boxes, which had just been delivered. Alice Swenson walked quickly toward the elevator bank, looking down at her feet, her shoulders drooping noticeably.

It had not been a good week for Alice. It started with her worrying where Carl could have gone; the worrying soon developed into anger, and the anger gave way to shock and remorse as the two investigators from the crime commission informed her that Carl Hoffman had died in a fiery crash in West Memphis, Arkansas. It had taken a while for the medical examiners to piece together enough information to know Carl's identification.

Their first visit had been basically polite and informative. However, before they left, they handed her a subpoena to appear before a federal grand jury in two days. That was when all the politeness and empathy disappeared. They had asked her so many questions about Carl, and then they went on to Frederick Sanchez at the Jolly Roger Bar and Grill and Orlando Perez, who worked at the Latin Imports company.

Alice had initially tried to profess innocence, saying she had accompanied Carl to the bar, but it was just to have drinks, and she didn't know anything about the people that owned the bar. The assistant federal prosecutor, however, reminded her that she was under oath and gestured to folders full of papers that he promised would make the grand jurors establish Alice as someone who knew much more than she was pretending. He also told her the length of time she would serve in federal prison for lying to a federal grand jury. Today, Alice was finishing her second day of testimony and felt sure she had told them everything they wanted to know.

Clint Parker and Amos Boudreau walked out of the jury room with the assistant prosecutor. The FBI crime lab had successfully matched the fingerprints of the stabbed man in Memphis with partial prints from the state police car in Mississippi.

The three federal men went into Amos Boudreau's office. Three cups of coffee were poured, and they sat down to review the procedure of that morning.

Amos Boudreau sat behind his desk, twirling a pencil. "What do you think, Randy, have we gotten everything Alice knows, or do you think we need to continue to lean on her?"

Randy Hamilton was serving his fifth year as assistant US attorney and, despite his youthful, boyish looks, had successfully put a record number of individuals out of business and/or in prison. He had sandy-blond hair and light-blue eyes, which accentuated his youthful look. But the criminals of the southeast district had learned that Hamilton was nobody to take lightly. "I don't think we're going to get any more useful information out of Alice, but I do think she's scared enough that threatening her with more charges might persuade her to become a confidential informant. I leaned on her pretty hard about Donald Simmons and got nowhere. I think Simmons is way above her pay grade, but it's possible she could learn things as time goes on, and I hope she would be persuaded to share those things with us."

Clint Parker stood up from his chair, set his coffee cup on Amos's desk, and said to Hamilton, "That's a very smart idea, Randy! We need to supply her with a scenario of answers to questions that she will likely be asked. The right answers should help her avoid ringing any alarm bells, and it just might lead to information that, if dropped in her presence, would be helpful to us. I agree that it's unlikely she moves in the same circles as Simmons—that's the frustrating part of this case. Simmons is like a ghost that floats into the picture, leaves no trace, and floats back out. It may help that we finally got a federal judge's permission to put a tap on his phone, but the events of the last week have probably put him in panic mode. If he's as smart as they think he is, he's going to be very careful about what he does and whom he talks to for some time."

Clint Parker was skeptical about Randy Hamilton's optimism regarding the effect they were having on Donald Simmons. Clint recognized that Simmons had done an effective job setting up his organization. He had multiple layers of people between him and the actual criminal deeds being performed on his orders. They now had a tap on his phone and two marshals watching his house. So far, these measures had produced zero results. It was obvious to any experienced listener that Simmons was being deliberately vague during any conversations on the telephone. Additionally, he had become a real recluse, rarely leaving the house, and on those rare occasions when he did, he went to a nearby grocery store and adjacent liquor store. Twice, he had encountered another car in the grocery parking lot; they had both stopped when the drivers' windows were next to each other. The exchange, each time, was so short that it was difficult to imagine any meaningful information was passed.

Tonight promised to be different. It was about noon when the postman came to Simmons's front door. Instead of dropping the mail in the box at the street, the mail carrier had gone up to the front door and rang the bell. The officers in the surveillance van speculated that there was postage due or something that needed to be signed for. At 1:00 p.m., Simmons made a local phone call. When a voice on the other end answered with yes, Simmons said, "I'm having some of the boys over tonight for cards. Are you up for a few hands of poker?"

"I'm always up for a good poker game" went the reply. "What time are you starting?"

Simmons answered, "Make it eight o'clock. The other fellows will be here shortly after."

The two US marshals turned in their cramped quarters and gave a thumbs-up to each other with smiles all around. One of the men called Amos Boudreau and gave him a report on the phone conversation. Amos said he and Clint Parker would arrive at the stakeout at about 7:00 p.m. and join the men in the van.

The rest of the afternoon was uneventful; in fact, it was so quiet that the two officers in the Land Rover alternately took naps to fortify themselves for the coming evening.

At 6:55 p.m., a dark-colored Ford turned the corner a block east of the Land Rover and killed its lights as it slowly eased up behind the van. Parker and Boudreau got out of the car and quickly entered the van. Once they were settled inside, Clint produced a bag of fried chicken, grits, and redeye gravy and a large thermos of coffee. While the two stakeout men worked on the food, Clint and Amos monitored the listening equipment. There was nothing to hear, and the two officers reported it had been that way since the phone call arranging the poker game.

It was precisely 8:00 p.m. when the Lincoln Town Car went slowly down the street and turned into the driveway at the Simmons residence. There were no outside houselights burning, and the nearest streetlight was half a block away. They heard the soft thud of the car door being closed and could see a shadowy figure walk to the front door, which was promptly opened, and the visitor was welcomed inside.

149

One of the agents put on a pair of night vision goggles, and he used them to scan the Lincoln Town Car. Despite the fact that the car appeared to be shiny and clean, the license plate appeared to be smeared with dirt, and the numbers could not be read through the goggles. Amos Boudreau told the others to sit tight and he would be right back. He went back to the dark Ford and opened the back door. When he stood up, he was holding a small dog; his wife had reluctantly agreed to let him borrow the poodle for the evening. Amos walked across the street and set the dog on the sidewalk. He had attached to the collar a self-winding leash, which let the dog roam with limited restraint. He walked toward the Simmons house, and as the dog stopped at a shrub near the street, Amos turned into the Simmonses' driveway, getting closer to the illegible license plate. The top of the plate identified it as being from Louisiana, but the rest of the plate was thoroughly covered with a gray substance that appeared to have been put on wet and then dried to a hardness that Amos could not remove without tools.

CHAPTER 28

Donald Simmons was a very nervous man when he opened his door to the visitor. He had wondered how long it would take for the organization to pay this visit. The syndicate had suffered internal strife and become a week organization in the southeast region, except for Florida. Everyone's attention had gone to the glitz and glamour of South Florida. For many years, it had become easier and easier to smuggle anything into Miami and the Keys, stretching on southeast from the tip of the peninsula—illegal immigrants, young women from the white slavery markets worldwide, and of course, drugs.

The Kansas City organization had monitored the degrading of the organization in the southeast region and had immediately spotted the new upstart that began operations in New Orleans twelve years ago. They warned the boys in Miami that New Orleans could become a real problem for them. The boys, wallowing in piles of money, disregarded the warnings and concentrated on their orders for the next new, bigger yachts to sit in front of their new waterfront mansions.

Marco Genelli was a patient man. He was a great believer in giving his *brothers*, who had paid their dues to the *family*, wide latitude to make their mistakes and then correct them. Marco had, however, lost his patience with the situation in New Orleans. The operation down there was sloppy and amateurish. Marco did realize that Simmons had recognized a no-brainer opportunity and had understandably gone after it. Simmons had made one critical mistake. He did not do his homework, and he either did not know or did not believe that he needed the blessings of a bigger organization before he could just land in a town and start doing business. Recently, Marco had sent emissaries to Simmons to explain where he had erred in setting up his business. His emissaries had suggested to Simmons that everything could be worked out. A percentage of the gross could be paid to Kansas City, and he could attend regular meetings, becoming educated to the rules and procedures for doing business. He could become part of the family. Simmons had foolishly told Marco's representative to take a flying fuck down the throat of an alligator. Such disrespect was totally unacceptable in Marco's world.

Two days ago, Marco had dispatched his most-special emissary to fly to New Orleans and meet with Don Simmons. There would not be any further offers to consider. There would be no detailed discussion of the business. Instead, the emissary would act as if everything was okay and acceptable. He would offer him friendship and camaraderie and suggest that they should have a drink with a toast to new friendships and new beginnings.

Don Simmons was feeling euphoric. The mail delivery earlier in the day contained a note that, by its tone, recognized Simmons's organization and accepted its authority in the states of Mississippi, Louisiana, and Arkansas. The note said if he wanted to accept their friendship, he should call a number in New Orleans and invite Mr. Perón to come to his house for an evening of poker. Simmons had eagerly made the call, and now, here was this man sitting in the overstuffed leather chair across from his desk. "What drink may I prepare for you, Mr. Perón?" Simmons's voice was so syrupy and patronizing that Mr. Perón felt his stomach move uncomfortably.

"A Manhattan on the rocks with a splash of club soda, if that's not too much trouble," Mr. Perón said.

"It is no trouble at all for me to be gracious to my special guest!" Simmons finished mixing the drink and set it on a small table next to the overstuffed chair. He then returned to the bar and made himself a martini. He opened the door of a small refrigerator and retrieved a bottle of olives, spearing two of them with a toothpick and dropping them into his martini. It was then that he realized he had failed to put a maraschino cherry into Mr. Perón's drink. He looked back into the refrigerator and then said, "Excuse me one moment while I get a cherry from the kitchen refrigerator."

Mr. Perón smiled understandingly and said, "But of course, that would be very nice. Thank you."

Perón watched Simmons go out of the room and down the hall to the kitchen. As soon as the man was out of sight, Perón rose and walked to the bar, retrieving a small bottle from his pocket. He held the bottle upside down over the martini and squeezed. One drop of crystal clear liquid came out of the bottle into the martini. Mr. Perón returned to his chair and picked up his drink, which he was holding when Simmons returned to the room. Simmons was holding a small crystal dish of maraschino cherries.

He held it out to Simmons, who selected two of the cherries and dropped them into his drink.

Satisfied with his performance as bartender, Simmons turned and raised his glass and said, "Here's to new friendships and two friends showing mutual respect. I am so happy to welcome you as my friend."

Mr. Perón raised his glass and replied with his own toast, "As a personal representative of Mr. Genelli, I am honored to bring you his words: 'New friendships make our world larger, and mutual respect holds our world together!'"

The two men raised their glasses in unison and drank to their toast. Mr. Perón's eyes narrowed and seemed to be recording every movement by Simmons. As Simmons's broad smile started to recede from his face, replaced by a faint grimace and a puzzled look forming in his eyes, Perón spoke, "Mr. Genelli wanted me to make sure you understand my toast. Mr. Genelli and men like him all over the world have sacrificed many things to build their organization. There are only two ingredients important in the structure of the worlds they have built: respect and loyalty. The fact that you could not show either quality disqualified you from being part of Mr. Genelli's world. In another few seconds, you will be dead, but he wanted you to know before why you had to die a foolish man."

Simmons heard the words but could not respond. His mouth was open, but his throat felt paralyzed, and now it seemed the paralysis was moving down through his body. He tried harder to speak, say one word, but his efforts only produced a bulging of his eyes, and as his brain began to shut down, the eyes had one more glimpse of Mr. Perón, who was now smiling. And that was the last thing he saw.

Mr. Perón carried his glass to the bar, washed it, and wiped it dry. He hung it back on the stem glass rack and took a handkerchief to wipe any places he might have touched with his fingers. The poison would produce all the symptoms of a heart attack, which the medical examiner would recognize and with which he could rule the death as a natural result of heart failure. He pulled on a pair of gloves and went to the front door, wiping the handles as he left. He backed the Lincoln out into the street and drove slowly away, paying no attention to the van and the dark-colored Ford one-half block behind him.

Inside the van, Clint and Amos decided they would follow the Lincoln and the guys in the van would stay until the lights went out in the Tudor house they had been watching. They had traveled about four blocks before they caught up with the Lincoln sitting at a red light. Amos moved over to the right lane to avoid being right on the bumper of the Lincoln. The streetlight at the intersection gave the two FBI agents their best look at the driver. The man appeared to have dark complexion, and his dark hair was combed straight back and had sideburns that came below his earlobe.

The traffic light turned green, and the two cars moved out at the pace of the speed limit.

Clint said, "From what I saw, it's hard to tell whether he's Hispanic or Italian. Let's just stay with him and see if he goes to a hotel. If he does, we may get a chance to work on the license plate and find out what name he's registered under."

The Lincoln continued a rather random pattern, but Clint was convinced the docks on the Riverfront seemed to be a probable destination. Twice, Clint pulled his car toward the curb and turned the lights off, keeping his eye on the taillights of the Lincoln, and, when an appropriate distance was between them, turned the lights back on and pulled back out on the street.

He hadn't gotten the impression the driver was trying to detect or shake a tail; instead, he was of the opinion the driver was just relaxing and taking his time to get to his next destination. When they came to Front Street, which ran parallel to the water, the Lincoln stopped, and after some hesitation, the driver turned right and proceeded west until he came to the Jolly Roger Bar and Grill.

"Well, well, well!" Amos said as Clint pulled the Ford to the curb five cars back of the Lincoln. It was only ten o'clock, and business was still pretty brisk at the Jolly Roger. The dark-complexioned man got out of the Lincoln and stood for a while, looking at the bar as if he were trying to decide whether or not to try to buy it. Appearing to have made a decision, the man walked to the front door and entered the bar. "You would think a man driving a fancy car like that would choose a nicer part of town to stop in for a drink!"

Amos and Clint got out of the Ford and walked to the rear. Inside the trunk, Amos retrieved two jackets that showed a fair amount of wear and was a little frayed around the neck. The two men removed their ties and suit coats and donned the used jackets. The coats fitted loose and came down below the hips, amply hiding the presence of their guns holstered at the hip. A New Orleans Saints baseball cap was retrieved from each coat and adjusted to fit. They looked each other over and gave a thumbs-up for the change in appearance. Amos grinned as he said, "Now the question is, can you handle a boilermaker without getting sloppy?"

They entered the bar and, for a moment, adjusted their eyes to the low-light, smoke-shrouded interior. Clint spotted the Lincoln driver toward the far back area of the bar, seated at a booth. The booths formed a line along the wall opposite the bar. Clint and Amos sat at the bar, the back mirror providing a good view of the man in the booth.

Clint looked around the room and observed that he and Amos fitted in pretty good with the crowd, as long as no one required them to open their coats and inspected their Wolf Brothers suit pants. "Well, it seems pretty obvious our boy isn't concerned about fitting in with the crowd."

A waitress brought an ordered drink to the man's table. It was in a tall glass, and they could make out small effervescent bubbles rising from the drink.

Clint added, "No, and I would guess his drink is the same thing he drinks when he's at home. Wherever home is."

The dark-complexioned patron talked with the waitress for a moment after she set his drink down. When he finished, the waitress responded, and when the man's demeanor changed to unfriendly, the waitress turned and went directly to the bar. She huddled with the bartender, who nodded his head and gestured for her to go back to work. She went around the bar to the two new arrivals. "What you boys hav'n?"

"Two shots of Hennessy with two beers back," Amos grunted the order. The girl turned and flounced back to the bar.

"Is that what we're supposed to drink to fit into this crowd?" Clint spoke as he looked the rest of the crowd over.

Amos chuckled. "It's a drink down here that won't raise any questions and won't tear your stomach up at the same time. I got acquainted with the combination while I was stationed in Paris after the war. Try it, you may like it."

The bartender poured the two drinks, and as the girl carried them on her tray and started toward them, they noticed the bartender make a quick trip up the back stairs. By the time she got their drinks on the bar, the bartender was already returning to his station.

In about two minutes, Clint and Amos recognized Frederick Sanchez coming down the stairs. This was the first time they had actually seen the man, but the photos of him left no doubt in their minds who he was. He walked to the booth where the Lincoln driver waited and spoke to the man. Clint noticed the bartender reach under the bar, and immediately, the volume of the music became louder. The two men alternated in their exchange with each other, but it soon became obvious that their conversation had gone from informative to confrontational. Sanchez held on to the back of the chair, facing the booth, obviously upset, and finally waved to the man in the booth to leave his establishment. Sanchez stepped back, and the man rose from the booth, threw a large bill on the table, and went to the door. Amos and Clint left their half-finished drinks on their

155

table and went to the door. They paused inside while they observed the man walk to the Lincoln.

For what seemed like a long time, the man just sat in the Lincoln, looking back at the front of the bar. Amos pulled his baseball cap low and said to Clint, "I'll pick you up at the door." Without another word, he went out on the sidewalk and walked toward the Ford. He kept his head down and shuffled his walk with an unsteady gait. The man didn't even look up as he staggered past the Lincoln. Amos got in the Ford and waited. Clint was still standing inside the door of the Jolly Roger.

Finally, the man started the Lincoln and pulled out onto the street. Amos rolled the Ford up to the front door and slowed for Clint to jump in; he kept it rolling and resumed the surveillance. It was obvious the demeanor of the driver of the Lincoln had changed. His driving became more aggressive. "Now he's got some place to go, and he's in a hurry to get there," Clint said as he fastened his seatbelt.

It was 11:30 p.m. when the man pulled into the long-term parking lot of the airport and parked in a slot near the shuttle bus pickup station. Clint and Amos stopped outside the ticket gate and watched as the man got on a bus to the terminal. At the terminal, the man entered at the door leading to the Trans World Airlines ticket counter. Clint got out of the Ford and followed the man as he checked in. The passenger clerk gave him a boarding pass and directed him to the gate. Clint had exchanged his frayed jacket and ball cap for the coat to his suit and no longer resembled the man in the bar. The men paused at a concession stand and bought a magazine, proceeding to the loading area just in time for the departure of the last flight to Kansas City until tomorrow.

Clint did not have enough information on the man to justify boarding the flight and following him to Kansas City. He returned to the entrance to the terminal, where Amos was waiting. "Well, did our boy sprout wings and fly?" Amos asked.

Clint replied, "Yes, he did. Last flight to Kansas City, but I decided we should stay right here and follow up on the contacts he made while he was in town."

"I'll drop you back at the hotel, and we can pick this up tomorrow morning. Maybe a good night's sleep will steer us in the right direction toward making some sense of what happened this evening." Amos drove back into the edge of the French Quarter, dropping Clint at the Hilton. "See you in the morning. Wanna have breakfast at seven in the hotel?"

Clint made a face. "Okay, slave driver, seven it is. Good night."

Clint went up to his room and made a quick call to his wife and apologized for waking her up, telling her he loved her and collapsing into the bed. He was asleep in seconds, which was an ability that had always served him well since he had been in law enforcement. Six hours of trouble-free sleep, and tomorrow morning would find him ready and able to sort out the events of this evening. He was starting to get that feeling that eventually came during an investigation. All the pieces were beginning to come together, even if he didn't yet know what they would look like when they actually came together.

It was 6:00 a.m. when the phone began to ring. After one short ring, Clint picked up the instrument and heard a recording wishing him a good morning and telling him it was time to get up. He showered quickly and ran the electric razor hurriedly over his face and dressed in a fresh shirt and the suit he had worn yesterday.

He made a quick call to Baptist Memorial in Little Rock and was advised that Ham Turner was still in intensive care, but the doctor categorized him as stable. He clicked the button on the phone and made a hurried call to Glenn Wiggs. "Glenn, this is Clint, and I'm calling you from New Orleans. I need you to go to Baptist Memorial Hospital this morning, get next to Ham Turner, and stay with him until I get there later today. When the doctor says it's okay, call my office and have my secretary come to the hospital. She can be with you when you talk to Turner, and she does shorthand, so have her take good notes on anything he says. There's a flight out of here at one p.m. and another at five. I expect to be on the one o'clock, and if that works out, I'll be at the hospital before two."

He finished the call, and when he hung up the receiver, he noticed the red light on the phone was flashing. He lifted the receiver, and the hotel operator told him she was holding a call and would put it through to him.

It was Amos, and Clint immediately caught the tension in his voice. "Clint, we've got a problem. The housekeeper for Donald Simmons showed up early this morning and let herself in the house as she does every week to do the laundry and housecleaning. She found Simmons in his study, slumped over his desk. He was still sitting in his chair, and from all appearances, he died of a heart attack. She called NOPD, and they have a detective at the scene, and an ME is on his way. I'll be in front of the hotel in about ten minutes. Stop in the coffee shop and get them to fix a couple of large coffees and munchies. We'll have breakfast on the way to Simmons's house."

Fifteen minutes after the call from Amos, the dark-blue Ford pulled up in front of the hotel, and Clint got in, carrying the coffee and two cinnamon rolls in a to-go tray. Amos pulled back into the morning traffic and parked the car north to Simmons's house.

Clint handed a cup of coffee to Amos and set the donut tray on the seat between them. "Did the police say what time the cleaning woman found the body?"

Otis sounded the horn as they passed two cars that seemed to be in no hurry to get to work. "Seven a.m. sharp, her normal time every Friday."

For the next fifteen minutes, the two men concentrated on the coffee and cinnamon rolls. When they arrived at Simmons's house, a police cruiser, a light-blue Ford LTD, and the medical examiner's car were all in the driveway. Amos parked on the street, and the two FBI agents walked toward the front door.

A uniformed cop directed them down a hallway to the study. The body was still seated in the swivel/tilt armchair, tilted forward, with the head resting on the desktop. The left hand was extended out beyond the dead man's head, while the right hand hung down at his side. The medical examiner picked up the right hand and looked at the fingers then performed the same exercise with the left hand.

The detective went over and shook hands with Amos, who turned to Clint and made the introductions. "Detective Sergeant Samson Belou, meet FBI Agent Clint Parker. Clint, this is Sam, NOPD, and the man in the white coat is Cecil Wrigley, county medical examiner." They all shook hands and exchanged greetings.

Clint looked at the body slumped over the desk and asked, "Anything interesting so far?"

Wrigley walked back over to the desk and gestured to the left hand of the deceased. "So far, there is not a whole lot to go on with. We'll know more when I get him downtown and do an autopsy. A preliminary checklist would include the fact that the man appears to be in excellent physical condition. There's a pretty well-equipped workout room next to the garage that would explain that. The cleaning woman tells me he was right-handed, so it may be nothing, but the way his left hand is extended across the desk while his right arm hangs down toward the floor suggests he might have been trying to do two things. There's nothing to confirm that there was another person in the house, but hypothetically, he might have been reaching toward someone with his left hand for help when he felt the attack coming on. If he was right-handed, I thought, why wouldn't he be reaching with his right hand? You boys come around the desk and take a look in the knee space near his right hand."

Amos walked around the desk, reaching in his inside pocket, pulling out a pencil flashlight, and squatted down. Five seconds later, he stood and handed Clint the flashlight. Clint squatted down beside the chair and pointed the little beam of light into the dark knee space. There, just three inches from the dead man's right hand, was a white button affixed to the dark wood of the desk.

Clint stood and swept the scene with his eyes, looking for any abnormalities that would suggest a closer look. He had always found that the scrutiny of a well-trained law enforcement officer frequently saw things that a medical examiner missed. Then his brain flashed a signal, and he looked again at the desktop. The man's skin was dark, suggesting long sessions beside his swimming pool and/or regularly scheduled trips to a tanning salon. When his gaze continued to the fingertips, he realized what the signal from the brain had been. The fingertips were abnormally white, especially around the nails.

The medical examiner had been watching Clint's gaze and spotted what he was looking. "See something puzzling, Mr. Parker?"

Clint turned to the examiner and said, "I'm not trained in medicine, Mr. Wrigley, but anytime I see extreme variations in skin tone and color on a dead body, I suspect it's an abnormality, especially when the body looks as fit and trim as Mr. Simmons's appears to have been before he died."

Wrigley looked at Clint with a quick smile that expressed a new level of respect for the FBI agent. "I'm impressed, Parker. I assure you it will be on the first list of things to be checked when we reach the lab. There are poisons in today's market that act so swiftly that in just seconds, the victim's muscles and auto reflex system is paralyzed. Death follows quickly and, oftentimes, leaves telltale marks of total discoloration on the appendages of the body."

Clint asked, "How soon can you let us know the results of that test?"

"No more than two hours from the time we arrive at the lab, probably sooner than that. I'll call you as soon as I know," Wrigley said as he began preparations to move the body.

Amos produced a card and, handing it to the AME, said, "Call me with the results. I think Mr. Parker's going to be on his way back to Little Rock."

Back in the car, both agents were quiet, processing the events of last night and this morning. Finally, Otis said, "It's kind of weird to think that the boy we were following last night killed a man right under our noses and then drove across town, cool as a cucumber, and had a pretty unpleasant confrontation with Frederick Sanchez. I'm not sure what all we're looking at here, but I think I just felt the ground move in New Orleans."

Amos pulled up in front of the airport and, as Clint got his small bag out of the backseat, said, "Call me when you get through with Turner. It would be so helpful if he were able to talk this afternoon."

Clint said, "The doctors felt pretty positive this morning that we could talk to him this afternoon. I'll let you know as soon as I have something. Thanks for the tour of New Orleans. I have a good feeling we were in the right place at the right time last night. Sure wish we knew who the guy in the Lincoln was."

They shook hands, and Clint grabbed his case and disappeared into the terminal.

Chapter 29

Clint had gone directly to the hospital from the Little Rock airport. Ham Turner was propped up in his bed, and though the doctor said he was much improved, Turner was still playing the sympathy card.

"You're looking better, Ham. How are you feeling?"

Ham Turner seemed to bring an effort to open his eyes and speak. "I'm hurting pretty badly, Clint. My head feels like it's going to blow up."

Clint reached out and placed his hand on Ham's arm. "Well, the doc says you're recovering better than he expected. Vital signs are good, and your luck was with you. An inch lower and you wouldn't have a headache to worry about. We need to talk about some things, if you're up to it."

"I don't know, Clint. I'm pretty weak. Maybe tomorrow, okay?"

"Things are moving pretty fast, Ham. I don't think we can wait. We need some answers so we can put a stop to the operation that I think got you shot. The sooner you answer our questions, the faster we can protect you and have the best chance of keeping you alive. I need to know just how you got your job at ABI and what role Bruce Caldwell played in hiring you. The operation of drug smuggling and distribution in Arkansas, Louisiana, and beyond is starting to unravel, and if Caldwell is involved, you can help us nail his ass. If you help us, I can help you. That window of opportunity won't stay open very long, and if you don't help us, I'll see to it that you'll go down hard. Are we clear?"

A tear welled up in the man's eyes and then slowly spilled over and began to wind down the deep furrow marking the joining of his nose and cheek. It slowly followed the path of least resistance, flowing down to the edge of his upper lip and threatening to drip. The man raised his left arm, grimacing from the movement's effect on the wound in his right shoulder. As he kept his arm over his eyes, a sob escaped, faint at first, then louder as his upper body shook with resignation. The pain increased and took his attention from self-pity to the reality of his condition; he was wounded, and he was void of any further pretense.

"Oh my god, Clint, I am so screwed. I've been a damn fool, and it's all coming down on me."

Clint Turner leaned forward and said, "You're also a very lucky man, Ham!"

"In a way, you may be right. I'm more lucky than smart," Turner spat the words as if they would choke him if he didn't get them out.

Clint waited without further comment.

Ham regained his composure and continued, "I always wanted to be a cop, but truth is, I was never very good at it. When Orville Carson offered me the job of town marshal at Carsonville, I thought my dream was coming true in spades! He needed someone to bring in the men that had been kicked off the trains by the railroad dicks and then help keep all the workers in line. I had more power over more people than I'd ever dreamed of. I soon learned the job had its dark side, but then, what job doesn't?" He paused thoughtfully. "The first man to try to run away was something I'll never forget. He lit out during the night, and nobody missed him till he didn't show up for breakfast roll call. Took me and three other men and four hounds most of the day to track him down. We found him hiding in a culvert about five miles from the bunkhouse. Tied him onto a horse, belly down, and made him ride in that position all the way back to headquarters. That poor bastard was hurt'n bad by the time we got back. Then Orville made us tie him to the whipping post, and he brought out the snake whip. He told me to give him a dozen lashes across the back with his shirt off."

Ham paused, his eyes glazing over as his mind went back to what he'd done. "I didn't think it would be as bad as it was. That whip sure cut that poor bastard up like slicing a beef roast. Orville had stayed and watched. He looked the man over when we were done, and after fifteen minutes of just hanging there while the workers looked on, he told us to cut him down and put him in the bunkhouse." He paused. "Four of the men carried him and put him on his bunk. When Orville went back to his house, I went to the tack room in the barn and got a jar of axle grease. I took it to the bunkhouse and told the men to put the grease on the cuts. We used that on the horses when they got cuts and scrapes, and it seemed to help them, so I figured it might help the man's back. It was still two days before he could go back to work."

Ham drifted off into his thoughts, causing Clint to clear his throat, then he began again, "I didn't like parts of my job, but Orville would tell me that all men needed authority over them or they would become a mob. He said that once that happened, my life wouldn't be worth the bullets it'd take to kill me. I did the work without complaining, and then when things started to go bad, he goes and blows his brains out and leaves me out in the cold!"

"How did you first make contact with ABI, Ham?" Clint asked.

"I got a phone call from Bruce Caldwell. That was a big surprise because I didn't even know Caldwell. Anyway, Caldwell asked me if I was looking for work, and I told him I needed a job. He said I should call Mr. Donald Simmons in New Orleans and see if he could help me. I was pretty suspicious because, like I said, I didn't even remember meeting Caldwell, and here he was, trying to help me get a job. Anyway, I called Simmons."

"Did he bring up the ABI job right away?" Clint asked.

Ham looked down and said, "No, not right away, but when I told him I really needed some income, he said there were some small jobs he needed done, and if I would help him with some of them, he would make it worth my time."

Clint asked, "What kind of things did he ask you to do?"

"Little things at first—courier work, like delivering things."

Clint asked, "Did you know what you were delivering?"

"Not at first. It was envelopes or small packages, and the recipients were all over the place. City officials in New Orleans to small-time government employees in Mississippi or Memphis. I was pretty suspicious that there was money in those packages because of the people receiving them. Law enforcement and key people that could control where the police were on specific days or nights. I was picking up pretty good payments for a delivery boy, so I didn't get too nosy."

Clint stopped scribbling notes, prompting, "The job with ABI?"

Ham, enjoying his story, would not be interrupted. "That happened right after I got back from South America."

Clint raised his gaze, and a new look of interest showed in his eyes. "Simmons sent you to South America?"

Ham frowned and said, "Yeah, I think he decided he could trust me and I was experienced at dealing with scumbags, knew how to handle a gun if it was necessary. I think I was riding shotgun, sort of. I met a man by the name of Frederick Sanchez at the New Orleans airport. He had the tickets to Bogotá, Colombia, for the two of us. We flew into Bogotá on the red-eye and went to a charter operator near the terminal. Arrangements had been made for us to go with a load of freight headed to Medellín back in the mountains. When we got to Medellín, a man was waiting with a Land Rover to drive us to a cocaine factory. It was only twenty kilometers, but it took about three hours to get there on the worst damn road I'd ever seen. Some places, there was no road, but the driver knew where he was going, and pretty soon we would be back on what looked a little like a road. We finally got to the factory, and Sanchez was greeted by the man in charge like they were old buddies."

Clint asked, "Describe the factory, and how long were you there?"

Ham was getting into the story. "It didn't look much like a factory, but that's what they called it. Mostly a bunch of canvas tent tops. They were opened on all sides to let the air flow through. If they'd been closed, the poor bastards working inside wouldn't have lasted a week. The boss gave us a tour and explained that the tops protected the cocaine from the rain and the opened sides vented the fumes and kept the temperature below a hundred degrees. I've never known it's so hot, and the humidity was always high. It was like taking a steam bath with your clothes on."

"Did the driver go with you on the tour?" Clint asked.

"No, he stayed with the Land Rover. That's a valuable piece of equipment out there in the jungle. If he'd left it alone for one minute, one of the peons would've driven it off. Assuming he knew how to drive. Anyway, we got the grand tour, from cooking, drying, and packaging the stuff. There must have been near a hundred workers there. Some had their wives or girlfriends, and they lived in little huts made of small trees and tied together with vines. That night, Frederick and the factory boss worked out the details on shipments. I just stayed close to Fred in case some peasant decided he couldn't live without Fred's shoes or wristwatch. I wore my gun where everyone with eyes could see what they would have to deal with if they caused any trouble."

"You stayed overnight at the factory?" Clint asked.

"Yeah, and we were just going to sleep when we heard a commotion outside. We went out to see what was going on."

Ham paused to remember. "What we found were two peasants, both trying to talk at the same time, and the boss looked pretty pissed that his sleep wasn't happening. The one peasant had gone to his hut after his shift ended and found the other one in bed with his wife. He wanted to kill the horny bastard, but there was a camp rule that said only the boss could kill, and if anyone did kill another worker, then the boss would execute the killer. The execution would be slow and painful and done in front of all in the camp. The camp boss made a quick decision that lover boy would be taken out of the factory area and shot and his body dumped in the river to feed the piranha. Frederick took the boss to one side, and they talked a few minutes. The boss then told two men to take the man into the woods and tie him to a tree where others had been dealt with. We walked over to the boss's hut and joined him in a shot of his rum, then he picked up his revolver and went into the woods. Frederick and I had just almost dozed off when the sound of the gun rang through the compound like a knife. I shuddered and looked at Sanchez. He didn't flinch, and I thought he was some kind of weird, cold SOB!"

Ham paused and took a drink from the water bottle then resumed, "Early the next morning, we got ready to start back to Medellín, and no one made any comments about the night before. I just wrote it off to men going off the reservation after being out in the jungle for so long. We drove about a mile from the factory until we came to a place where the trail veered to the right. Off to the left, I could make out a row of small tree trunks tilted at a thirty-degree angle. The driver stopped the Land Rover, and Sanchez hopped out and walked through the undergrowth. The line of small logs formed a crude roof of what had served as a guard post when needed. In thirty seconds, Sanchez came back out of the trees with the little Romeo right on his heels, a big smile from ear to ear. That was my introduction to Orlando Perez. He came back to Bogotá with us, and Sanchez pulled a few strings and got him into New Orleans. The factory boss charged $200 not to shoot a guy. Anyway, Sanchez got himself a loyal manager to run the operation on Gulf Street."

Clint reread his notes on the yellow pad and said, "You said it was right after this trip that you got on at ABI?"

"Within a few days, Simmons arraigned for me to go in and talk to Bruce Caldwell. Caldwell was nervous as a cat during our first meeting, but he eventually decided I could be trusted. I made an application, and within a couple of weeks, I was an ABI agent."

Clint was getting the information he needed to hit Bruce Caldwell with a conspiracy charge under the organized crime statutes. But he had to scare Ham out of having any second thoughts about which side he was on. "Ham, are you aware that Donald Simmons is dead?"

Ham Turner's jaw dropped like a rock as his head shook sideways, as if that would cancel what he'd just heard. "No—I mean he can't be. I just talked to him last week. How did he . . . ugh, did he have a car wreck?"

Clint's voice was flat and crisp, "No car wreck. He was poisoned in his own home."

A shudder swept through Ham's body as he struggled to find his voice. His voice squeaked, "Poisoned! Are you sure? I mean, Simmons was a careful man, and he lived alone. Who could have gotten to him in his own home?"

Clint leaned toward the stunned man and lowered his voice. "It's becoming pretty clear, Ham. There's a struggle going on in the drug-running community. Someone is not happy with the footprint Simmons has made in the region. My hunch is that Simmons, being a very smart man, figured a new method for shipping the drugs into the country and distributing to the supply network. He did his research and identified who needed to be paid in the law enforcement community to intervene when intervention was needed and look the other way when it was necessary. He just had one blind spot. He forgot to ask permission from the capos, who always want a piece of the action when a newbie wants to start a new operation. *Free enterprise* is not a term with which they are familiar."

Both men were silent for what seemed like a long time. Clint let Ham digest his predicament. Ham was still trying to be in control, but everything was breaking apart, spinning out of his control. He muttered, "Any idea who killed him?"

Clint knew he had Ham on his heels. He needed to be asking the questions, so he ignored Ham's query and asked, "Did Simmons ever talk about Kansas City while you were around? Did he ever mention a name in connection with Kansas City?"

Ham tried to focus, but it just seemed that his world was falling apart. "I think I may have heard Simmons mention the Kansas City people, but no names. I can't help you with that angle. Damn it, Clint, if this is a fight between two gangs, they must be coming for me."

Clint spoke in a stern voice, "That's God's truth, Ham. If you want to stay alive, you have to put your trust in the law and me. Any other choices you may think you have have a probable chance of success of slim to none."

Ham replied with a whine, "Yeah, but I didn't come out so good. Last time I depended on you!"

Clint stood close to the bed and looked at Ham. "The difference is, before, we weren't expecting any attempts to kill you, but when it happened, we were able to protect you and get you to a hospital quickly to save your life. Now we are on full alert and will use all means available to protect you. If you reject us and refuse our help, the bad guys will still have you on their hit list, and you'll be standing naked in the rain. How long do you think you'll last in that scenario?"

Another involuntary shudder went through Ham's body, and when he looked up at Clint, he said, "Okay, what do we do now?"

CHAPTER 30

Clint's plan went into high gear. He met with the hospital administrator, who agreed to do his part. He prepared the paperwork for a "deceased" Hamilton Turner, knowing a local reporter would be all over the story before the day's end. A hearse from a small funeral parlor would pick up the body this afternoon and take it to their crematorium. Clint would arrange compensation plus an extra amount for their confidentiality.

After dark, Cam would arrive at the funeral parlor and park in the covered ambulance stall in the back. Ham would get in the rear of Cam's station wagon and lie down on a makeshift bed and ride back out to the cabin on the Current River. In a few days, he would resume his fishing lessons and write in his diary.

Clint called Amos in New Orleans and got an update on activities at the Jolly Roger Bar and the warehouse on Gulf Street. Otis reported that the warehouse had started posting a guard at night.

The alert status had been moved to high, and the FBI would have to be especially careful. From now on, surprise was the essential ingredient.

* * *

New Orleans . . .

Amos Boudreau sat patiently in the three-fourth-ton Dodge van, watching the front door of the Jolly Roger. He had been on the stakeout for two hours, and the only light inside seemed to be a single fixture mounted on the wall behind the bar. He had talked to Clint Parker ten minutes ago, and the news from Little Rock had helped him shake the boredom that was so common on stakeouts. The success in Little Rock and Memphis was helpful in reinforcing his mind-set while keeping his vigil on an empty bar on New Orleans's waterfront. His attitude wasn't improved by the slim chances anyone would show in the wee hours of the morning.

Clint had assured him it was worth the effort if he could stay awake. They needed to get their hands on Frederick Sanchez, and they feared he was sure to rabbit out of New Orleans sooner or later. Otis speculated that Sanchez would head for Texas and then slip across the border into Mexico. Once he blended into the population there, the odds of finding him were very slim, even if the local authorities cooperated, which was doubtful.

Clint agreed with the theory, but they both knew that Sanchez would need money once he got into Mexico. Lots of money would be required for the protection that Sanchez would need. They speculated that any significant cash available to Sanchez would be in the safe at the bar. After all, Donald Simmons had not been around for a few days to collect surplus funds. There could be a significant buildup of receipts, enough to buy some favors in Mexico. They decided to watch the bar 24-7, and Otis had the night-owl shift. They had a US marshal watching the apartment where Sanchez lived, but so far, nothing.

Amos looked at his watch for the umpteenth time. It was 3:00 a.m. He was reaching for his thermos to pour fresh coffee when the movement caught his attention. He focused on the front entrance of the bar, but by all appearances, the place was empty.

Amos had done enough surveillance work that he knew it was natural to imagine activity when there was none. When you concentrated on a scene long enough, the brain was capable of creating the image.

He rubbed his eyes and gazed again at the entrance until he was sure there was no human form in his field of view. He shifted his attention to the street for two seconds and then back to the front door of the bar. There it was again, an almost-imperceptible movement. The dark clothing and bronze skin made the man almost invisible, but Amos was sure the figure of a man had just moved out of the alley and was inching along the front of the bar toward the door.

Amos saw the figure's head swivel and imagined the eyes darting left and right to spot anyone watching from the street. The van Otis was driving had large lettering that read Caribbean Outfitters. There were three other vans on the street, and all looked as if they had been put away for the evening.

The figure reached the door and stood for a moment, apparently fumbling with a ring of keys. With a quick movement, he opened the door enough for him to slide through and then closed the door behind him. Amos waited for a count of ninety then eased out of the van and moved across the street and hugged the front of the bar as he approached the door. Amos looked through the frosted glass of the front window. He couldn't make out anything specific, but as he approached the door, a shaft of light shone down the stairs in the back. Sanchez was upstairs in the office. Reaching the front door, Amos gripped the handle and tried it; it turned easily.

Obviously, Sanchez was satisfied he was alone and was interested in getting the money quickly and had not thought it important to relock the door. Otis pushed the door, and it swung easily and made no sounds of protest. He squeezed through and closed the door. Otis debated with himself whether to go upstairs or wait for Sanchez to go down. Sanchez made the decision for him. The upstairs door opened, and momentarily, a shaft of light shot across the head of the stairs and then disappeared as it was flipped off.

Amos stepped back along the side of the stairwell and waited while Sanchez went hurriedly down the steps, carrying a briefcase in his left hand.

"That's far enough. This is the FBI. Put the case on the floor and raise both hands high!" Amos stepped behind the man. "Take two steps forward and stop." Amos reached for the man's left hand and brought it down, clicked a handcuff on it, and repeated the process on the right. Amos moved his left hand up until he had Sanchez's collar; he gripped his hand around the material and pushed against his neck, guiding him toward the bar. In the dim light, he found the bank of switches on the wall and flipped two of them up. Light flooded the bar area, and Frederick Sanchez ducked his head, squinted against the light.

Amos swung the briefcase onto the bar and released the two latches. He lifted the top and saw the neatly stacked bundles of $100, $50, and $20 bills filling most of the case. "Planning a little vacation, Frederick?"

"That's my money, and there's no law against carrying it in a briefcase."

Amos closed the case and said, "Well, we have to determine whose money it is and then where it came from, Frederick. Mr. Simmons will probably be pretty unhappy with you helping yourself to his money."

Sanchez jerked his head around sharply as he blurted, "He's d—I mean, I don't know what you're talking about."

Amos smiled at the man as his dark eyes darted toward the door.

Amos, taking advantage of Sanchez's confusion, asked, "So you think your boss is dead? I didn't think you would fall for the story in the news. While Simmons was down in the federal building, telling us what a loyal and dedicated manager you are—innovative and creative, I think, was how he described you—you were on your way down here to steal his money. He is going to be very upset when I tell him."

Sanchez was squirming in his shoes. He wanted to run but knew he wouldn't make it to the front door. "Listen, I just run a bar for Mr. Simmons. Anything more, I don't know anything about it."

Amos shifted the gun, and Sanchez's eyes locked on it and started to get larger. Otis asked, "Did Simmons ask you to come for the money and maybe bring it to him?"

His eyes opened wide. "Yes, yes, that's exactly what he did. I came to get the money and take it to his house."

"At three o-clock in the morning, Frederick? Simmons was right, you are one dedicated bar manager. But like I said, Mr. Simmons is not at home. He's downtown. He was so exhausted from talking to us for two days we let him go to bed and get some sleep. It helps a man's memory to get a good night's sleep. We might do the same for you if you start telling the truth about this money and some other questions we have. Tomorrow, Mr. Simmons can remember more ways you have helped him build his drug business."

"I don't know what he's telling you, but he lies. I just take care of the Jolly Roger. You know, pour drinks and fix food for the customers. I don't know anything about other business. Did you say drugs? I know nothing about drugs. You have to believe me!" Sanchez was getting the shakes, and Amos asked him if he needed something to drink.

"A little taste of rum, *por favor*," he muttered

The charade was going too well to stop just now. Amos reached for a half-full bottle of rum from the backbar and poured a generous amount into a glass. Sanchez eagerly grabbed the glass and gulped the amber liquid in two swallows. "*Gracias*, senor. You are very kind."

"I can't remember what Simmons called the man from Kansas City," Amos said, scratching his head. "What is his name?"

Sanchez's eyes widened and looked like they might fall out of their sockets onto the bar. He protested, insisting that he did not know anyone from Kansas City. "I tell you, I'm just a simple bar manager."

Amos took Sanchez out to the car and put him in the backseat. Tossing the briefcase in the front passenger seat, he got behind the wheel and drove toward the federal building. The sun was just going up over the Gulf of Mexico, and Amos drank in the postcard scene.

At the federal building, Otis turned his prisoner over to a US marshal, who would do the booking, and headed to his office. He stopped at the machine and bought a cup of black coffee and called Clint Parker at home.

The two men shared the events of the past twenty-four hours, and Clint said, "My congratulations on the arrest. You can hold him as a material witness temporarily and try to keep him isolated from any news about Simmons's death. Keep hammering him for the name of the guy from Kansas City. The commission is scheduled in there day after tomorrow. I'll fill Glenn Wiggs in on these developments and alert him that he's going to have a number of people to question. Get some sleep, and we'll talk tomorrow."

CHAPTER 31

Blake took a sip of the sweet pineapple-based rum drink from the tall, skinny glass and was trying to figure out all the ingredients in the concoction. Gabby had become very creative with the varied juices and rum mixtures. Blake looked down at his growing waistline and made a mental note to wean himself off the calorie-laden delights. Much of their food supply was brought into Little Cayman by boat from Grand Cayman. The off-the-beaten-path nature of the smallest of the Cayman Islands was a major attraction to the couple. Here, they felt they would be able to relax without being suspicious of every newcomer. There were few newcomers since most of the residents were here before Blake and Gabby arrived. The tourists mostly went to Grand Cayman or the smaller, much more exclusive Cayman Brac. Little Cayman was very underdeveloped and had little to offer to the service-demanding American tourist.

Blake had used a property manager connection through Ross Mathews, the banker in Little Rock. He had arranged for them to lease the little house with a thatched roof sitting right on the beach. It was off the beaten path, surrounded on three sides by groves of banana trees, and faced a small cove just north of the main road going back into Cayman Brac City. He smiled as he remembered Gabby being apprehensive about moving into a house she had never even seen a picture of in an island she had never heard of before. Ross Mathews passionately urged her to put aside her worries and trust his assurance that it was the perfect house in the perfect place for the two of them.

It had taken about two minutes for Gabby to admit Mathews had understated the charm of the place, and she fell madly in love with it. The house was small, one bedroom on the south side and a kitchen on the north. In between was a large open room separated from the kitchen by a long bar built with bamboo cane and topped with a beautiful mahogany slab that must have had ten coats of lacquer. There were six barstools at the bar, and the thatched roof rose in a conical shape to a height of twenty feet. The heat rose into the cone and escaped through the downward construction of the roof.

The east wall of all rooms had sturdy panels of bamboo, which could be removed for fair weather—which was most of the time—and quickly replaced when a tropical storm brought wind and torrents of rain. On the outside wall, the windows framed the bay leading out to the Caribbean waters, which moved gently as far as the eye could see.

Movement in the corner of his vision caught Blake's attention, and he turned to watch as Gabby emerged from the turquoise waters of the bay and walked to one of the beach chairs, wrapping an oversized towel around her shoulders and continuing toward the cottage. Blake was sure he would never tire of looking at her, and he reminded himself again how lucky he was.

He called out to her. "Hey, gorgeous, don't you know that you are supposed to have a bodyguard when you walk around on the beach in a swimsuit that small?"

She looked up and asked, "Is that a public service announcement, or are you looking for employment?"

"I can't apply for the job. I'd have to lie about my motives on the application."

Suddenly, she screamed and ran toward the house, and as she approached him, she leaped through the air, and Blake reached and caught her in midflight.

Gabby flashed a coy smile and purred, "Your pretty quick, mister! Maybe you should apply to be my bodyguard. You have the right instincts."

Blake held her close and answered, "I had this terrible intuition that you were about to be attacked."

"But there isn't anyone else around to attack me. Just you, sir!"

Blake's eyes flared wide. "Curses, foiled again." He turned and ran toward the bedroom, both of them laughing and screaming.

They made love with abandon, and afterward, they fell into a sleep that was without fear or concern. They woke just as the shadows were getting long over the bay, but an oversized moon was rising over the waters of the Caribbean, and they decided to ride their bicycles into town for dinner.

They had been on the island for eleven months without incident. Just before they had flown out of Florida on a private charter, Blake had seen an article in the *Miami Herald*, dateline, New Orleans, reporting the murder of Donald Simmons. A shudder ran through his shoulders and down his back, prompting him to walk faster to the twin bonanza awaiting him and

Gabby. By chartering the plane and buying an eighteen-foot boat with twin mercury outboard engines, all under the same name as the bank account in St. Louis. Blake felt his tracks were pretty well covered. Simmons's death was reassuring. That was one less person that would care where he was and what he was doing.

For the last month, it seemed that Gabby recalled more incidents about Hot Springs and Kansas City. She had learned to appreciate the beautiful hills of the Ozarks, especially their vivid colors in the fall, and the good times they had with friends and acquaintances at the casino. They had deliberately avoided making any close friends here on the island, as Blake was well aware of the long arm of the syndicate. Their tentacles could well reach into the Cayman Islands. He had no doubt they used the unique banking laws to keep prying eyes away from their financial dealings, just as he and Gabby were doing.

The idea of living on a tropical island had initially been very appealing, and at first, it delivered every fantasy they'd had. However, after about six months, they started to miss the familiar things back home.

It certainly wasn't that they had gotten bored with each other. If anything, their passion for each other seemed stronger than ever. The weather and minimal clothing seemed to drive their sexual appetites for each other to higher levels.

As their passion grew, they began to want to experience other things together. Back home, there would be short trips to Kansas City to have dinner on the Country Club Plaza and then long walks along the festive streets under the millions of small lights that outlined the enchanting recreation of Seville, Spain, block after block.

Another shorter drive would have them on Lake of the Ozarks, where they could cruise for weeks without seeing the same shoreline that stretched 1,750 miles through the picturesque valleys of the Ozark Mountains.

* * *

Blake went to the bar and mixed two fruity drinks and carried them to the long deck. He just had a minute to watch the water gently lap against the sand when Gabby joined him.

Blake handed her a glass and said, "You know, a little earlier, I watched a beautiful woman swim in from the lagoon and walk out of the water. She picked up a towel and sponged the water from her hair and started walking toward me. I remembered seeing that same scene in a movie a few years ago, so I looked around but couldn't spot the camera crew anywhere. I'm sure it was the same actress that made the movie. It was so exciting to think I was the only man watching her, and the closer she got to me, the more I could see how stunning her beauty was."

Blake stopped, keeping the incredulous look on his face.

Gabby reached out and touched his face. "You, poor man, I'm afraid you have been in the sun too long. That and the rum are producing delirium and hallucinations. We may have to move you to a cooler climate and keep you indoors more."

Blake shook his head and murmured, "I'm afraid it's too late. The image is burned in my brain. I'll never lose the picture of her walking out of the surf like she did." As he finished talking, his head slumped forward and his eyes closed.

Suddenly, he felt Gabby jump onto his lap and squeal as she began to tickle his ribs. "You are such a terrible actor, and you must hire a better writer. Your lines are too predictable."

Gabby paused; her hands came up from his ribs and cupped his face. "But whatever you do, don't change your heart. I don't want you to ever stop loving me."

Gabby moved back to her chaise lounge and took a sip of her drink. Looking out at the turquoise water, she got a faraway look in her eyes. "You know, Blake, sometimes I feel like we could stay here for the rest of our lives, but then I wonder, what for? I think we both are overachievers. We need to be accomplishing something or we will slowly doubt our value, our purpose.

Blake reached under the cocktail table and retrieved a folded envelope. He opened the envelope and pulled out a handwritten note. "Let me read a short message from Ross Mathews. I picked it up yesterday when I went over to Cayman Brac for supplies. Your comment reminded me to share it with you."

> Dear Blake and Gabby, got your letter last month regarding real estate investing. I have checked around the area for low-profile communities that have healthy economies and good future prospects. Two strong candidates would be Camdenton, Missouri, on Lake of the Ozarks or Branson, Missouri, on Table Rock Lake. Both are quiet communities, but they are the largest towns on the lakes, and each has a slow, steady growth. As more people have money for recreational purpose, the lakes could have a strong upside for appreciation in value. The 1,700 miles of frontage on Lake of the Ozarks provides a wide selection of sites where you might build a home. I have a friend that owns the Farm and Home real estate franchise in

Osage Beach, Lake of the Ozarks. He does very well up there and knows the area better than anyone I know. His name is Walt Ferryman, and he's totally trustworthy. Let me know if I can be of further assistance. Hope you're both healthy and tanned.

—RM

Blake handed the paper to Gabby. She took it and gazed out at the water and said, "It's a tough decision, isn't it, babe?"

Blake was quiet for a few seconds then said, "In a way, yes, but the lake sounds good. I wouldn't mind having a house on the lake and a houseboat tied to the dock. We could go out on it for a week at a time and never see the same shoreline twice. The fishing's supposed to be great, and when winter comes, we can just fly down here or somewhere else for three or four months and stay warm."

Gabby looked at Blake, shaking her head. "You're sounding like some old man. Fishing, houseboats—are you trying to get old on me, Mr. Stevens?" She laughed mischievously as she got up and started into the house.

Blake went after her. "I'll show you who's getting old!" Her squeals carried out to the beach, but no one was listening.

CHAPTER 32

Clint Parker was winding his way home after a very satisfactory day. Ham Turner was very much alive despite the depressing story issued to the press of the valiant but unsuccessful fight to save him. The doctor had been most cooperative in the deception, having Turner fully covered with a white sheet and taken down to the morgue on a gurney. Cam Wilson arrived after dark and laid Turner in the back of his old station wagon and covered him with a blanket and then a tarpaulin. Two garbage bags at the rear completed the picture just in case someone was watching from the parking area. Cam drove out of Little Rock and headed northeast toward the cabin on the Current River. Thanks to Governor Lorna Summers, an Arkansas State policeman would be waiting at the cabin to assist Cam in looking out for Turner's safety. Between the three of them, the fish population in the river was endangered.

Turner's time in the hospital had not been spent entirely on recovery from his wound. A team of investigators from St Louis had spent hours extracting in a cohesive form all that Turner knew about the criminal organization that ran from New Orleans to Little Rock and Memphis with the key man in the ABI itself.

The latest development, the murder of Donald Simmons, strongly indicated a squabble within the syndicate. More probable, Clint and Amos suspected, was a squabble between two competing groups. The Kansas City FBI office had sent two interrogators down to assist Amos with questioning Sanchez and the others arrested in the warehouse on Gulf Street. Together with what Turner had told them, the picture was coming together, except for one item.

They still didn't know the name of the man from Kansas City.

Clint's theory was pretty simple: Simmons was so busy making a huge pile of money that he forgot to play by the rules. He didn't ask permission; hell, Clint thought, he didn't even raise his hand.

When the operation was small, the big boys didn't pay much attention, but it grew rapidly and it was pretty clean from a law enforcement angle. That aspect got attention from Kansas City. Who were these guys?

Anthony Civella was the big man in Kansas City. He was the power broker for the OUTFIT, but he was also the political kingmaker and the go-to guy for the unions. Nothing much happened in Kansas City without Civella's fingerprints on it. Unfortunately, Civella wore gloves most of the time. He owned the territory and had the control, but he had very trusted officers to enforce his laws.

Simmons's death was a complete surprise, Clint thought. As the saying goes, "I didn't even know the other guy was upset until I looked down and saw my shoes were full of blood and my testicles were hanging from his belt." A very appropriate illustration of how a guy like Civella exercised his authority. There were no second chances with Civella. You only got to be wrong once.

Donald Simmons was too smart for his own good, Clint thought. He probably thought his visitor wanted to congratulate him on his genius. He might want a piece of the action, and Simmons might be friendly and cut him in in return for some favors out of Kansas City.

"Poor stupid bastard," muttered Clint. "He never saw it coming! Just have a nice drink with the stranger from the cow town up north."

It seemed obvious to Clint that Simmons thought he knew the visitor well enough or found his credentials acceptable enough for him to lower his guard and invite him in for a drink in his study. No alarm bells were going off when Simmons was fixing the drinks.

When did the visitor have the opportunity to drop the poison into the martini? In his mind, Clint put himself in Simmons's study. There had to be more time than just a turn of the head. The visitor must have found an excuse for Simmons to leave the room or at least divert his attention to some task that would require a prolonged time of inattention to the drink. The man probably had a plan B for killing Simmons if the poison weren't possible. Clint played the question game until he turned onto the street to his house.

One thing was obvious; the unknown man from Kansas City was a cool operator. An ordinary hit man would have pulled out a large gun and put at least two holes into Simmons. The standard formula for assassination was one shot in the stomach and one behind the ear. It didn't matter which ear; the one closest to the gun was just fine.

Sometimes the shooter would deliver a final message for the condemned man to hear before the second shot turned off the lights.

Clint thought, with poison, there would have been an opportunity to make such a delivery once it was clear the poison was going to work. He turned into his driveway and entered his garage, closing the overhead door as he stopped.

CHAPTER 33

In North Kansas City, a dark-blue Buick was turning through an opening gate and moving slowly along the winding drive that meandered through lush landscape on either side and ended in front of the two-story English colonial brick structure. The house sat on the back half of the five acres, and the winding drive through the heavy landscape changed direction often because of uneven terrain. The pattern was to prevent a motorized vehicle from achieving any speed over ten to fifteen miles per hour and making it to the front door at high speed.

Motion-activated floodlights and motion sensors signaled the car's approach. A security hut just inside the heavy iron gate made the initial approval for admission. Then a second sentry hut with two guards was halfway between the gate and the house. One man checked the car's occupants' IDs and any irregularities, while the other waited inside the hut behind bulletproof glass. When the all-clear thumbs-up was given, the steel cable suspended eighteen inches above the drive was lowered, and the car was allowed to proceed. Inside the house, a third guard watched the procedure and checked the occupants against his guest list for the evening. In the event of an alarm, a second cable would be raised just behind the car, and a squad of heavily armed men would converge on the car with armor-piercing weapons.

No alarms were sounded as Marco Genelli's car pulled under the tall portico and stopped.

A large German shepherd and a Rottweiler came from opposite sides of the house and waited for Genelli to step out of the car. They recognized his scent at once, and the hackles on their necks relaxed. Genelli spoke to the dogs, calling their names, but made no effort to touch them. He then walked up the stairs to the opened door.

Genelli entered the spacious library and approached the oversized mahogany desk. Vincent D'Oro rose to greet Genelli and extended his right hand. Genelli took the hand and bowed his head and kissed the large ring on the third finger. "Vincent, it is a good day when I am in your company." The two men walked to the end of the desk and embraced and kissed each other on the cheeks.

They stepped back, each man looking carefully at the other.

D'Oro spoke, "Marco, my friend, you are looking well and appear to be in good health. I trust you had a successful journey to New Orleans."

"Indeed, I am well and honored to be in your beautiful home and in your service." Genelli released his hold on D'Oro and went to the chair across the desk.

D'Oro waved him back to his feet and directed him toward two Italian leather chairs facing each other over a low table; a fire burned in the fireplace behind the table.

A maid in a black-and-gray uniform appeared with an antipasto tray and a large bottle of red wine. D'Oro poured the wine and held his glass in salute. "We will drink to your excellent service, and you must tell me about your visit. This is a great wine from Southern Italy. Enjoy!"

An hour later, Marco had completed his report, including his final words to Donald Simmons and his inability to respond with his paralyzed vocal chords. That brought joy to D'Oro, who clapped his hands and rocked back and forth in the overstuffed chair. "Congratulations, Marco, you are my best emissary to those that show me no respect. I think others who have thoughts of taking advantage of my good nature will have second thoughts, eh!"

Marco clapped his hands again and took a mouthful of the wine.

"The truth is, I hate the town of New Orleans! It is a filthy nest of perverted descendants of French pirates and whores that we would be better served with all of them hanging from the gallows."

Marco took a sip from his glass and nodded his agreement then leaned toward D'Oro and said, "You are very wise, my capo, when you describe the animals as you do. However, your wisdom also tells you that this sewer and its vermin make it the ideal place to receive the cocaine, marijuana, and the heroin coming in from South America and the other southern suppliers. I have visited the people in Colombia and was received with total respect. They are ready to do business with you when the pretender is eliminated."

D'Oro smiled. "And you have eliminated him permanently, yes, Marco? But I am being too happy. Now, you must tell me about our new business in Arkansas."

When Marco was finished with his report on Hot Springs, Vincent was glowing. "The casino is a natural to fit into our business. We will drive more business to it from the northeast operations as well as the Midwest. I haven't told you, but one of our affiliates has purchased the spa next to the casino. We have concluded the transaction and will coordinate the advertising and promotion of the three businesses. I noticed your report hardly speaks of the small motel and tavern called Blake's Place. Do you think it is not important for our business?"

Marco smiled. "You are always wise beyond all others. It is my opinion that we do not need or want this business. It doesn't make enough profit, and it stands out too much. In a small community like that, everything that goes on attracts the neighbor's curiosity. The next thing that happens is a visit from the local sheriff. Too much risk and not enough reward."

D'Oro reached out and patted Marco's hand. "You are also wise, compadre, maybe that's why I like you so much. I must warn you not to become smarter than me. Okay! Now tell me your recommendation for this place."

Marco paused, digesting the words from the crime boss. "While I was there, I visited with the manager and the whores that work there. They have been there since the man Stevens bought it. The manager would like to buy the place and would be happy to just keep it operating. They are not wise like you. They are simple people who just want to make a little money and have a place to live. The woman said to me that she would like to buy the place if it is for sale."

"And what did you tell her, Marco?" Vincent spoke slowly.

"I told her that our company rarely sold anything but that I would pass on her interest to my superiors."

D'Oro slapped his knee and rocked back in his chair. "I must say, my friend, that you are my best representative to help me with the family business. I need you to return to New Orleans and begin the process of building the system of bringing the merchandise in from the south. You know how to open the doors to the politicians there, and in both capitals, you must make friends and identify our enemies. You know how we operate. We love our friends and pray for our enemies."

They raised their glasses once more and finished their wine.

Marco stood and said good-night, kissing the ring once more, and he could hear Vincent D'Oro still chuckling at his own humor as the huge oak door closed behind him.

CHAPTER 34

Glenn Wiggs was driving the boring long road through Arkansas. He was anxious to get back to his beautiful home and check on the Mississippi River to make sure it was still moving. It had been three long days in New Orleans, and even though the trip was faster through Mississippi, he'd taken the route through Arkansas. The scenery was better this way, or was he just emotionally prejudiced toward his home state? Either way, he felt the tension move from his body as he drove.

The grand jury was about ready to wrap up the investigation, and indictments would be handed down before the end of the month. He was disappointed that their number-one target had been taken out before they had a chance to question him. His death had followed the garroting of the truck driver in Memphis and the presumed killer dying in a fiery crash with a double tanker of gasoline that night. The US attorney and a large contingency of US marshals had hit a brick wall in trying to track down the man from Kansas City, as he was now referred to. The FBI office in Kansas City had their suspicions, but busting the syndicate in Kansas City was like eating a hard, frozen ice cream cone. You had to take one lick after another. Trying to eat it too fast would give you a terrible pain in the side of your head.

CHAPTER 35

Ham Turner jumped from his folding chair as soon as he heard the sound of the little bell. He'd tied the bell to the end of his pole after failing to hear the sound of the reel on two occasions. His difficulty with his hearing was mostly in the lower range of sounds. The end of his rod was bouncing up and down, and as he reached for it, the tip went down and stayed.

"You've got a big one, Ham! Let him run, but not too easy or too far." Cam was coaching from the far side of the dock. The end of the rod began to straighten, and Ham decided to take charge. He pulled the rod back to turn the fighter and began to reel in and pull back as he moved the fish closer to the dock.

"Watch out for him to make another run. That boy's not ready to quit." Cam put his rod in a holder and reached for the dip net. Suddenly, the fish turned and began to pull the line from the reel.

"Let him run, loosen the brake a little. You don't want him to break the line."

The line started to slack.

"He's coming back, reel in—reel in, don't let him spit the hook out," Cam hollered as he brought the net to the edge of the dock and held it ready.

The fish made one more feeble attempt at running, but he was too tired. Ham reeled him up near the dock, and Cam slipped the net under him and lifted the fish out of the water.

Cam put a finger through one of the gills and lifted the fish out of the net. It was a beauty, with a healthy splash of colors decorating each side. He handed the fish over to Ham, who took it with pride bursting out of his wide smile.

"That's a beauty, Ham," Cam said. "I'd say about two and a half pounds. Three pounds is about the biggest you'll find in the Current River. They stock these fish up north, and this big boy was smart enough to avoid the anglers up north, or he was lucky enough to be caught in the catch-and-release areas back when he was smaller. Anyway you got yourself a nice fish. Congratulations. I know a fella up the road who's pretty good at getting a fish like this ready to hang on your wall."

Ham furrowed his brow. "Yeah, I just hope it'll be hanging on my office wall, not the one in my jail cell!"

Cam grabbed the gear and started up to the cabin. "From what Clint tells me, I think you've got a better than fifty-fifty chance of avoiding jail time. Your testimony to the grand jury has been a great help in the case against Bruce Caldwell. It's a big deal to remove a cancerous bastard like Caldwell before he does any more damage."

Little Rock

Alvin King felt like a man with his shirttail on fire. The faster he ran, the hotter it burned. If he stopped and stood still, the fire would surely consume him.

King thought back on how it had started. He had worked hard at ABI, sure that he had the edge on becoming the boss of the top law enforcement agency in Arkansas. He was involved in all the extra activities within the agency, joining the ASIS (American Society for Industrial Security), positive that rubbing elbows with the top cops at Arkansas's major corporations would indirectly earn him a favorable nod from their CEOs when the position of director opened. He attended all the seminars for law enforcement officers and conferences dealing with every aspect of public safety. He showed up at major social events and tried to be in every picture that included key political power brokers, positive he would be remembered when the governor sounded them out for advice on top appointments. Unfortunately, his best connections were made during the time Charles Williams had been governor.

Williams had been a master of political power management. They had first met when Williams was a state senator, and he seemed to recognize the talent and ambition in this young lawman. In truth, Williams recognized a man who was driven by a quest for importance and knew that such a man could be manipulated to serve his own ambitions.

During Williams's two terms as governor, King had enjoyed a meteoric series of promotions until he was assistant director. He had performed every request for special service and had easy access to the power circle around the governor. Then it was as if the whole world blew up, at least his world did.

Orville Carlson was exposed in his slave-labor camp on his farm. He even faced arrest for kidnapping and murder. If Orville ever went to trial, King feared that his role in taking homeless men out to Carson's farm and turning them over to Ham Turner in exchange for contributions to his retirement fund would be exposed. Fortunately for King, Carson took the coward's way out and killed himself. Before the dust settled, Charles Williams's career came apart like a cheap suit, and all of King's contacts evaporated like early morning fog.

After Glenn Wiggs became governor, a whole new group of access regulators moved into the governor's office, and Alvin King became known as Williams's cop, and his career moves were frozen. At first, King speculated that when the director stepped down, Wiggs would have to move him into the job. He wouldn't dare pass over someone with his longevity and track record. That was the way politics worked.

Unfortunately for King, Glenn Wiggs was a reform-minded governor who resisted playing by the old rules of politics. He was committed to reviving the purpose of ABI, fighting crime in Arkansas, and all his information convinced him that Alvin King was not the man.

It was after he was passed over as director that he had received a call from a man named Frederick Sanchez. Sanchez presented himself as a citizen who was sick and tired of seeing good men being dumped on by politicians, especially good men in law enforcement. King's bruised ego was very receptive to the righteous indignation on his behalf. After King agreed with everything Sanchez had said, Sanchez invited him down to New Orleans for a weekend. A group of concerned citizens were gathering to have a little fun and figure out ways to take care of people like Alvin King, who gave their lives protecting ordinary people and then get their throats cut and left on the streets to die.

It was stupid, demagogic bullshit, but King bought it hook, line, and sinker. The following Friday, he left work early and drove to New Orleans.

The gathering of the self-righteous took place in a beautiful home west of New Orleans. It sat on about twenty acres in Bayou Country. Two deep inlets came in on two sides of the property, the road on the third, and the swamp occupied the back property line. The house was a sprawling plantation-type building with a wide porch around three sides. The grounds were manicured, with walking paths meandering through the lawn, stopping at four separate gazebos equipped with chaise lounges and small bars stocked with ice and beverages and attended by young women who were stunningly beautiful.

Sanchez had greeted him and escorted him into the house. They stopped at the kitchen, where one of the young women, with long blond hair, wearing a pale cream-colored knit dress that left nothing to the imagination, greeted him and asked what he would have to drink. She said he should call her Yolanda and that he should definitely call her for anything he would like to have. She stepped close to him, handing him his drink. Her eyes were so blue, and she looked straight into his without blinking. He took the drink, and she squeezed his arm, pressing her ample breast against him.

"Well, Alvin, let me show you around and meet a few people. We'll catch up with Yolanda later. I'll have someone take your suitcase upstairs and put it in a bedroom we've reserved for you. It's at the end of the hall to your left. Looks out toward the marsh, if you're into nature."

For the next fifteen minutes, Alvin met an interesting assortment of people. They were from all over Louisiana, Mississippi, and Florida. Some did not say where they were from, and he did not ask.

The sun was low over the bayou, and Sanchez asked him if he would like to go up to his room to change. He said dinner would not be served until eight, but in the meantime, there were platters of shrimp and crayfish to nibble on. Alvin excused himself and went back into the house. As he neared the stairwell, Yolanda appeared from the kitchen.

"Well, I suppose you've met all the VIPs and now you're going to change into something comfortable," the woman said in a soft, purring voice. "May I show you to your room?"

Alvin spoke in a voice slightly higher than normal, "That is very kind of you to offer."

They went up the stairs, her hand on his arm. "I understand you had a long drive down from Arkansas. When I drive a long distance, I get a tension in my shoulders. If you want, I could give you a massage, then you can dress for the evening and we'll rejoin the party."

"That's a very nice offer, Yolanda. I do feel a bit of tension in my neck and shoulders."

They went into the bedroom at the end of the hall. His suitcase was sitting on a bench against the wall. The king-size bed had been turned down. Yolanda went into the bathroom and came back with two drinks. She handed one to Alvin and sat the other on the nightstand.

She pushed him toward the bed and said, "Please sit on the bed and have some of your drink. It will help you relax." She knelt down in front of him and began removing his shoes. Setting the shoes aside, she began massaging his feet. He was surprised by the strength in her hands. She was deliberate in every move, and he began to feel the effects of the massage. She stood and reached for his belt. Alvin started to help her, but she brushed his hand away and said, "It is very important that you relax and let me do everything for you." She pulled him to his feet and lowered his trousers to the floor. She then began to unbutton his shirt and reached around him as she pulled it over each arm. At one point, while removing his shirt, his right arm came over her shoulder, and he started to pull her against him.

"No, no! You must not be in a hurry. We have plenty of time. I want you to turn over on your stomach and relax." He got on his stomach, and she got on the bed, straddling him on her knees, and began to work the muscles across his shoulders, neck, and back. After about ten minutes, she rolled him onto his back and began to work on his arms and then his legs. When she came to his thighs, she reached back with both hands and slid her knit dress over her head. She wore nothing under the dress.

He lay there for a while, drinking in her beautiful, perfectly shaped body. She smiled at him and bent down to kiss him. He felt her breasts against his chest; they were firm but, at the same time, soft and full. Her nipples grew hard, and she explored his mouth with her tongue. He reached for her, carefully taking a breast in each hand, and moved across them. She reached down and found his erection and slid it into her warm wetness and began to move on him. She was so slow and deliberate with every movement that his climax was postponed longer than he had ever experienced. Finally, she thrust herself down on him then up and down again and again. He groaned as he exploded inside her, and she responded with her own noises.

They lay still, his arms around her, and she curled up against him. Finally, she looked at him and asked, "Are you relaxed now, Mr. King? I think I should start the shower, and we should get ready to rejoin the party."

It was a large walk-in shower, and they cleaned each other, playing like kids. Bruce had never experienced a woman like this, and he wondered if they would make love again later tonight.

Downstairs, Yolanda escorted Alvin to a group of people.

As they approached the group, Alvin saw Sanchez was the center of attention. He turned and welcomed King to join them and made introductions. After a while, Sanchez took King's arm and steered him over to one of the gazebos, where a man sat by himself. Sanchez said, "May I present Mr. Alvin King. Mr. King, this is Mr. Simmons, our host."

"I'm pleased to meet you, Mr. King, and welcome to my home. 1 trust you are being well cared for. It is important to me that my guests receive the full hospitality I can offer."

"Mr. Simmons, I assure you the hospitality thus far is superb, the finest I have known anywhere. May I compliment you on your beautiful home and express my gratitude for your kind invitation?"

"It will be my pleasure to have you as my guest, and I hope it will be the beginning of a relationship that will be beneficial to us both. Mr. Sanchez represents me in many of my business interests, and there may be times when you can do a favor for me. He will call on you on my behalf and explain what small thing we may need. You will be well cared for when you render these small favors. We pride ourselves in the level of care we provide to our friends for their favors."

"I am already impressed with how you care for your guests here at your beautiful home. I hope I can be worthy of such care in the future."

Simmons looked at King and said, "I feel certain that we are going to have a very beneficial arrangement. Now, enough talk. Mr. Sanchez, take Mr. King back to the party. Tomorrow, we will talk again, but tonight is for pleasure."

They walked back toward the house just as a three-piece group started to play something with a lively beat. As the two crossed the room, a striking woman King had not noticed before got up from a table and came toward them.

"Whatever he is having, make two of them." She turned to face him. "Hello there, and where have they been hiding you? I am Deloris, but I would be pleased if you would call me Dee."

She had a head full of red curls that stood up, and tiny ringlets of red curls seemed to flow in all directions, framing the tan complexion of her angular face, accentuated with proud cheekbones that sheltered her finely chiseled nose and full, ripe lips.

"Welcome to the party. May I get you something to drink and maybe something to snack on?"

Alvin took her offered hand and smiled. "You can do both if you'll just call me Alvin."

He followed the redhead over to a small bar. The band was playing a variety of Frank Sinatra and Nat King Cole, and three couples were clinging to one another and moving to the music and other urgings.

"Would you like to dance, Alvin?" Dee asked, catching his gaze toward the patio.

He turned back to the red hair and the well-endowed hostess. She was wearing a mint green knit dress that seemed to be a duplicate of the one Yolanda wore earlier, only different in color.

Must be the standard uniform, mused Alvin, thinking that he couldn't have made a better choice.

Alvin said, "I'm not a very good dancer, but maybe after a drink or two, we could give it a try. The music is great. Makes a poor dancer like me want to try."

Dee threw her head back, moving her flaming hair in response, and said, "Yo was right. You do have a sense of humor and are easy to be around."

"Yo?" Alvin queeried, not tracking on the name.

"Yolanda, your friend this afternoon. Don't tell me you have already forgotten, you naughty man."

King could feel his face redden with embarrassment. "No, I certainly haven't forgotten Yolanda. I just didn't connect the nickname right away. You probably have the ability to make men forget other women. That will be my excuse."

Dee reached out and hugged Alvin, letting him understand that everything he imagined the dress emphasized was true and all hers.

"Speaking of Yolanda, I haven't seen her this evening. Is she here?" Alvin spoke without taking his eyes off her green eyes for a second.

Dee, still holding Alvin against her, said, "Yo had a previous dinner engagement, but she told me to take good care of you tonight. Let's find a place where we can sit and get better acquainted. They'll call us for dinner in a half-hour." She slipped her arm through his and led him to a wicker love seat under a willow tree.

The music wafted over the garden area, setting a romantic mood across the party.

Dee set her drink on a small table and settled next to Alvin, cuddling close to him. He looked down at her amazing eyes and bent to kiss her. She responded with opened lips that welcomed his, and the kiss lasted until they were both satisfied that the promise of the night would not be disappointed.

When dinner was called, Dee guided him around one end of the house to a courtyard, where a five-foot brick wall surrounded five tables draped with white linen cloths and four-place settings each. Alvin and Dee went to a table in the rear. Don Simmons was at a table in front, and Sanchez hosted a table near the entry to the courtyard.

Four waiters dressed in black slacks and white short-sleeve shirts moved among the tables with military precision. The food was served at the right temperature, and as each guest finished, the waiter appeared and removed the plate and replaced it with the next course.

Finally, he could eat no more and pushed back the small quantity of cherries jubilee and reached for his wine.

The dinner would have rated five stars in the finest restaurant in New Orleans. When he expressed this opinion to Dee, she smiled and informed him that one of the finest Creole restaurants in the French Quarter had supplied the food and staff to serve them. They got up and went out of the courtyard and walked out to the bayou and went along the waterway. The music was coming from the patio, and Alvin knew he was making a major change in his career in law enforcement.

Dee had been a perfect companion for the evening. Beautiful by any man's standards and the most attentive any woman had ever been to him. In fact, King had never been much of a ladies' man. In his youth, he had always been unsure of himself with the girls and was mostly not accepted in the circle of the macho boys.

King had attended the community college, and though his grades were mediocre, he graduated. He married right after graduation to the only girl that he'd ever had sex with.

Janet had proven to be the worst decision he'd made up to that point in his life. She was negative in her outlook on life and frigid in the bedroom. They had stayed in the marriage for ten years, her because she could just ignore him and him because he feared the prospect of looking for someone all over again. Janet finally filed for divorce, and it was quickly finished. The last contact with her was when a mutual friend told Alvin she had moved in with another woman, and they were pretty happy together. Alvin King went into the toilet and threw up his lunch. A short time later, he was hired by ABI.

CHAPTER 36

The three-piece combo had picked up the tempo, and Alvin snapped back from his memory trip. A few couples were dancing on the patio, and Alvin realized that Dee was not sitting next to him. In fact, she was out there, writhing and moving to the beat of the music and motioning for him to join her. The drinks, dinner, and memories of Janet had mellowed him into a "who gives a fuck" attitude. He stood, a little wobbly, and made his way to the beautiful woman, who beckoned him to join her.

"She wants me," he said to himself. "Fuck you, Janet." He began to join in the beat that fueled the dancers, and in seconds, he saw himself as Fred Astaire, and this gorgeous redhead wanted him. "Alvin King. Eat your heart out, Janet!"

They must have stayed on the dance floor for an hour or more through fast tempo and slow, sexy music, when Dee would wrap her arms around his neck and move against him until his legs would barely hold him erect. In fact, something else was erect and hard as a tree limb.

Dee guided him to the back door of the house, and without a break in her movement, she took his right arm and led him into the house and up the stairs. She was humming the tune "Walkin' My Baby Back Home" while she undressed him and bent to pull the knit dress over her head, the red curls tossed and settled back in place. He reached out to fondle her breast, and she let him. They went into the bed as if they were one, and the foreplay continued until she moved under him.

Alvin had always been a "quick on the trigger" man in his limited experience. This was different from any experience he had ever known. Dee held his face and kissed him long and deep, and the pleasure he felt kept him strong and focused on giving her the same pleasure he felt. She guided his mouth to her full breast, which pointed up toward him. He kissed one and then another until she began to moan, telling him not to stop. They both reached their climax together and kept the motion going until they were drained.

Dee got a towel and wiped them both dry and then curled up next to him and said, "Yo was not lying when she told me you are a man with a big appetite."

They slept for a few hours, and Alvin woke to find her running her hand over his body. He fondled her, and soon they were searching each other. She rolled over on her stomach, and he moved on top and had his first sex in that position. He couldn't believe the powerful pleasure that surged through his body.

When Alvin woke up the next time, the morning sun was streaming through the window, and he realized Dee was gone. He looked in the bath and noticed the knit dress was not on the floor where she had dropped it the night before. He stepped into the shower and let the hot water pound on him, bringing him awake and refreshed. He dressed and went downstairs.

A black woman in a white apron over a black dress was in the kitchen. She said good morning as she poured a cup of steaming black coffee.

"Cream and sugar are on the table, sir. Fix it to your taste. And how many eggs would you like, scrambled or fried?"

"Three would be great. Fried, please."

By the time he had drank half of his coffee, the maid set a plate in front of him. Three eggs, hash browns, and toast. There was a bottle of Cajun sauce on the table, and he applied it to the eggs.

"Where is everybody? Did I sleep so long they all left?"

The woman kept putting away the dishes in the sink. "I don't know where, but I think they all left about an hour ago. My husband, Jim, is outside. When you are ready, he will fetch your suitcase and put it in your car. Mr. Simmons said for me to tell you he was glad you came to visit, and he will be in touch in a day or two."

This was the first time Alvin had met Donald Simmons, and he wondered how much he'd obligated himself to the man during this brief time as a guest in his home. He didn't mind doing some favors for the man; maybe he would get invited back for another visit. He smiled and went up to get his suitcase packed.

* * *

The special favors in the beginning were minor and seemed harmless in terms of right or wrong. As time went on, however, the requests became more questionable and, ultimately, downright criminal, constituting malfeasance of his office and the oath he'd taken. An occasional phone call from Yolanda or Dee took his mind off legal technicalities and set him contemplating his next visit to New Orleans.

CHAPTER 37

Alvin King paced the floor of his private office, growing more agitated by the minute because his calls were being ignored. That had been his third call to Sanchez with no response.

He had spotted a copy of a Teletype on Kondraky's desk informing him and the ABI director of the death of Donald Simmons in New Orleans. There was a notation at the top of the page that read "Your eyes only," but Kondraky was out of the office this morning, and the stupid girl from the communications office had brought the message to Kondraky's desk without putting it in a sealed envelope, thus giving King an opportunity to read it while snooping around Kondraky's office.

He was hungry but didn't dare leave the office until he had an idea how serious the problem of Simmons's death might be for him. On the way back to his desk, he heard the buzzing sound announcing a call, and he hurried to his desk. King picked up his phone carefully as if it might blow up in his face. "King here."

A strange voice he didn't recognize, sounding like a poor connection, spoke, "Mr. King, this is someone you've never met, but we do share mutual friends. One of our friends suggested I call and invite you to lunch. If you haven't eaten yet, I thought we might meet today, say, in about a half-hour. Does that work for you?"

King sputtered, "No—I mean, I'll have to check. What did you say your name was?"

"Actually, Mr. King, I didn't say, but I'll clear that up and a few other questions you may have when we meet for lunch. Let's say in thirty minutes, at the Cracker Barrel."

Alvin hastily glanced at his watch. It was 1:15 p.m. He had a bad feeling about this, but he could either say no to this man and wait for Sanchez or forget waiting and see what this man had to tell him. He wouldn't have to say anything; he could just listen, and then he would know more than he knew now.

Panic was starting to freeze his brain, so Alvin said, "Okay, but make it two thirty at the Cracker Barrel." He clicked his phone and dialed the number in New Orleans for the Jolly Roger. After three rings, a man answered, "Jolly Roger. What can I do for you?"

"Long distance for Frederick Sanchez." Bruce tried to imitate an operator.

The voice sounded irritated. "Look, I told you before, Mr. Sanchez is not here, and I haven't seen or heard from him since Monday. Can I deliver a message or get your number and ask him to call you?"

Bruce hung up the phone without another word for the irritated bartender. He grabbed his coat from the coat tree and put it on as he headed for the parking garage.

* * *

"Able to Baker, our subject has left his office and should be coming to the garage for his car."

Baker said, "Ten-four, Able. We are on the car. Did you get a destination?"

"Affirmative, Baker, we're lunching at the Cracker Barrel. Over."

Baker said, "Let him come out of the garage solo. We'll pick him up when he hits the street."

Able responded, "Ten-four, Baker. We'll let him clear the garage and then catch up. We know where he's going, so no need to crowd him."

King stopped and looked right and left as he crossed the garage and, once in his car, checked his rearview mirror. Satisfied he was clean, he turned right. He saw no suspicious cars moving too slow or parked on the street. He picked up speed slowly, checking his mirror, and suddenly slammed on the brakes as a pedestrian cut across the street in front of him. The pedestrian pulled his hat tight and held it as he hurried to the sidewalk.

"Fucking idiot," King screamed and concentrated on slowing his rapid heart rate. He proceeded east on First Street, not noticing the pedestrian jump into a tan Ford that had come to the garage entrance. The driver of the tan Ford let another car pass and then pulled out, turning east on First. A blue Chevy van pulled out of its space on the street and did a U-turn, heading east.

At First and Lee Streets, King turned into the Cracker Barrel parking lot. The tan Ford drove past the lot and made a left turn at the next corner.

As King approached the front door of the restaurant, he didn't notice the blue van with white lettering that read Fresh Produce turn into the lot and drive to the rear door, where a sign read Delivery.

The Cracker Barrel was a favorite among big eaters across the southern states. The chain bragged about the barrels near every booth. They were filled with individual packets of saltine crackers and salty roasted peanuts in the shell. Diners could help themselves to the tasty morsels until the soup and salads ran out. A man at a back booth stood as Caldwell entered the main dining room and, when he had Alvin's attention, motioned him to the booth.

"Mr. King, please join me if you will. I haven't ordered, but the waitress tells me the chicken and dumplings are delicious. The table help in restaurants are usually a good source of the best dishes, I've found."

The man's mannerisms threw King off-balance. He picked up a menu and, after a brief glance, said, "That sounds good."

Alvin looked at the man in the tropical tan suit, who looked up at the waitress and said, "Two of the lunch specials and iced tea. That all right, Alvin?"

"Yeah, uh—that will be fine." King picked up a napkin with Cracker Barrel printed on it and spread it across his lap then nervously adjusted its position.

"I suppose you're wondering about this meeting. You're probably asking yourself, who in hell is this guy, and why am I having lunch with him?"

Alvin squirmed. "Something like that. I mean, I don't know your name and I don't know you. However, as a law enforcement officer, I am naturally curious." King was playing with his fork and spoon, trying not to appear nervous and failing miserably.

The man appeared to notice Alvin's nervousness. "Some names are not important, while other names are essential. It was essential for me to know your name and a lot more about you. My name, on the other hand, would be meaningless to you, but for today, to help us communicate, you can call me Joey. The important thing for you to know is that I represent a principal that is merging with a number of business entities in the region. They have become aware of your services to these enterprises in the past and would like to arrange for your services to continue in the future. It makes perfect sense from your point of view since the failure to extend your agreement would, at best, mean a loss of income for you."

"You said *at best*. What would be the *at worst*?" King asked.

"If we had to discuss that, I'm afraid you might lose your appetite," Joey answered, his expression hardened.

"You don't beat around the bush, Joey. Why don't we both quit dancing and just say what we're here for, aside from the chicken and dumplings."

Joey put his knife and fork down and his hands in his lap. "Very well, Mr. King. For a few years, you have had, let's call it, an extraemployment arrangement that has supplemented your income from the state of Arkansas quite nicely. Your benefactor in that arrangement has become, shall we say, inactive and will not be able to continue his agreement with you. However, my clients would like to continue the agreement. As a gesture of our sincerity, I have with me what we might refer to as a signing bonus of $5,000. As I said, it will just serve as a good-faith deposit. Then, we will consider your previous arrangement to be extended with all understandings unchanged."

King relaxed a little. He did not feel comfortable with "Joey" and his nameless principal, but this could be a safe landing after a horrifying flight.

King said, "I am aware of the death of a man in New Orleans, and one could assume it's possible we both knew him. My arrangement with him had certain conditions. You seem to say you know about that agreement and want to keep them unchanged. The difference between that agreement and what you're proposing is that I knew whom I was dealing with and you imply I would not know the person or persons you represent. I don't feel very comfortable about being in that position."

The man across the table narrowed his eyes and leaned forward as he spoke. "Look, Mr. King, I thought we were going to quit dancing. The point you need to understand is, I don't give a fuck whether you're comfortable or miserable. You need to understand that your previous agreement was based on serious miscalculations on your part. You were dealing with amateurish upstarts that were trying to play a game without following the rules. Now, you are being given a chance to stay in the game and deal with the rule makers. Do you understand what I'm saying to you?"

Alvin's voice came out as a whisper. "Yes, I think I understand, and I appreciate your candor."

The waitress brought their lunch, and they ate in silence. Finally, the man called Joey pushed back his plate and wiped his mouth with the cloth napkin and said, "That has to be the best chicken and dumplings I've ever tasted. You guys in the South do know how to eat, but I have to say, a steady diet of your foods could cause a man to have a heart attack. You have to be careful to not overdo a good thing, or the old ticker might just quit on you. You agree?"

Joey reached in the inside pocket of the tan suit coat and withdrew an envelope. Sliding the envelope across the table, he said, "Do you have any questions, Alvin?"

"No, not at this time. I assume I'll be hearing from you."

The man stood and said, "You'll be hearing from me, but you'll want to stay under the radar until this grand jury finishes its sideshow. We'll be in touch if you can help."

The man called Joey put on his hat, turned, and walked to the cash register. When he was finished, he turned and walked out to the street without looking back.

CHAPTER 38

While Joey paid his bill at the Cracker Barrel, Clint Parker watched and waited to pay his own check. Two of the officers that had followed King to the Cracker Barrel had left earlier and gone to their radio cars to be ready to resume their surveillance. Clint would go in the lead car, the second car would team with Clint to follow the man in the tan suit, and the remaining two agents would keep their eyes on Mr. King. Clint hurried to the waiting car and grabbed the mike and keyed the radio. "Charley, this Able, what is your ten-four?"

"Charley here. I'm still parked in the row behind the suit. He's sitting still in his car. Don't know if he's waiting for his lunch partner or making notes on their meeting. Hold on, he's backing out. He's coming your way. We're moving."

"Ten-four, Charley. We'll let you both pass, then we'll move."

Clint scooted down in the seat as the car passed by them, then Clint slid back up and they joined the parade.

After two blocks, Charley faded back and Able's car moved up, all the while keeping each other informed of their movements prior to execution. Clint looked at the agent driving his car. "I'd bet a week's pay this is our boy from Kansas City."

* * *

Marco Genelli left the rental car in the drop-off lane at the airport and walked into the terminal. He had his return ticket, so he proceeded to the TWA boarding gate. It was a small turboprop feeder plane that would take him to Kansas City. The counter agent at the gate thanked him for checking in early and gave him his boarding pass. He walked across the corridor to a concession stand. He eyed the magazine rack, and being a

200

serious cook when he had the time, he picked up a cooking magazine to be read in the plane. He paid for the magazine and a pack of breath mints with cash and went back to the boarding area.

Clint Parker was sitting off to the right side of the boarding area, reading a copy of the Little Rock gazette. He peered over the top of the paper, watching the man return to the boarding area. He had been able to call the office in Kansas City and arrange for two agents and a car to tag the man as he came off flight 84 at the terminal in Kansas City. If the suit were driving his personal car from the airport, then they would get started on identification. Clint was sick of calling him the Man from Kansas City or the Man in the Tan Suit.

The speaker called for boarding on flight 84, and everyone lined up to get a seat. When the subject showed his boarding pass and disappeared down the inclined ramp to the plane, within a few minutes, flight 84 was pushed back into the Jetway and began to taxi toward the runway. Clint walked to the loading ramp and confirmed it empty. He stopped at the boarding counter and showed his credentials, persuading the agent to share the suit's name as Joey Walker.

Clint had no doubts it was an alias as he walked to a nearby pay phone and called Kansas City to confirm the subject, Joey Walker, was on his way. Photos of the subject had been sent by wire. Clint started to relax as he headed out to catch his ride back to the office. It had been a pretty good day, he told himself.

CHAPTER 39

The flight had been short and routine. Marco Genelli stood and retrieved his tan suit coat, pulled it on, and pulled his overnighter bag down. Downstairs, he walked out and stepped into the parking-lot bus and sat down. He kept his bag next to his seat and kept a lookout for his parking section. Reaching his nearly new Cadillac Coupe DeVille, he pressed two buttons on his remote, opening the trunk and unlocking the driver's door. He drove out of the airport lot and, few blocks later, turned north onto a street that ran past a collection of small homes, mostly bungalows built twenty-plus years earlier. Unknown to any but a handful of people, the occupants of the small residences all worked for the same enterprise. They were the soldiers for the multitiered conglomerate that ran most of the political and criminal life of the metropolitan area and a sizable portion of its economy. Two blocks later, what appeared to be a dead-end revealed a well-paved street that ran off to the left at thirty degrees before being blocked by a gate of heavy steel controlled by an electric opener. He stopped at a speaker box and inputted a code on the numeric pad. A voice from the speaker verified his password and matched his picture on a CCTV monitor with his file photo and buzzed him in.

He wound his way to the portico and handed a valet his keys and entered the massive door. In the foyer, a second man told him Mr. D'Oro was waiting in the study. He opened the tall heavy oak door, and as he entered the elegant library, D'Oro turned away from a massive brick fireplace. He held out his right hand with the oversized ring.

Finished with the formalities, D'Oro settled back in his high-backed chair and smiled as he said, "Well, my friend, preliminary reports say you had another successful journey to the southern territory. I always like to hear the story from the lips of the man who makes things happen for my benefit."

Genelli began, "The process in New Orleans is coming along nicely. We will resume shipments from Colombia in two weeks. I was unable to make contact with Frederick Sanchez. He is probably panicked over Simmons's death and may have gone back to South America. My lunch with Alvin King went well. He accepted your goodwill gift, and after I lectured him on rules, he softened his arrogance. I think he is an idiot, but for now, he's our idiot."

"You continue to be the most-effective mechanic in my machine, Marco. I want everyone to look for Mr. Sanchez. I don't care what country he is hiding in. I want him working for us, or I want him dead. Is that understood?"

"It is clear to everyone that Sanchez must be found, dead or alive," Genelli answered.

"I have briefed our political arm on most developments down there, but I want to deal with Sanchez until he is no longer a problem."

* * *

Nicholas Civella had become the godfather of Kansas City's criminal family following the downfall of Mayor Tom Pendergast, the mayor that combined politics and criminal activities in a very transparent manor. Pendergast was also the owner of the Redi-Mix concrete company, which many had speculated offered a quick way to dispose of the bodies of his opposition and/or traitors.

It had, at one time, become one of America's most notable and successful criminal-political organizations. Tom Pendergast had been one of the most cold-blooded politicians who controlled the criminal elements of his city while enjoying the support of the voters as a larger-than-life folk hero.

Finally, one of his lieutenants had a falling-out with the mayor. He cooperated with the federal investigators, resulting in the mayor being convicted on tax evasion, a popular charge in that day, and sentenced to federal prison.

Civella had dramatically expanded the activities of the mob, preferring to elect people to political offices who were loyal to the family, while he concentrated on building the mob's power through more outright criminal behavior.

D'Oro was a favored *prince* in the Civella family, but no one was above being disciplined for incompetence or disloyalty. His beautiful home was one of five on the private drive that received protection from the soldiers living in the small bungalows and were connected by a system of tunnels that allowed servants, or residents, to move undetected from the street from one house to another—or receiving an unannounced visit from Civella when he wanted to look in the eyes of a suspected traitor or an incompetent.

Genelli lived in a luxury condominium on the Country Club Plaza. His condo was on the twenty-first floor of the twenty-three-story building. The top floor was shared by three large units that belonged to Civella, the boss of the Fireman's Union and a second-in-command of the Teamsters Union. The tower was the tallest residential structure in Kansas City, and the view of the plaza from a balcony of the building was the envy of many.

Marco Genelli entered the small lobby adjacent to the basement parking garage that served the condo's owners and guests and punched the elevator for the twenty-first floor. He was feeling pretty good about himself and the success of his trip. D'Oro was a little disappointed he had not located Sanchez but seemed satisfied that Alvin King was under their control and had indicated at the end of their meeting that they might move on a plan for King to become the director of ABI. D'Oro had not expanded on the subject, but Marco assumed that when the time came, it would be up to him to remove the present director, and the way he felt tonight, he was just the man who could do it.

In his euphoric mood, Marco had dropped his guard (which he rarely did) and failed to see the black Ford that had followed him since he left the airport that afternoon. Had he been more alert and not enjoying his feeling of invincibility against mere mortals, he might have detected the same car was now parked across the street from the garage entrance, and the man who walked into the garage as Marco stepped into the elevator noted that the elevator had not stopped until it reached the twenty-first floor.

The FBI agent walked back to the Ford and picked up the mike to his radio. A voice on the other end acknowledged the report, and they agreed the agent would stay until 10:00 p.m., and if there was no further activity, he could go home. Another agent would resume the watch at six tomorrow.

Genelli took a long shower and, after he finished his second drink, decided to go upstairs, where the secretary treasurer of the Firemen's Union was having a party. There was always a supply of girls at his parties, and tonight, that was just what Marco needed to bring himself down from the high he'd had all week. He took the elevator to twenty-second and heard the music and laughter as soon as the door slid open.

CHAPTER 40

Little Rock

Alvin King was walking down the hall that connected his office and the larger office of Chester Allen, director of ABI. Their meeting had been routine, but it did seem that Allen was more inquisitive than normal. Allen was a pain in the ass, in King's opinion. King had been sure he was going to get the job of director four years earlier. When it was announced that newly elected governor Lorna Summers had selected Allen, he was stunned. It was true that Allen had a long record of managing Arkansas State agencies. He was known as the hired gun in Arkansas politics. He'd served as ABI director now for three years—longer than normal for him. "He's bound to leave soon," mumbled King as he sat down at his desk.

In a larger office down the hall, Chester Allen was still sitting at his desk, gazing out through the large window in his office that viewed most of the city of Little Rock. His mind went back over the meeting with Alvin King, looking for telltale signs of evasion and misleading answers that King had given to his questions.

Governor Summers had supplied the questions and a briefing on the concern that came from the FBI and the crime commission. She promised that Clint Parker would fill in the blanks for him in the very near future. In the meantime, he should conduct business as usual. He respected Clint Parker completely and knew the governor would not hang him out to dry. If there were skunks in his woodpile, his job was to flush them out, or at least help the good guys in the white hats. He dialed the governor's private phone, ready with his report.

---

* * *

Frederick Sanchez paced the floor of the holding cell in the basement of the federal building. He was not a prisoner, but he had signed a waiver of his right to an attorney and a prompt hearing before a federal judge. The end of the road had come for Frederick, and he was betting his future on the FBI's fair treatment.

The cell wasn't home, but it beat the amenities at the jail across town as a guest of the Little Rock police. The most important thing now was to stay off the radar of the people who'd killed Simmons and were making serious efforts to find him. He had considered going to them and offering his services just as he had performed them for Simmons, but as he had that thought, something caused the hair to stand up on the back of his neck. He decided a deal with the FBI was better than an insurance bullet from some Pisano from Kansas City. Clint Parker had a reputation of being a tough but fair cop, and Sanchez had made the trip to Little Rock to turn himself in. So far, Parker was living up to his reputation.

His thoughts were interrupted by the sound of the elevator bringing a marshal to take him upstairs for some lunch and more questions. *Well*, he thought, *I may as well help them. They have the power to keep me here in this country, send me to prison or back to Colombia. Here in the United States, with a new identity, I could have a life. In prison or Colombia, or in the hands of the cartel, I would be a walking dead man.*

* * *

Clint Parker had just hung up the phone and, for a while, looked at the instrument that had delivered the best news he'd received in days. "Marco Genelli is his name," the caller had said, excitement in his voice.

The agent had painfully admitted they'd had Genelli on their top-five list for months but couldn't put specifics to their suspicions or keep the verifying witnesses alive long enough to make a case before a federal grand jury.

The agent said he would say a prayer that Clint would be able to tie a murder around Genelli's neck.

Clint told the agent he would welcome all the help he could get.

He called home to tell Jean he was leaving the office and she should prepare the kids to go to her mother's for the evening. They had an invitation for dinner at Glenn's, and their grandmother had thoughtfully invited the children to her house for an overnighter. Thirty minutes later, they were driving east, and both felt as if they'd shed some of the tension that had been gripping them lately.

Mary had prepared a delicious catfish dinner with a special wine from New York, a Riesling that removed even more of the tension. After dinner, Glenn opened a second bottle of the wine, and he and Clint walked out onto the deck that looked down at the Mississippi River.

Glenn walked to the railing and set his glass down. "You can't see much of the river at night, but the channel markers and navigation lights are always on, and it's thought provoking to an ex-minister to watch the boats make the turns and hold to the channel just the way this new radar instructs them." Glenn picked up his glass and raised it in salute. "Here's to the navigation lights to us all, and may they burn bright and keep us safe in the coming days."

Clint drank to the toast and said, "Amen to that. I was thinking on the way over how many miles you and I have traveled together. The state of Arkansas was a real mess back then, and after the scandal of Orville Carson and his suicide, I believed we'd turned things around and everybody would settle down and things would return to normal. Now, I realize how perceptive you were when you congratulated me on joining the bureau. Your words were 'We were going to need all the good soldiers we could get on the front lines.' I thought then you were just talking like an old preacher, but now, look at us, fighting the same battle, only against a bigger and smarter enemy, decades later."

Glenn smiled and said, "Those were the ramblings of a former preacher. The predictions I relied on for my comments were written down for us two thousand years ago, and they're proven correct over and over throughout man's history."

"Do you think we'll ever win the war?" Clint asked.

"No, Clint, I don't. But we will win some of the battles, and we must fight the war. Our children will be sorely disappointed if we don't."

Jean and Mary went out on the porch, and the conversation turned to families and subjects that all normal people contend with as they strive toward a better tomorrow in their communities. The similarities were not lost on Clint as he drove back home while Jean curled up against him and slept like the innocent she was.

The next morning, Clint was at his office early. He and Amos had finished a long phone conference. The identification of Genelli was a big help in piecing events together. It was also troubling to know the mob in Kansas City was involved. Arkansas's crime was challenging, but adding the Kansas City family to the mix presented a new learning curve and more directions to defend against. By Arkansas standards, Genelli signaled a much tougher job for Clint and the crime commission.

Agents in Kansas City were monitoring Genelli 24-7, and a wiretap on his phone would be connected tomorrow. Clint wanted notice if Genelli was coming back to Arkansas or New Orleans.

CHAPTER 41

Kansas City

Marco Genelli hung the phone back in its cradle and took a minute to organize his thoughts. The killing of Chester Allen had just been ordered. The note, unsigned, had been delivered by one of the bodyguards of D'Oro. The note was written in a code used by the family. If it should fall into the hands of the FBI or other nonauthorized recipient, it would be meaningless. The last line, telling him he should go and visit his gravely ill mother before she died, was an instruction to call D'Oro for confirmation.

Marco had dialed Vincent and told him he would be visiting his mother and that he had called his cousin, who would meet him at his mother's house. The cousin, Sammy Belou, was from New Orleans and still had good connections there even though he had lived in Kansas City for five years. Sammy was a car guy who could make any car start or break down when he ordained. He specialized in car wrecks that looked like accidents. Belou would meet Genelli in Little Rock tonight.

When Genelli's car came out of the parking garage that afternoon, a pale-blue Ford pulled out from a driveway across from the entrance, stopping long enough for a man coming out of the garage entrance to get in the passenger side, and followed Genelli's car.

"Central, this is unit 6. We are mobile, heading north on Broadway. My friend is traveling with light baggage. Probably going to midcontinent. We'll advise you as we know."

The private line lit up at FBI HQ, Kansas City. The operator answered with a four-digit number. The caller spoke a different four-digit number and was put through to the agent that matched.

Little Rock

Clint pulled into a parking slot reserved for airport security and watched as a tan Ford sedan proceeded to the TWA sign and pulled over. A man wearing tan slacks and a light-blue short-sleeved shirt, not tucked in, got out and entered the terminal. Fifteen minutes later, Marco Genelli came out of the terminal with another man. The second man had dark skin and unruly black hair, cut long, and bushy black eyebrows. He was dressed in black—pants, sweatshirt, and lightweight jacket. He and Genelli were talking to each other, never looking around for anyone observing them. They got into the tan Ford after loading their bags in the trunk, and the Ford began to weave its way out of the terminal traffic. Two cars cautiously followed as it headed toward downtown.

Short of city central, the Ford turned into an area of light industry and pulled into a property with a high board fence and a sign that read Acme Auto Wrecking—Parts for Sale.

Clint pulled his car up against the fence and got out. He walked past the open gate and saw Genelli and the dark man talking to a third man.

The driver waited in the Ford.

Their hands were gesturing as if completing a description. Clint walked past the gate and waited a couple of minutes then turned and walked back. The three men had raised the hood of a nearby car, and they were bent over a fender, looking down into the engine well. Clint, not wanting the men to notice him, returned to his car.

Ten minutes passed, and the Ford came out of the wrecking yard and turned back the way it had come. When the Ford came to a small commercial center, it turned in and stopped in front of the first business. The two anchor stores facing the street were a small car rental and a discount auto parts. Genelli went into the car rental, and the man dressed in black walked into the auto parts store.

A few minutes later, Genelli went out and nodded to the driver of the tan Ford, which drove away. Genelli walked to a black Pontiac in a row of rental cars and got in. He pulled out of the row of cars and stopped in front of the auto parts store. The man in black exited the auto parts store and got in the Pontiac.

Clint and the light-blue Ford followed the two men. When they turned into the garage building that served the State Office Building, Clint's heartbeat increased noticeably.

Clint picked up the mike to his radio. "Bravo, this is Able. Bravo 2, take a walk through the building, looking for your car. Bravo 1, go to the exit on Second Sreet and wait. I'll wait here."

The agent reached in the glove box and retrieved a small walkie-talkie and went into the garage. Clint was nervous and was about to go into the garage when the agent went out. He walked to Clint's car and got in. He pulled a small spiral notebook from his pocket, tore out a page, and handed it to Clint. "Looks like a license number," said Clint.

"Yeah," answered the agent, "and the car is parked in a slot that says it's reserved for Chester Allen—Director."

"He's the boss at ABI," Clint said. "What was the man doing?"

"I almost missed him, but I noticed the driver's door wasn't closed tight, and then I saw someone sit up in the seat. It looked like he had been in the floor under the dash. I hid behind a car in the opposite row. I was trying to decide how to leave when the other guy came scooting out from under the car. They picked up some tools and walked to where their car was parked. That's when I slipped down the ramp and got back here."

Clint stared back at the garage. "What do you think?"

"A bomb—that's what I think! They're pretty gutsy doing this in broad daylight, but I don't think those two have started a new auto service business. Fix your car while you work."

The radio cackled, and the agent at the exit said the subjects were driving out onto Second Street. Clint told the agent to continue surveillance and Able would join him. He got out and instructed the agent to take his car and join Baker. Clint turned and walked to the entrance of the State Office Building.

The elevator seemed unusually slow getting to the ABI floor. Clint showed his badge to the receptionist and said he had to see the director immediately. She said that Director Allen was in a meeting and could not be disturbed. Clint had been in the offices and knew there was a conference room to his right. He bent down at eye level with the young girl and said, "Miss, I'm sure you're good at what you do, but unless you buzz Director Allen this second and tell him there is a life-threatening emergency in the lobby, you will be interviewing at the unemployment office this time tomorrow!"

The girl's face was drained of color, and her hand shook as she dialed the conference room and spoke to Director Allen, who appeared in the lobby with a security man right behind him.

Allen stopped as he recognized Clint and looked around the lobby for the emergency. Seeing no sign of an event that warranted his issuing orders, he walked up to Clint and asked, "Agent Parker, can you explain what's going on out here?"

Clint spoke in a hushed voice, "In your office, Director."

Ten minutes later, Clint had finished his summary of events of the morning that had brought him to Director Allen's office.

Chet Allen, despite his crisp, almost-elegant appearance, was no stranger to situations that called for quick decisions and action. He absorbed the situation as fast as Clint related it. He knew Clint Parker's reputation and decided to follow Clint's lead. "What should we do at this point, Clint?"

Clint did not hesitate. "Thank you, Chet. We need a forensics team and a bomb\-disposal unit to record the scene and clean your car. I have two cars following the perpetrators, who will report to me as soon as they stop somewhere. They may have other targets, so we don't want to alert them that we're onto them yet. There is another issue involving your office that I should brief you on."

An hour later, Clint had finished filling the director in on two of his high-ranking officers, including the assistant director and a special investigator.

Chester Allen was visibly shaken by the revelations. Clint assured Allen that he was not considered a principal in any conspiracy and would be read in on any further investigations. Obviously, Alvin King could not be privy to confidential operations, and extreme care would be taken to conduct any actions aimed at organized crime so as not to create suspicion on King's part.

"It's going to be a little tense for a few days," Clint said. "There's no way to know exactly how many days, because I want a stronger case against King than what we presently have. How soon the case will be strong enough depends on when the mob makes an overt move, especially moves involving King."

Allen looked up from the notes he'd made and said, "From what you have told me, they're feeling pretty sure of themselves. A day or two is probably as long as they'll want to wait. Anything we can do to push their button?"

"Let me think about that." Clint stood and started toward the door.

Down the hall, Alvin King looked at a case file that had been opened for an hour. He had not read the first line of the report but wanted to look busy to anyone that came into his office. The man who came to his home last night said he should expect a major announcement regarding Director

Allen. "You may want to brush up on your statement of sympathy and reassurance of your determination to continue the fight for law and order." The man had left before Caldwell could ask for clarification, but he had been alerted that the assassination of Allen was imminent. This time, he was sure the director's job would be his. Why hadn't someone burst into his office with the terrible news?

Looking out his window was no help. His view was toward the industrial area, and every building was low and dingy. The good view was on the opposite side, filling the large window in Allen's office. *Oh well*, he thought, *it will be mine soon enough.*

CHAPTER 42

Marco Genelli paced back and forth from the bathroom to the outside wall and back. He had checked into the Canal Motel two hours ago and spent most of the time since on the phone, to no avail. None of his contacts were able to help him in his search. It was as if a spaceship had swooped down and carried a group of individuals off to Mars. His sources were pretty sure Ham Turner was dead. They had put together the report from the coroner along with the log at the hospital and the record of cremation at the funeral home, convincing Marco the man had not survived the hit at the cabin on the Current River. Fortunately, from his viewpoint, the assassin had been killed in the aftermath.

Marco's man in New Orleans had come up empty in his quest for Frederick Sanchez. NOPD received a complaint of a burglary at the Jolly Roger Bar, but someone had later called and said it was just a mix-up and there never was a burglary to begin with. The new crew in New Orleans were moving at all engines full throttle, reorganizing the operation to bring in the drugs and distribute to the key cities in the Midwest. That didn't settle his frustration over the missing people.

That little voice in his head kept telling Marco to lower his profile in the area and play defense. D'Oro, on the other hand, was pushing to get the operation in gear. "Strike while the iron is hot, Marco" was his reaction to Marco's gloomy report and cautious assessment.

D'Oro had ordered him to go to Alvin King's house and remind him whom he worked for before he began to think it was the state of Arkansas. Vincent wanted King locked in when he was promoted at the ABI. Marco knew what a big deal it was going to be for the mob to have their own man in charge of the top law enforcement agency in Arkansas. Then things could get back to the way they were before all the reformers started taking over.

It was 9:30 p.m., and the FBI agent watching King's house was on his second cup of black coffee. King had arrived home at 7:15 p.m. after stopping at a fried chicken place and having a quick dinner. Upon King's arrival, the agent stopped half a block back and waited for the garage door to close. He then pulled his car past the small bungalow, where his rearview mirror could afford a full view. He watched as lights came on in the back. *Probably the kitchen,* he thought. Then a light came on from upstairs. When the upstairs lights went back off and the dim light came on in the front area of the living room, the agent assumed it was going to be TV time until he called it a night. He adjusted his outside rear mirror to give him a full view of the bungalow, and should a neighbor take a night stroll and see him, he would not automatically associate him with Caldwell's house. He slid down behind the steering wheel, making himself mostly disappear.

It was 10:30 p.m., and most houses on the street had gone dark. The agent was surprised when the headlights appeared two blocks back and eased toward him. He scrunched himself deeper into the seat, keeping his eyes on the rearview mirror. As the car neared King's house, a flashlight began to send its beam across the yard, seeking the metal numbers confirming the address. The car stopped in front of King's house, and after a moment, the driver turned the car to the curb, parking on the wrong side of the street. The headlights went off, and a moment later, the figure of a man got out and walked up the steps to Caldwell's front door. The light on the wall next to the door came on for a moment, and the door opened. The man talked with King briefly and turned the porch light off. Both men went back inside the bungalow.

Even though the agent could not identify King's visitor, he sensed that it was an important one. He got out of his car, shook out a cigarette, and lit it as he walked across the street. From his jacket pocket, he retrieved a small penlight, and as he casually strolled past the improperly parked car, he read the license plate. It was Arkansas plates, and a decal in the rear window indicated it belonged to Razorback Rentals. He returned to his car and wrote down the number and name of the car rental and waited.

It was near eleven thirty when the man emerged from the bungalow and got in his car. The agent had thought about the decision he had to make: stay on his stakeout or follow the stranger in the rental car? He weighed the different potential consequences. He felt that King had not expected the visitor, and the visit had lasted nearly an hour. He had to assume that the visitor had a message for King that could not be relayed in a short phone call or a short visit at the front door. He concluded the visitor was someone important, and that meant he had to know his identity.

The rental car pulled away from King's house and turned right at the next street.

The FBI agent started his car and followed. The rental car went through three blocks until it reached the main street and turned left toward downtown. The agent accelerated to catch up and saw the taillights. Fortunately, there was little traffic this time of night, so the agent gave the black rental car lots of room until they approached a traffic light.

A few minutes later, the black car entered a parking lot with a sign that read Rest-Over Motel—Vacancy. The agent pulled his car to the curb and killed the lights. The black Pontiac continued to the back of the lot and parked. The agent got out of his car and walked quickly into the lot and observed the driver of the black car get out and walk to a door in the far back corner. A light came on inside the unit, and a man opened the door. The two men exchanged a few words, and both went back into the room. Fortunately, they were not paying any attention to the man who appeared to be intoxicated, fumbling for his key two doors away.

Chapter 43

As the agent heard the room door close, he straightened and walked by the room the two men had entered, making a note of the lettering on the door: 128.

He went to the motel office. As the bell over the door announced his entrance, the night clerk jerked his head erect and frowned his irritation at the interruption of his nap. "What can I do for you?" the man asked through an exaggerated yawn.

The agent flipped his badge case in front of the clerk. "I want the names of the guests in 128, please."

The clerk, scratching his head, replied, "Don't you need a warrant for that kind of information?"

The agent leaned over the counter and looked the clerk in the eye. "This is an urgent request from the United States government, and if I have to wake up a federal judge, I will. Then, I will roust every guest in this fleabag and get names and addresses for each person. There will be follow-up inquiries at their homes and places of business. So unless you want your occupancy to drop 50 percent over the next months and your boss to fire your incompetent ass, just show me the registration for room 128."

The clerk reached under the counter and retrieved a five-by-three box of cards. He thumbed through the tabs and pulled out a card. "Yes, sir, that's Mr.—"

The agent took the card from the clerk and read it, copying the information. "M. Genelli, Kansas City, Missouri." Handing the card back to the surly clerk, he said, "Put this back where you found it. If the men in 128 begin to act frightened or spooked, I will be back with more FBI agents than you can imagine living in Little Rock. They will search every room, including yours, and turn everything they find over to a United

217

States attorney for prosecution. Do you understand?" The trembling clerk nodded his understanding.

The agent went back to the parking lot and got in his car. He spent the next thirty minutes watching room 128 and glancing at the clerk, using the time to make notes in his book on the time line for the events while the details were fresh in his mind. The lights went out in room 128, and the night clerk was sitting behind the counter, head slumped forward, unmoving and apparently asleep.

At 7:00 a.m. the following day, the agent, Bud Smith, was standing in front of a select group of law enforcement officers in the FBI conference room, giving a verbal account of the previous evening. Clint, Ken Kondraky, Glenn Wiggs, and two other FBI agents listened and made notes.

When Smith finished his report, Clint thanked him and complimented him on using good judgment in leaving his stakeout and following the man who had visited Alvin King.

Clint walked up to the blackboard and talked as he wrote a name. "Marco Genelli is a name we have finally tied to the man who has been a busy boy all over our region. Kansas City has wired a dossier on Mr. Genelli, which tells us he is one of the top enforcers in the Civella crime family. The bureau has had this guy in their sights for a long time, and while they will feel somewhat cheated out of bringing him down, they have pledged their total support of our efforts down here in Podunk-land." A chorus of chuckles went around the table.

Clint continued, "Bud's quick thinking last night not only gave us a name but also an address here in Little Rock. He and an unknown associate are staying at a flophouse motel, the Rest-Over, room 128, on Myrtle near the river. We have a team on them now and will have three teams watching them until they make a move or leave town. Genelli is driving a rental car, a black Pontiac. If he goes to the airport, one team member must follow and determine his destination. My hunch is, he is here for a specific task and will stay until it's done.

"We have two men in custody that are fully cooperating with us. As soon as we think we have enough for Glenn's group to get a true bill from the grand jury, we want to move fast on cleaning these bastards off the street. Amos Boudreau will be in charge of operations in New Orleans. They have identified the subjects they will snatch when we're satisfied we've got the main spokes in the wheel in our sights.

"I do not want to fail to thank Ken Kondraky for representing the ABI in this investigation. Director Allen is fully briefed and will help in any way he can. The action plan, objectives, and assignments are spelled out to the extent possible in your handout. A final word of caution: Do not discuss this task force with anyone outside of this group without clearing it with me. At the same time, use your ingenuity and skills that every one of you posses. Those traits are one of the main reasons you're on this task force. Now, let's get out there and mop up this mess. Good luck!"

Chapter 44

Little Rock

Alvin King sat behind his desk, twirling a pencil and glancing at the door to his office. One more trip to the water cooler or restroom and someone might be curious. He'd already made too many trips, checking on activity in or around the lobby.

Chester Allen had been at his desk all morning and appeared to be doing his normal routine. He'd been on the phone a lot and had one visitor that was unknown to King, but that was normal for Allen. He was always politicking with a legislator or VIPs of one stripe or another; that was his job.

The layout of their floor was simple—private offices around the perimeter for management, agents, and investigators and a conference room, two interview rooms, kitchen and break room, restrooms, and an open room filled with clerical and secretarial staff. As Alvin returned to his office from the last trip, he walked around the west hall, which ran by Ken Kondraky's office. The drape was pulled across the tall, narrow glass next to the door. Normally, a visitor could peer through the glass to verify the person inside was in and not busy. It was unusual for the narrow drape, which usually hung beside the glass as part of the décor, to be pulled across the glass, preventing the ability to look in.

Now, King was consumed with questions. "Why would Kondraky close his drape? Did he have a visitor whose identity was to be kept from others in the office?"

Then another question occurred: "Was Kondraky not in his office? If not, where could he be, and why wasn't he in the loop on any investigation involving an agent that he was supposed to directly supervise? After all, he was the assistant director and, as such, should be aware of all investigations going on in this jurisdiction. He picked up the phone and dialed three numbers.

"Shirley? This is Assistant Director King. Do you know if Agent Kondraky is in his office?"

There seemed, to King, to be an unusual pause before the girl said, "I don't think so, sir. I believe he's on sick leave today. Bad tooth, I think. Someone told me he was going to the dentist. Can I do something for you, sir?"

King's mind went back to yesterday. He had left a little after six, and Kondraky was still at his desk and seemed quite normal. "No, it can wait till tomorrow. Maybe the dentist can help him and I can go over this file with him when he gets back."

King shuffled papers and played with his pencil. He was sure he had rearranged everything on top of his desk. He felt the anxiety rise in his neck muscles and claw its way down his back. He finally made the decision. He had to get out of the office and talk to someone he could confide in. He grabbed his coat and hat and headed for the lobby.

Alvin King stopped at the front desk and waited for the girl to look up from her typewriter. "I have some things to check out in the field, and I'll be out of the office the rest of the day. If anyone needs me, tell them I'll be back in the morning."

The girl put on a forced smile and said, "Yes, Mr. King, I certainly will. You all have a nice afternoon."

Alvin King decided to pass the elevator and went to the stairs, taking two at a time from the second floor to the lower-level garage. He glanced around the rows of cars before he went to his. Everything looked normal, whatever that was, he thought.

King calmed himself and tried to drive out of the garage normally. "Don't want to attract anyone's attention," he muttered. Despite his effort, he did apply the accelerator too quickly, and the tires squealed momentarily. He hit the brakes and then repeated the acceleration. Finally, he held his breath and got his right foot under control and drove the car slowly to the entrance. Alvin looked both ways, finally going right onto to Second Street. A glance in the rearview mirror revealed he was the only car on the street that wasn't parked and empty. He turned his attention back to his driving, not noticing the tan Ford pull away from the curb and follow about six car lengths back.

King drove west on Second until the city gave way to scattered commercial businesses and vacant lands waiting for development. He approached an intersection controlled by a stoplight, then he remembered the Sundowner Restaurant and Lounge on the southwest corner of the intersection. The one-story building sat on the southernmost portion of the property, with ample parking out to both streets.

Alvin slowed and turned into the parking lot. There were only six cars scattered near the entrance. A big neon sign scrawled across the edge of the roof read Sundowner Restaurant and Lounge—Fine Food.

He walked into the dim interior, pausing to let his eyes dilate and adjust to the low light level. Finally, he could see a couple on the dance floor, not really dancing, but moving to the rhythm of Nat King Cole doing "Answer Me, My Love." Another couple was in a booth along the back wall. If they went any further, they would need a motel room. There was a cluster of men at the far end of the bar, telling the stories they had all told before, but they all laughed as if they had heard them for the first time. Alvin sat at the bar opposite the quartet of storytellers and ordered scotch on the rocks.

The first drink went down fast, and he took a pull of the fresh drink and asked if they had a pay phone. The bartender pointed him toward a sign that said Restrooms. In the hall leading to the restrooms was a black wall phone. He pulled a paper from his wallet and dropped a handful of coins in the top of the phone. He heard four buzzing sounds indicating another instrument was ringing. Finally, Dee answered a sultry "Hello, this is Dee."

"Dee, this is Alvin, Alvin King. How are you?"

"Al, it's good to hear your voice. Are you in town?"

"No. Actually, I'm in Little Rock, but I needed to hear your sexy voice, so I left the office, stopped for a drink, and called. God, it's good to hear you. I could drive down there this afternoon and take you to dinner tonight. How about it?"

Dee was slow in answering him. There was a pleading tone to his voice that alerted Dee. "I don't think I can do dinner tonight, Alvin. I'm going with some friends over to McAllen, Texas, for the weekend, so I won't be here. I'm sorry."

"Where the hell is McAllen, Texas? Sounds like some hick town to me. Why go to a place like that when you already have New Orleans?"

Dee laughed. "It is across the border from Matamoros, Mexico, and the two of them together is the best party town you've ever seen. Anything goes, and I wish you were here. You could go with us."

"Well, I could be down there in three or four hours." Alvin had not heard any invitation from her, and his depression was gaining on him again.

"I'm really sorry, baby, but we're just about to load up and hit the road. Is everything all right?"

He couldn't control his emotion. "No, goddamit, everything is not all right. Some pretty strange shit is happening, and I'm feeling like I'm standing naked in the rain."

Dee's voice lowered and took on authority. "Listen to me, Alvin. You need to be calm, and if you're by yourself, don't drink too much. Get a bottle and go home. I will have someone call you in an hour. Will that give you enough time to get home?"

"Who's going to call me? Genelli?"

"Don't worry about that. The guys will take care of you. You're an important man, Alvin. They will protect you. Now, hang up and drive home slowly. No tickets, ya hear?"

"I hear you, Dee. God, I wish you were here with me. You make me strong, and I . . . I love you!"

"I love you too, Alvin. Now pay your bar tab and go home. You don't want to miss that phone call when it comes. Bye-bye now. I love you!" The phone clicked, and she was gone.

Alvin tossed some bills on the bar and went out to his car. He drove home like a robot. Talking to Dee had taken his mind off his fears and focused him on her. He was sad she was going out with other friends and not him. He had idealized his experience with her, and his fantasies did not recognize the reality of who and what she was and how much she was paid to be her. Anyway, she had talked to him and told him she loved him. He drove home carefully without stopping. He had whiskey at home.

CHAPTER 45

The FBI agent had waited in the parking lot. He didn't want to go into the bar too soon after Alvin. About twenty minutes went by with no one coming or going. He took off his suit coat and tie and grabbed a nylon jacket and a baseball cap from the backseat. He walked into the darkness of the bar, and after his vision adjusted, he sat at a table near the bar. He panicked when he'd finished his inventory of the patrons and did not see Alvin King. He saw the restroom sign and headed for it. Just as he approached the narrow hall running back to the restrooms, a man stepped out, and the two men almost collided. He realized it was King, who was bent over as if he were in pain.

"Watch where you're going, man. You're going to hurt somebody if you're not careful."

Alvin steadied himself and muttered, "I'm sorry, it's just the way this fucking day is going. You okay?"

The agent kept his head down, moving away and continuing toward the men's room door, waving Alvin away.

Alvin King walked to his car as a rain shower began to soak Little Rock. He was so deep in his self-pity that he drove out of the parking lot and down Second Street back toward town, never exceeding the speed limit and never looking back at the car shadowing him all the way home.

Alvin pushed the door opener before turning into his driveway and again as soon as the car cleared the garage door opening.

Inside, Alvin went straight to the bar in his study and began to pour a generous helping of scotch over three ice cubes.

The phone on the desk emitted a muted ringing sound, still causing Alvin to jerk the bottle sideways, spilling the amber liquid on a stack of cork coasters.

"Damn," he shrieked, reaching for a bar towel and hurriedly wiping up the spill. He sat at the desk, watching the phone until it stopped ringing. He continued to sit at his desk, trying to calm his nerves while looking out the rain-spattered window at the street in front of the house. He could detect no movement of cars or pedestrians.

"You're letting your nerves run away with your reasoning, Alvin!" he cautioned himself. "Don't forget who you are and the power you exert in the state. Whatever problems there are to deal with, you can handle. You know who swings the weight in local politics, and they will move to cover your ass if you make the call!"

He moved to the bar and freshened up his depleted drink. As he turned back to his desk, his eyes scanned the street in front. Everything was quite; nobody was moving.

Suddenly, the desk lamp went off, leaving the study and the house in darkness.

Alvin knew the house well enough to navigate in the dark. He headed, cautiously, to the breaker box in the kitchen closet.

As King entered the kitchen, he felt cooler air brush against him. Alarm seized him as the light from a neighbor's patio revealed the opened kitchen door.

Alvin King had enough experience in his profession to know danger even when he couldn't see it.

He turned back toward the study, but he was too late. A hand from behind covered his mouth, and he felt the knife penetrate his side. He coughed as the air involuntarily escaped from his left lung, then there was a stinging new pain from his heart, leaving him unable to draw a breath.

The unseen person behind him continued to hold him upright, and the man slowly let him slide to the floor. Alvin could still hear the man whisper as he gently laid his head down, "Should have kept your cool, Alvin. Your friends still cared enough to send their very best."

CHAPTER 46

FBI agent Murphy had noticed when the dim light went out and left the house in darkness. *Probably going to the kitchen for something to eat*, he thought.

Two minutes later, warning bells in Murphy's head alerted him that it was too long in the dark. He made a decision and walked briskly to the front door and rang the bell. The door was locked, and no light came on in response to the bell.

The sense that something was seriously wrong prompted the agent to take the small flashlight from his coat pocket and walk cautiously around the house to the back door. It was standing open.

The agent drew his pistol and stepped quietly through the open door.

The beam from the flashlight revealed a man's legs protruding around the corner of the cabinet. Murphy's heart accelerated as he raised the gun, holding his breath as he focused his senses on the room. To his left was a doorway connecting to a hallway.

He turned toward the opening, sensing rather than seeing the movement in the darkness. A flash of light and the bark of a gunshot resulting in a numbing sensation on his left side accompanied the sense of falling. The beam of the flashlight caught the image of a man moving toward him.

His last sense of awareness was the sound of his gun matching the kick against his right hand. His vision faded as the flashlight skittered across the floor.

Consciousness returned with a searing pain in his left shoulder radiating down his left arm. Murphy could make out a dim light a few feet away from his feet, then he realized it was the flashlight, and his memory came back in a flash. The memory was followed by the fear that someone had taken a shot at him and had apparently been partly successful. He scooted to the flashlight and then located and retrieved his gun. Alert to further attack, Murphy waited with his gun ready, but there was total silence.

Murphy tucked the flashlight under his injured left arm and, holding the gun in his right hand, stood and scanned the kitchen. The flashlight beam landed on a body lying on its back with part of the face and the side of its head torn away. Another sweep of the light revealed the pair of legs he had seen when he first entered through the back door. A quick check of that body revealed the face of Alvin King.

Satisfied there was no further threat in the house, Murphy flipped on the kitchen light. There was a wall-mounted phone near the refrigerator. The night operator at the bureau told him she would alert Clint Parker and an ambulance to his location.

Murphy told her, "Better call the coroner as well."

* * *

The EMT pulled the needle and inspected the bandage. "There you go, Mr. Murphy. That was your lucky bullet. Nothing but tissue and probably a little nerve damage. We'll give you a free ride to the hospital and let the doctor do a more through exam, but needless to say, you were much more fortunate than the other two."

Clint Parker nodded in agreement. "That's for sure, and there were two lucky bullets at work here tonight. Your reflex shot as you were falling caught your attacker under the left jaw and didn't exit until it was above the ear. That angel on your shoulder was working overtime tonight."

The ambulance screamed off to the hospital as the local police were preparing to load the other two for a trip to the morgue.

CHAPTER 47

That night signaled the beginning of the collapse of the overly ambitious effort to import illegal narcotics into the Southeastern United States via the Mississippi corridor.

The following days were a blur of grand jury indictments and FBI-led raids from New Orleans to Memphis. Throughout four states, there became a shortage of beds in short-term jail facilities.

Clint Parker, Amos Boudreau, Glenn Wiggs had never been so busy in their lives. They were pretty sure they had dealt severe blows to the drug business in their tristate area.

"The question was, how long would it take for someone to pick up the pieces and start over again?" Clint asked. Amos and Glenn nodded their heads affirmatively.

The three were having an early dinner at Arnaud's in New Orleans after a final session with the grand jury. Their work had been successfully brought to a close, and the jurors had been dismissed.

Clint raised his wineglass. "Here's a toast to a job well done. Amos, I specially appreciate your good work here in the NO office, and, Glenn, you did your usual outstanding public service, and I know the governor will have more on that in the near future. Salute to you both."

Both men drank to the toast, and Glenn responded, "Well, Clint, thank you for the kind words, but you and Amos did all the heavy lifting. I did what political appointees do—attend a lot of meetings, make a few phone calls, and shake a lot of hands."

Amos spoke up, "I think we made a damn fine team, and I'm very proud to have worked with both of you. It feels good to win a war."

Clint cleared his throat and said, "I'm reminded of some words of wisdom Glenn said to me as we watched the Mississippi River about a year ago. Glenn, you told me we never win the war against evil, but we have to fight the battles. We won this battle, and I love the feeling of victory, but except for the guy we killed in Little Rock, I regret that we couldn't bring the hammer down on the organization in Kansas City."

"Well, that's another battle, and it will be fought on another day," Amos said as he raised his glass in another salute. "Here's to the never-ending battle against evil."

Glenn raised his glass. "You fellows are learning that evil has always been in our midst, and as we defeat portions of it, new players will pick up the cause and commit new atrocities. As soldiers in the fight for good, we cannot allow that force to go unchallenged. I'm happy to say that as long as men such as you stay in the fight, the good people will back our efforts to suppress the efforts of those that yield to their evil nature."

With looks of solemn recognition in their faces, they drank to the toast.

Halfway between Little Rock and Kansas City, the bow of their houseboat ploughed steadily through the calm waters of Lake of the Ozarks, and another toast was being raised.

Gabby handed one of the fluted glasses to Blake, who held the wheel of the forty-foot craft with the other hand. "Here's to the most handsome captain with whom I have ever cruised the seven seas."

Their laughter floated across the still water and climbed the forested hills into the Ozark Mountains.

Author's Note

The story of my first book, *Arkansas Knights*, and this sequel, *Southern Justice*, was inspired by actual events. I grew up in Southeast Missouri and, after college at the University of Missouri, lived in Kansas City for seven years. The most memorable time in Kansas City I spent as an agent for a prestigious private detective agency, aiding in the conviction and sentencing of seven people to Leavenworth Federal Prison.

I witnessed the impact of criminal activity that moved into the rural areas of Arkansas, Missouri, and Mississippi and the ways it changed the area and too many of the people. Kansas City and New Orleans had their history of criminal activity, but the rural areas and smaller towns suffered through painful transitions as the criminal element infiltrated their society.

Their struggle against crime is not unlike all of America—valiant, noble, but never finished.

OTHER BOOKS BY
BILL KINKADE

Arkansas Knights

A drama set in rural Northeast Arkansas filled with colorful characters seeking to control the development of a growing country. Some brought the law, while others made their own law.

Two Minutes to Live—Ten Seconds to Die

A police drama set in the Dallas-Fort Worth metro area.

Arkansas Knights: Southern Justice

The continuing drama of the struggle to make the Mississippi River states into a vital part of a growing country against those that would turn it into a corridor for illegal drugs and criminal enterprise.

Edwards Brothers Malloy
Thorofare, NJ USA
January 28, 2016